Thomas Babington Macaulay

Biographies

Thomas Babington Macaulay

Biographies

ISBN/EAN: 9783337012502

Printed in Europe, USA, Canada, Australia, Japan

Cover: Foto ©Raphael Reischuk / pixelio.de

More available books at **www.hansebooks.com**

LORD MACAULAY'S BIOGRAPHIES.

BIOGRAPHIES

BY

LORD MACAULAY

CONTRIBUTED TO THE

ENCYCLOPÆDIA BRITANNICA.

WITH

NOTES OF HIS CONNECTION WITH EDINBURGH,

AND EXTRACTS FROM

HIS LETTERS AND SPEECHES.

EDINBURGH:

ADAM AND CHARLES BLACK.

MDCCCLX.

PRINTED BY R. AND R. CLARK, EDINBURGH.

CONTENTS.

———

PREFACE.

THE following Biographies are selected from the Encyclopædia Britannica. It was intended to publish the contributions of Lord Macaulay in a separate volume when the work was completed; but as the lamented and unexpected death of the noble author cuts off the possibility of any further contributions, it has been considered advisable to publish them at once. It is to be regretted that they have not been again revised by the author as he intended, before they appeared in a separate volume; but as they were carefully corrected by him when passing through the press for the Encyclopædia, there is ground for believing that they would have required little alteration. When these articles were written for the Encyclopædia

A

Britannica, Lord Macaulay had ceased to write for the reviews or other periodicals, though often earnestly solicited to do so. It is entirely to his friendly feeling that I am indebted for those literary gems, which could not have been purchased with money ; and it is but justice to his memory that I should record, as one of the many instances of the kindness and generosity of his heart, that he made it a stipulation of his contributing to the Encyclopædia that remuneration should not be so much as mentioned ; and I know it was his intention, had he enjoyed sufficient health and opportunity, to have even increased the number of his contributions.

Some of the circumstances attending Lord Macaulay's connection with Edinburgh excited much interest, and I embrace this opportunity of giving a short notice of the transactions of which I was cognizant, with extracts from his letters and speeches.

ADAM BLACK.

EDINBURGH, FEBRUARY 1860.

NOTES

LORD MACAULAY'S CONNECTION WITH EDINBURGH.

———◆———

I WAS first introduced to LORD MACAULAY in the summer of 1839, and had the honour of his uninterrupted friendship till his death. During his connection with Edinburgh, I was his frequent correspondent, and had an opportunity of learning his views on many of the public events of the time; his opinions are so just and instructive, and so eloquently expressed, that I am led to believe that extracts from his letters, and from his speeches on public measures, especially as affecting Scotland and Edinburgh, will not be uninteresting.

When Mr. Abercromby, one of our representatives, was called to the Upper House, and we had to look out for a successor, our attention was drawn to the eloquent advocate of parliamentary reform and ardent friend of civil and religious liberty, T. B. Macaulay; and I was authorized by the Liberal

Committee of Edinburgh, to invite him to offer himself as a candidate for the representation.   To this
communication I received the following answer :—

" London, May 15, 1839.

" Dear Sir—I have seldom been more gratified
than by your letter; and whatever may be the result
of our correspondence, I shall always reflect with
pleasure on such proofs of esteem and good will from
such a quarter.

" Unconnected as I am with Edinburgh, I should
never have thought of offering myself as a candidate ;
and when my friend Napier first mentioned to me
your suggestion, though I was pleased with it as a
compliment, I considered it as nothing more.   If,
however, I could be seated in the House of Commons
as the representative of your noble city, I should be
in the very situation which, of all situations, would
be most agreeable to my feelings.   I should be able
to take part in politics, as an independent Member
of Parliament, with the weight and authority which
belongs to a man who speaks in the name of a great
and intelligent body of constituents.   I should during
half the year be at leisure for other pursuits to
which I am more inclined, and for which I am perhaps better fitted; and I should be able to complete
an extensive literary work which I have long meditated.   If I were member for Edinburgh, I should,
I assure you, be quite as unwilling to be in place, as

my constituents could be to see me there. I have already, since my return from India, declined one lucrative and honourable office, that of Judge-Advocate. And, I think, I may safely venture to promise that I will never hold any office, however high, except under circumstances under which it would be wrong and dishonourable to decline it. I dislike the restraints of official life. I love freedom, leisure, and letters. Salary is no object to me, for my income, though small, is sufficient for a man who has no ostentatious tastes. And I have no doubt that, at the present moment, my public duty and private inclination coincide, and that I should be of more use to the Government out of place than in it.

"I shall be glad to hear what course things take. The Speaker, I believe, has, after some hesitation, made up his mind to go to the House of Lords. Mr. Fox Maule and the Marquess of Lansdowne have just assured me of this. If so, the new writ for Edinburgh will probably be ordered on Friday week, the 24th. On one point it is fit that I should explain myself with the utmost clearness : I mean the pecuniary part of the business. I cannot spend more than five hundred pounds on the election. When I name this sum, I go to the very farthest limit, perhaps beyond what is proper. If, therefore, there be any probability that the candidate will be required to pay more than this, I hope that you will

without delay look round for another person.—
Believe me," etc.   " T. B. MACAULAY."

On the 29th of May he addressed the electors
in the Music Hall, which was crowded by a most
attentive audience, who were captivated by the
manly eloquence of the candidate. The speech he
delivered on that occasion is printed in the volume
of speeches which he published in 1854.

The 4th of June was fixed for the city election
when Mr. Macaulay, on the motion of the Lord
Provost (Sir James Forrest), seconded by Mr. John
Wigham, a member of the Society of Friends, was
declared duly elected, after a feeble opposition by
the radicals, who were disposed to bring forward Mr.
Sharman Crawford.

In November 1840, he was inclined to pay a
visit to his constituents, but at that time a great
ferment prevailed on church polity, a subject which,
from the time of the Reformation, has occasionally
agitated Scotland to the very depths of society;
Churchmen were arrayed against Dissenters, and Dissenters against Churchmen, and the two sections of
the Established Church were in deadly conflict with
each other—that section, which was then called the
Church Extension party, and after the Disruption,
the Free Church, claiming co-ordinate jurisdiction
with the courts of law, and the moderate section
opposing them. He was therefore dissuaded by his

friends from visiting Edinburgh at that time, as there was danger of his being assailed by all parties, and giving satisfaction to none.

On that occasion I received a letter dated November 20th, 1840, from which I give the following extract :—

" My confession of faith is very simple and explicit, and is at the service of any body who asks for it. I do not agree with the High Churchmen in thinking that the state is always bound to teach religous faith to the people. I do not agree with the Voluntaries in thinking that it is always wrong in a state to support a religious establishment. I think the question a question of expediency, to be decided on a comparison of good and evil effects. I do not think it necessary to inquire whether, if there were no established kirk in Scotland, it would be fit to set one up. I find a kirk established. I am not prepared to pull it down; I will leave it what it has, but I will arm it with no new powers. I will impose no new burdens on the people for its support. I will make no distinction as to civil matters between the Churchman and the Dissenter. There are some questions which relate purely to the internal constitution of the church. Those questions ought in my opinion to be decided with a view to the efficiency and respectability of the church. The veto question is one of these. Whether the congregation ought or ought not to have a voice in the

selection of the pastor, is a question which will bear
a good deal of argument.   But this I say, that however it be determined, the Dissenter is not aggrieved.
He would have a right to complain if any tax or
any disability were imposed on him for the purpose
of adding to the wealth or credit of the church.
But if without any tax laid on him, without dis-
qualifying him for any office, the legislature can
make the church more useful to the country, the
legislature is bound to do so.   And on these grounds
I am favourable to a settlement of the non-intrusion
question on the basis of a popular veto.   But to the
high pretensions put forth by a portion of the church,
I am decidedly opposed.   I think that the veto or
some similar measure may be a desirable measure,
but I deny the claim to independence which the
Established Church sets up against the state.   These
are my views, open to correction, but sincerely entertained at present.   I do not expect them to please
the violent men on either side.   But I shall not on
that account disguise them."

In September 1839, on Mr. Macaulay becoming
Secretary at War, he was re-elected without opposition.   The Parliament being dissolved on June 23d,
1841, and his colleague Sir John Campbell having
accepted the office of Lord Chancellor of Ireland,
Mr. Macaulay was again brought forward for the
representation of the city, along with William Gibson

Craig, the son of Sir James Craig, a veteran and staunch Whig, to •whom Scotland was indebted beyond all others for resistance to Tory domination. In the darkest days of the reign of terror in Scotland, Sir James, with sound judgment and determined resolution, had encouraged and headed every movement for deliverance from political thraldom, till at length he was gratified by seeing, what was his anxious desire, though faint hope, the hustings erected at the cross of Edinburgh, for the election of their representatives in Parliament by the people themselves, instead of by the old self-elected thirty-three Town Councillors, who met in their own room to choose for representative of Edinburgh whoever was dictated to them by the house of Arniston.

The election on this occasion was carried without opposition.

Edinburgh, like some other towns, annually provides, for the amusement of its inhabitants, a week of horse-racing, to which her Majesty subscribes one hundred guineas, and before the reform of Parliament, the member for the city usually subscribed fifty guineas for the same purpose.

Shortly after the election of 1841, some persons wrote to Mr. Macaulay requesting him to sanction and continue this practice, but his abhorrence of anything in the shape of corruption was so great that he at once addressed me on the subject as follows :—

"London, July 14, 1841.

"My dear Mr. Black—I am much gratified by what you say about the race cup. I had already written to Craig to say that I should not subscribe, and I am glad that my determination meets with your approbation. In the first place, I am not clear that the object is a good one. In the next place, I am clear that by giving money for such an object in obedience to such a summons, I should completely change the whole character of my connection with Edinburgh. It has been usual enough for rich families to keep a hold on corrupt boroughs by defraying the expense of public amusements. Sometimes it is a ball; sometimes a regatta. The Derby family used to support the Preston races. The members for Beverley I believe find a bull for the constituents to bait. But these were not the conditions on which I undertook to represent Edinburgh. In return for your generous confidence, I offer faithful parliamentary service, and nothing else. I am indeed most willing to do what I can towards assisting your registration. I am willing to contribute the little that I can spare to your most useful public charities. But even this I do not consider as matter of contract. Nor should I think it proper that the Town Council should call on me to contribute even to an hospital or a school. But the call that is now made is one so objectionable that I must plainly say, I would rather take the Chiltern Hundreds than comply with it.

"I should feel this if I were a rich man. But I am not rich. I am on the point of laying down my carriage; leaving my house; breaking up my establishment, and settling in chambers. I have the means of living very comfortably according to my notions, and I shall still be able to spare something for the common objects of our party, and something for the distressed. But I have nothing to waste on gaieties which can at best only be considered as harmless. If our friends want a member who will find them in public diversions, they can be at no loss. I know twenty people who, if you will elect them to Parliament, will gladly treat you to a race and a race-ball once a month. But I shall not be very easily induced to believe that Edinburgh is disposed to select her representatives on such a principle. I will see whether the Home Office is inclined to do anything about pauperism in Scotland. I am rather apprehensive that Lord Normanby may be averse from taking any important step at a time when it is so clear that he is on the point of retiring from office.—Ever yours truly," etc.

"T. B. MACAULAY."

During the Parliament which lasted from this time till 1847, he took an active part in all public measures, especially those that were discussed in the House of Commons, where he spoke in favour of the motion for a committee to take into considera-

tion the state of Ireland. He warmly supported the
Dissenters' Chapel Bill against its bigoted opponents.
He likewise supported the motion for the equaliza-
tion of the Sugar Duties.

In 1845, when Mr. Ward moved, as an amendment on the Maynooth College Bill, that any provision for the purposes of the bill should be taken
from the funds applicable to ecclesiastical purposes
in Ireland, he argued that the amendment ought to
go much farther, and embrace the whole question
whether the Irish Church, as now constituted, should
be maintained or not; and he said—"I am prepared to
support my opinion, that of all the institutions now
existing in the civilized world, the Established
Church of Ireland is the most absurd."

In the same year he took charge of the bill for
abolishing Tests in the Scottish Universities, and,
with his colleague, faithfully attended to the local
interests of Edinburgh.

Till the repeal of the Corn Laws in 1846, the
discussions on this subject were carried on with
unexampled keenness in Scotland, and especially in
Edinburgh. At one time the repealers would have
been disposed to submit to a small duty; but when
this was resisted, the people of Edinburgh were
earnest in agitating for the total abolition of the
Corn Laws. As long as Sir Robert Peel opposed the
alteration of the law, it appeared to the Free Trade
party in Parliament that the utmost that could pos-

sibly be gained was a small fixed duty, and to this they resolved to direct their combined efforts ; had these been successful, they would have secured a great boon to the country at the time. Many who had joined in this policy were as friendly to complete free trade as Mr. Cobden. Among these was Mr. Macaulay; but he was persuaded that at that time to urge the total repeal of the Corn Laws, would be to risk the only benefit to the country within reach, and at the same time to embarrass those friends with whom he acted in this measure.

In February of that year, I wrote to him on the question, and stated the views of the Edinburgh Free Traders, and pressed on him, perhaps too strongly, the desirableness of his supporting them in Parliament. The following is his reply :—

"London, February 22, 1843.

"My dear Sir—I have delayed answering your kind letter till I received Mr. Wigham's communication. My mind is quite made up. I am certain that the only chance of our getting any mitigation of the existing evils is to act together cordially against the sliding scale. If the party of the Anti-Corn-Law League choose to separate themselves from the supporters of a moderate fixed duty, and to run down Lord John and those who agree with him, I am inclined to believe that we shall have to wait many years for any real improvement. The truth is, that the friends of perfectly free trade, of whom I am sincerely one, are in general quite mistaken as to their own strength. They live in towns; they herd together; they echo and re-echo each other's sentiments; they are accustomed to see large meetings collected, all animated by the same feeling; and they have got into a habit of repeating that public opinion is for free trade, that monopoly is detested by all except the aristocracy, and so forth. One would think, to hear them, that the United Kingdom had no rural population at all. Take such a county as Essex, with a population and a constituent body more than twice as large as that of Edinburgh; or Devonshire, with a population and a constituent body nearly four times as large as that of Edinburgh; and let any candidate for those counties talk Cobden's language on the hustings: nay, let him talk Lord John's, or even Gladstone's, and see how he will be received. He will be an object of as much detestation to the body of the farmers and yeomen as the Duke of Cleveland would be to our friends of the High Street. The Irish county members form, as you well know, a great part of the strength of the Liberal party in the House of Commons. There is hardly one of them who, whatever his opinion might be, would dare to vote for total repeal. He would infallibly lose his seat. It is to no purpose to say that this is ignorance and prejudice. I know it well; but I also know that you must work with such tools as you have. You are a minority of the people, told by the head. The higher and higher you go, the smaller is your minority. What, under such circumstances, is your clear policy? To consider all as with you who are not against you, to sink as much as possible all differences which exist between people sincerely desirous of extending the freedom of trade, and to supply, by prudence and union, the deficiency of strength. Instead of this, the members of the Anti-Corn-Law League seem to be determined to drive support from them. As if it were not enough to have against them the Government, the Church of England, the Peers, the House of Commons, the majority of the elective body—the majority, I firmly believe, of the people of the United Kingdom, they must attack the very persons by whose help alone they can hope to get any thing at all. Can any man seriously think that any improvement can be made in the Corn Law till some government shall take the question up? Now, what materials are there for a government among the total and immediate repealers? To imagine that we shall have a cabinet excluding Peel, the Duke, Stanley, Graham, Lord Aberdeen, on the one side; excluding Lord John, Lord Palmerston, Lord Lansdowne, on the other, and consisting of leading members of the Corn-Law League, is quite idle. From an appeal to physical force all good men shrink with horror, and all judicious men know that if such an appeal were made, the Anti-Corn-Law League would come by the worse.   But if there is to be no appeal to physical force, you can obtain no part of what you have in view, except by the support of one at least of the parties in the state.   One of these parties is much nearer to you in sentiment than the other; but your policy, I mean that of the League, seems to be to treat them both alike with every species of indignity and contumely.   Some purposes this course may answer.   It may fill the bellies of itinerant spouters; it may circulate reams of bad writing; it may very likely put Mr. Sharman Crawford or Colonel Thompson into my seat at Edinburgh; but it will not strike off a farthing from the price of the quartern loaf. These are my opinions.   I express them to you without the reserve which might be proper in a letter intended for the public eye; but I have only one story for you, for Mr. Wigham, for the Cabinet, for the hustings, and for the House of Commons, though I may vary the phrase according to time and place.   You see that, in my opinion, you are all in the wrong—not because you think all protection bad, for I think so too; not even because you avow your opinion and attempt to propagate it, for I have always done and shall always do the same; but because, being in a situation where your only hope is in a compromise, you refuse to hear of compromise; because, being in a situation where every person who will go a step with you on the right road ought to be cordially welcomed, you drive from you those who are willing and desirous to go with you half way.   To this policy I will be no party.   I will not abandon those with whom I have hitherto acted, and without whose help I am confident that no great improvement can be effected, for an object purely selfish.   How could I ever hold up my head, if I did ?   What change has taken place since last year, when I refused to vote with Villiers.   The Corn Law has grown no worse ; the arguments against it are the same.   The only difference is, that the feeling at Edinburgh is stronger ; and that I may hazard my seat.   Be it so.   I am quite resolved to run the hazard ; and of this I am certain, that if, holding the opinions which I have expressed, I did not run the hazard, you would despise me heartily. —Ever yours," etc.

He alludes to this subject in a speech which he made at Edinburgh on the 2d December 1845, for the purpose of petitioning her Majesty to open the ports for the free admission of corn.   He there says :—

"With respect to the past, gentlemen, I have perhaps a' little to explain, but certainly nothing to repent or to retract.   My opinions, from the day on which I entered public life, have never varied.   I have always considered the principle of protection to agriculture as a vicious principle. I have always thought that this vicious principle took, in the Act of 1815, in the Act of 1828, and in the Act of 1842, a singularly vicious form. This I declared twelve years ago, when I stood for Leeds : this I declared in May 1839, when I first presented myself before you; and when, a few months later, Lord Melbourne invited me to become a member of his Government, I distinctly told him that, in office or out of office, I must vote for the total repeal of the corn laws.

"But in the year 1841 a very peculiar crisis arrived. There was reason to hope that it might be possible to effect a compromise, which would not indeed wholly remove the evils inseparable from a system of protection, but which would greatly mitigate them. There were some circumstances in the financial situation of the country which led those who were then the advisers of the Crown to hope that they might be able to get rid of the sliding scale, and to substitute for it a moderate fixed duty. We proposed a duty of eight shillings a quarter on wheat. The Parliament refused even to consider our plan. Her Majesty appealed to the people. I presented myself before you; and you will bear me witness that I disguised nothing. I said, 'I am for a perfectly free trade in corn : but I think that, situated as we are, we should do well to consent to a compromise. If you return me to Parliament, I shall vote for the eight shilling duty. It is for you to determine whether, on those terms, you will return me or not.' You agreed with me. You sent me back to the House of Commons on the distinct understanding that I was to vote for the plan proposed by the Government of which I was a member. As soon as the new Parliament met, a change of administration took place. But it seemed to me that it was my duty to support, when out of place, that proposition to which I had been a party when I was in place. I therefore did not think myself justified in voting for a perfectly free trade, till Parliament had decided against our fixed duty, and in favour of Sir Robert Peel's new sliding scale. As soon as that decision had been pronounced, I conceived that I was no longer bound by the terms of the compromise which I had, with many misgivings, consented to offer to the agriculturists, and which the agriculturists had refused to accept. I have ever since voted in favour of every motion which has been made for the total abolition of the duties on corn."

The acceptance of the office of Paymaster-General of the Forces, in July 1846, caused a new election. Since he was re-elected in 1841, the struggle between the two parties in the Church of Scotland had ended in the Disruption of 1843; and many who, before that event, were uncompromising supporters of the Church, were now its vehement opponents, assuming that they were the true Church of Scotland, as modelled by Knox and Henderson, and suffered for by the Covenanters; the latter parties gave prominence to the peculiar views of the early Presbyterians, especially on the non-intrusion of ministers, and hatred of popery; and in their opinion to refuse to vote for the repeal of the grant to Maynooth, was in a Member of Parliament an unpardonable sin. Though he supported every good measure and opposed every bad, yet if he failed in this one point he could not escape condemnation. So strongly did this feeling influence many of the Free Church party, that even Sir James Forrest (then Lord Provost), who moved Mr. Macaulay at the first election in 1839, was now his most strenuous opponent on religious grounds. I should however observe, that many of the more moderate members of the Free Church publicly protested against the propriety of opposing Mr. Macaulay. It was, however, not only the Free Church, but a large body of the Dissenters, who were dissatisfied with Mr. Macaulay's votes on the Maynooth grant. The Dissenters were also desirous of a representative from their own body, or one holding their opinions, and such a one they thought they had found in Sir Culling Eardley Smith.

The election took place on the 14th July 1846. Mr. Macaulay was moved by the Lord Provost (Black), and seconded by Mr. Moncreiff; Sir Culling was moved by Sir James Forrest,* and seconded by Dr. Beilby.

The following is an extract from the speech of Mr. Macaulay on that occasion :—

" I thank you, my Lord, for the kind manner in which you have introduced me to this great assembly ; and I thank the electors of Edinburgh, as I have

* A ludicrous circumstance occurred while Sir James Forrest was speaking from the hustings in favour of Sir Culling. On the Queen's first visit to Edinburgh in 1842, the citizens were caught napping. It was not expected that her Majesty would arrive till nine or ten o'clock. She, however, landed at Granton before eight, and passed rapidly through the city on her way to Dalkeith; the magistrates, who were to receive her Majesty at the gate, in their robes, were sitting quietly in the council-chambers; the platforms that had been raised in the line of the expected procession were empty, and parties coming to town to welcome the sovereign on her first visit to Scotland were all grievously disappointed; all were indignant, and vented their rage on the Town Council, and especially on the Provost, whom they blamed for sleeping at his post, and causing this disappointment. He was the subject of the popular merriment and song. During his speech, in moving Sir Culling, he was frequently jeered by the mob for not being awake on the memorable morning, and a wag had procured a Kilmarnock night-cap, which was for some time tossed about among the mob and then thrown up to the bustings to Mr. Macaulay, who handed it to the Provost, by whom it was presented to Sir James, who received it with ineffable disgust, and then threw it with all his might at the mob, exciting a universal guffaw of laughter, which continued for some minutes. It is only justice, however, to Sir James Forrest to say, that he was punished for a sin which he did not commit. I was cognizant of the whole circumstances of the case, and fully acquit him of all blame.

had reason before to thank them, for the kind manner in which they have received me. They are aware that her Majesty has been graciously pleased to appoint me one of her ministers. They are aware that, by that appointment, the connection between them and me has been terminated; and that it is now for them to decide whether or not they will renew it. I hope when they calmly review the state of public affairs, the state of public parties, and the past conduct followed by myself and by those with whom I have been in the habit of acting, they will think that I have not forfeited their confidence, and that, by accepting a place in the service of the Crown, I have not disqualified myself for the service of the people. It is impossible, gentlemen, for me to see you thus assembled before me without feeling my mind carried back to the time when I last stood before you as a candidate for the same high and important trust. It was, I think, to a week, almost to a day, five years ago. Since that time we have seen great changes. Many predictions, many calculations, by the ablest.men, from the strongest appearances of things, have been utterly falsified. What seemed to us at one time defeat, has produced more than all the benefits which we could expect from victory. Good has been wonderfully brought out of evil. At the same time we have seen ties indissoluble, sundered. We have seen great and strongly organized parties melted down and re-cast. Amidst all these changes, who have changed I do not pretend to say. I have changed in nothing. My principles are the same as when I formerly stood before you; and of the opinions which then recommended me to your approbation, I have recanted, and wish to recant, none. It is necessary, perhaps, that in determining how far you can trust me in future, I should carry you back to the time when I last stood before you as a candidate. I was, as I am now, a member of the Government; but I was a member of a Government in a very different situation from that which has just been formed. The administration of Lord Melbourne, after many struggles, was then at its last gasp. Of that administration I can now speak with perfect impartiality. I can speak of it as calmly and freely as I can speak of the administration of Sir Robert Walpole or Lord North. I believe I say only what posterity will confirm, when I say that that administration, amidst many difficulties, did mean well and endeavour well,—that it effected some useful reforms,—that it indicated the path of the other great reforms which it was unable to effect,— that it showed lenity where lenity was possible,— energy where energy was necessary, and that, under that Government, Great Britain and Ireland formed for the first time one truly united kingdom,—united not only by statute and treaty, but also by kindness and affection. That Government doubtlessly committed faults, but its weakness and its fall were the

effects, I believe, not of its faults, but of its merits.
I believe that the most eminent of those who
thwarted and assaulted that administration, and who
at length overthrew it, and rose to power on its ruins,
if they had now to write its history, they would find
themselves constrained to admit, that the very acts
against which they raised the loudest and fiercest
clamours have the best titles to the public gratitude
and esteem.   If I revert to the manner in which this
administration was assailed, I revert to it because,
without such reference, it would be impossible that
I should distinctly explain the principles which
guided my conduct in opposition.   I do not do so
from any feeling of personal malevolence,—not from
any wish to attack those ministers who have just
retired from office.   As to the Right Hon. gentleman
who a few days ago was at the head of her Majesty's
Government, I have, in what seemed to me to be
the proper place and the proper time, said of him
that which I think—I have not shrunk in his
presence, and when at the height of his power, from
censuring those parts of his conduct which seemed
to me to be censurable : and it is not in his absence,
—it is not when he has just quitted power, and at
the moment when he has rendered a great service to
the country, that I feel inclined to throw any imputa-
tion upon him.   I would willingly pass by his errors,
and would willingly dwell only on his reparation.
I would willingly forget what were the means by

which he rose to power, and remember only for what ends he has used it. If I revert to parts of his conduct which it would be injurious to him not to suppose that he remembers with regret, I do so only because, without such reference, it would be impossible to render that clear and full account which I owe to you. When I entered Parliament—when I was sent thither by you in 1839—the administration of Lord Melbourne had still two years to live. During these two years it was strenuously attacked, but chiefly attacked on three points. When first I entered Parliament, the cry which met my ears against the ministry was, That they have engaged in pushing forward a plan of godless education. That cry was raised with such vehemence, and such assiduity, that it deceived many well-intentioned minds. In the House of Commons, on one occasion, the Government was run so close that I think the majority was only two. I remember when a long procession of carriages, with the Primate at their head, went up to Buckingham Palace, conveying to the Queen an address against the system of education supported by that ministry. The cry at the time was also raised against them that they were flattering and courting Popery in Ireland. That cry was raised during the whole of 1839. It rose still louder in 1840. It was raised as high as it had been raised in the time of Oates,—it was raised as high as it was raised in the time of Lord George

Gordon. Nay, for the purpose of rendering vain
that favour which it was said the Government of
Lord Melbourne were disposed to show to the
enemies of Popery, a measure was introduced, and
supported by the whole strength of the Opposition,
nominally for the registration of Irish votes, but
practically disfranchising the whole body of Irish
Roman Catholic electors. Well, then, the two cries
of 'No godless education' and 'No Popery,' in 1839
and 1840, did, as you can well recollect, grievous
injury to the Government that then existed. But
all these cases were, in fact, slight, when compared
with the storm that burst forth in 1841, when at
length the Government took their stand upon the
principle of free-trade. To the principle of free-
trade that Government had always been generally
favourable. Some of the members of it—as myself
for example—always distinctly declared it as their
opinion that free-trade in corn was the wisest and
the most just policy. Others did not quite go that
length; but I believe that in that administration
there was no person who was not disposed greatly
to relax the old protective system, and to admit
the necessaries of life at a lower and more steady
price, and, by so doing, to open up new markets
for English industry. Certainly, in the House of
Commons there was not a single member of that
Cabinet, to the best of my recollection, who had not
voted already for the motion that was made by Mr.

Charles Villiers on the subject. But the state of our finances in the year 1841 made it necessary that the Government should decide this question,—new taxes or free-trade. They made their choice. They declared that they were against monopoly. Monopoly instantly raised a cry against them. With the cry against their education system, and with the cry of 'No Popery,'—there was now joined louder than either of these cries the cry of 'Protection.' Under these circumstances, they were compelled to appeal to the nation.—They appealed—they were defeated; they retired—vanquished, but neither degraded nor depressed. They knew that a delusion could not last for ever. They knew that a time would come when full justice would be done them. How short the time that delusion would last—how it would be dispelled—how completely justice would be done them, and from what quarter it would come, I own we did not fully foresee. · Our successors had it now in their power to govern England, if so it seemed good to them, according to the principles which they professed when in opposition. For a time, they showed some inclination, in some measure, to act up to these professions. Official men in the House of Commons did still for a few weeks repeat the old common-places against the Whig system of education. Some appointments, justly displeasing to the Irish nation, were made; and when Irish discontent broke forth, and was strongly expressed, it was encountered

by an Arms bill and State prosecutions.   For a
time, you know, an attempt was made to uphold,
with some modification, the system of protection ;
and a new corn bill was put forth upon a new sliding-
scale, differing in details, but retaining the old
principle.   But in a little while the heavy responsi-
bilities of office began to calm and sober the minds
which ambition and faction had heated when in
opposition.   No choice was left to the rulers of this
country except this—inconsistency or public ruin.
They chose well.   One after another, all the principles
which, when we professed them, they assailed, were
by themselves adopted.   The Whig system of education went on efficiently under Tory management.
Attempts which the Whigs could not safely have
ventured, were made to soothe and court the great
body of the Irish people.   And lastly, in the present
year, a measure of free-trade, such as even the Whigs,
who thought it most desirable, would not have dared
to introduce, believing it to be impracticable, was
brought in and triumphantly carried by the Ministry
that was formed, as you know, on the principle of
protection.   Well, then, and what, through these
eventful years, was the course which it behoved us
to take—us undoubtedly who had much of which
we might fairly complain—us, who were driven from
power on pretences which we think no person can
now pronounce to have been justifiable.   Were we
to watch for opportunities of thwarting, frustrating,

and obstructing those whom we justly consider greatly to have aggrieved us ?—or were we, throwing away all recollection of the past, in no degree to allow it to interfere with the discharge of our duties to the country, but to come manfully forward and strengthen the hands of those whose study it had been, when we were engaged in the same cause, to weaken ours? Our choice was made. We determined to give a full and conscientious support to those measures which were in accordance with the principles which we always avowed. We gave it, and I myself gave it on one occasion, which I know has excited much difference of opinion here and throughout the country. My conduct in the matter I refer to has displeased many of you. I cannot ask pardon for it. I cannot ask pardon for being in the right. I come here to state it clearly, and to defend it. I speak of the Maynooth grant. It might be not altogether useless to a fair and ample discussion of that interesting subject, if all who express an opinion strongly respecting that grant, would take the trouble to inform themselves a little upon the subject. The opinion held on that subject by many respectable persons, I believe to be, that, in the year 1845, the Parliament of the United Kingdom committed a great violation of the sound principles of Protestantism, and endowed an institution for the propagation of Popery. The truth is this. Fifty years ago, when Ireland was an independent kingdom, governed by its own King, Lords, and Commons, and when those who preceded you here in Edinburgh had no more voice in the regulation of the affairs of Ireland than of the affairs of France, and when the Irish Parliament was strictly and exclusively composed of Protestants,—that Parliament thought it right to establish this institution for the education of the Roman Catholic clergy. Thus this institution was bequeathed by the Union to the United Kingdom; it came to us as an institution older than the Union, set up by an Irish Parliament, and being, moreover, the only act which the Irish Parliament, during the hundred and twelve years which followed the Revolution, had ever passed giving any sign of sympathy with the body of the people. I do not say—nay, I repudiate the argument —that we are bound to maintain that institution by anything of the nature of a technical treaty; but I say that, when a great and powerful country enters into a treaty on terms of mutual benefit, with a country much smaller and weaker,—when 100 Irish Members are sent to sit along with 558 British Members, it does become a grave question,—a question of high responsibility,—a question of justice,— how far the stronger of these powers should act against existing institutions in a manner strongly opposed to the sense of the great body of those constituting the weaker nation. I say that your own fathers felt this strongly. When they joined with

England, they took every species of precaution against the English introducing a Church professing such doctrines as those held by Laud, and since held by a school I need not name now existing in the Church of England,—they took every precaution that the United Legislature should not lay its hand on those religious institutions which your ancestors prized more dearly than their lives. When they sent 45 Scotch Members to sit with 513 English Members,—when they sent 45 Presbyterians to sit with 513 Prelatists, they took precautions that the 513 should in no way abuse their power. Though there existed nothing of the nature of an absolute treaty, the strongest considerations of justice ought to have induced the Parliament of the United Kingdom to pause before abolishing the institution which the Irish Parliament had bequeathed to them. Is it possible that so intelligent a body as the electors of Edinburgh can believe that there was any question of principle involved in what was actually done regarding this matter last session? It is a mere popular delusion to say that there was any question of principle about it. (Cheers and great hissing.) Principle! when those hisses are interpreted into intelligible sounds, we shall perhaps hear some orator who will attempt to show that the difference between £10,000 and £20,000 is a question of principle,—that the difference between a College, white washed and repaired, and one in ruins, is a question of principle,—that the difference between a half-filled larder and a full larder is a question of principle,—that the difference between a vote passed regularly every year for fifty years, and one which Parliament may rescind whenever it thinks fit, is a question of principle. Is it not monstrous? We hear a good deal of talk about the homage that has been paid to idolatry, but that is not the ground of attack. You object to us offering a hecatomb to idolatry, but not to us offering a lamb, —you exclaim against a pound being laid on the altar, but you have no objection to a pennyweight. I ask, if such an institution is to be maintained at all, ought it not to be maintained in such a manner as befits an institution which the State does support? This is the principle about which you exclaim,—the principle that the State may support a Catholic institution which has servants with arms out at elbow, but not in decent livery,—that it may support an institution which has grounds for the recreation of the students, but you will not let it keep a roller, —that the institution may keep professors to teach languages and science, provided you pay them lower than a village dominie,—and that it might lodge students, provided it put them three in a bed. This is what I call, and will call, a popular delusion. And then look at the other side of the account. When this bill was brought in, wisely or unwisely, what were to be the consequences of rejecting it?

Have those who clamour so loudly against it ever calculated the cost of throwing it out? Have they considered whether this difference of £13,000 a year was worth a civil war?   *   *   *   *   *

To such a course as this I trust the attention of the new Government will be directed. Whether I shall be honoured by bearing a part in those noble and beneficent measures that shall engage its councils, it is for you to determine. I shall await your determination with little doubt, and with no fear. The contest which we are told is at hand can have no issue for which I am not perfectly prepared. Seven years ago, at your spontaneous invitation—an invitation neither directly nor indirectly sought by me—I re-entered public life, which, till then, I thought I had left for ever. While I retained your confidence, I was determined that I would not quit my post. If you now reject my services, it is not my intention to tender them to any other body of electors. I shall consider myself as having received a legitimate and honourable dismissal, such as will authorize me to return to pursuits from which I have derived far more happiness than ever I enjoyed in the affairs of the British Senate. To hold office under an administration, or to be in Parliament, ought not to be necessary to any man's happiness; and I bless God that it is not necessary to mine. I do not think any man an object of pity who can with a character and conscience unsullied, exchange politics for the pleasure of literature and domestic life—which has a pleasure and distinction which the Government can neither give nor take away. I shall carry with me to my retreat one only regret,—a regret of no selfish kind. It will deeply pain me to think, that at a time like this,—a time when the prospect of good government and repose was opening before us,—a time when, after so long a period of gloom and tempest, the dawn of a bright and tranquil day seemed to be breaking upon Ireland,—when, throughout Great Britain, all passions seemed to be strangely lulled,—when the constituent bodies of the empire, to which a solemn appeal was made, were everywhere answering that appeal in a manner honourable to their good sense and their good feeling, —that there should have been one place under the dominion of senseless clamour and malevolent prejudices worthy only of a dark age. Yes; for such clamours and such prejudices might well become a dark age,—they might well become a rude and barbarous nation, but it will be to me a subject of deep regret if I have to carry into my retreat the thought that I found it dominant in the liberal and enlightened city of Edinburgh in the nineteenth century."

The polling was carried on languidly, and ended with 1735 for Mr. Macaulay, and 832 for Sir C. E. Smith.

The majority was so decided, that his friends

considered themselves justified in calculating that the hold which Mr. Macaulay had on the representation of Edinburgh was so strong that there was little danger of his being disturbed, and this may have been one reason why sufficient precautions were not taken before the disastrous election of next year.

The election of 1847 was most discreditable to Edinburgh. It rejected a representative who had proved himself the faithful guardian of their interests, a man of downright honesty, a valuable minister of the Crown, distinguished as an eloquent and sound constitutional senator, a historian, critic, and poet, whose writings were admired wherever the English language was read; in short, one of whom Edinburgh, Parliament, and the kingdom might be proud. His defeat on this occasion took not only his friends, but the nation by surprise.

It was known that he was to be opposed, but no one contemplated the possibility of his being defeated. His rejection was owing to the combination of several heterogeneous parties, pandering to the prejudices of the times.

The opposition which was engendered among the Free Church and Dissenters, at the election of last year, was fostered and had gathered strength; his fearless honesty, and the too free expression of his sentiments, the unscrupulous misrepresentations of his opponents, who turned with great effect against him his unguarded expression of the " braying at

Exeter Hall," all operated injuriously against him.
Then there was the standing reproach of worshipping
"the Beast," by supporting the Maynooth Bill; and
to add to the other objections of a religious character,
on which Scottish Presbyterians are particularly sensitive, the Government had shortly before appointed
a new Bishop for Manchester, thus strengthening
Black Prelacy.

To these objections on ecclesiastical grounds, was
added one of an opposite character, at least according
to the views of his religious opponents—the con-
tinuance of undue restrictions upon the publicans and
spirit-dealers, especially in regard to their licenses.
It was this last that brought the combined opposition
to a head.

Candidates, when disagreeing with their constituents, or with deputations from them, generally get
rid of unpleasant questions by polite evasions, or
promising to take them into consideration; but so
sensitively honest, and withal so acute in discerning
the weak points of a case was Mr. Macaulay, that
instead of soothing those who thought they had
a grievance to complain of, he plainly told them
where they were wrong, and argued the point with
them, even though he agreed with them in the
main.   The consequence often was, and particularly
in this Excise case, that they considered they were
not only to receive no help from their representative,
but that he would oppose them.

This happened to a deputation who waited upon him from the publicans and spirit-dealers, who returned and reported to their constituents, that Mr. Macaulay would not support their views. This consequently arrayed a large and influential body against him, these joining the No-Popery men, the Godless-education men, the extreme radicals, and the crotchety coteries, formed a very powerful phalanx, who had recourse to every artifice to damage Mr. Macaulay in the eyes of the electors.

They had now to look out for some one to use in opposition to their former member, and at length prevailed on Mr. Charles Cowan, the son of one of the most respectable citizens of Edinburgh, but who, though of excellent private character, had not in any way distinguished himself in public affairs before. It was evident that they were acting under the influence of cabal and caprice, and not from any preference for him whom they had selected as their instrument of offence. At a meeting with the electors in the Music Hall, Mr. Macaulay ably defended his conduct while in Parliament. The following is the conclusion of his speech on that occasion:—

"In reference to all questions in respect of my conduct, it is for you to decide. If your decision shall be adverse, I shall submit to it without a murmur. That decision, if it be adverse, will probably deprive me of some things which may be thought enviable; of some things which few persons who had so little pretension to them from their fortune and social position have attained to in our time. But my estimate of happiness does not agree with those who place it on such objects. I can truly say I never sought for those things by any crooked course—that I found them only because they lay in the way of duty, and honour, and virtue —that I never solicited them, and that I can relinquish them without a pang. Exclusion from public life may have terrors for the man who is conscious he has brought it upon himself by unworthy conduct towards his country. It may have terrors to the man who has no tastes and no occupations to supply the place of public business; but as for me, my conscience reproaches me with no wrong. On my integrity, malice itself has never thrown a stain. I have no fear that my hours will pass heavily in retirement; and I do not altogether despair of being able to show, that even in retirement, something may be done for the greatest and most lasting interests of society. Feeling this, I assure you that if you shall think fit to pronounce my dismissal, I shall accept that dismissal not only with tranquillity, but with unaffected cheerfulness. I assure you that no bitter feeling will mingle with the gratitude with which I shall always remember your past kindness; and the very worst wish that I still have for the gentleman who may succeed me is, that he may find in politics as much satisfaction as I shall hope to find in letters and repose."

The excitement continued to increase on both sides, but his opponents, by the use of the popular cries then prevalent, gathered strength hourly, while his friends were discouraged and alarmed.

Thursday, 29th July, being fixed for the nomination, the candidates were Macaulay, Gibson-Craig, Cowan, and Peter Blackburn, who was brought forward by the Conservatives, in the hope that in the scramble among three Liberals, they might slip in a Tory.

Mr. Macaulay was moved by the Lord Provost (Adam Black), and seconded by William Tait, publisher of Tait's Magazine. During the proceedings at the hustings, an effigy of a bishop, dressed in full canonicals, was hoisted up and exhibited to the mob, and then handed up to the Provost, and every interruption was given to Mr. Macaulay and his supporters; the voices of both the candidate and his movers were drowned in the hootings and yellings of an excited mob. Still it was not believed that the electors would act under the same frenzy.

The polling was fixed for Friday the 30th; by this time fears were entertained for the result, for while the enemy were united, and confident, our party was disorganized and disheartened by the desertion of many who had acted with them on former occasions. I waited with Mr. Macaulay in a room of the Merchants' Hall, to receive at every hour, the numbers who had polled in all the districts. At ten o'clock, we were confounded to find that he was 150 below Cowan, but still had faint hopes that the next hour might turn the scale; the next hour came, and a darker prospect; at twelve o'clock, he was 340 below Cowan. It was now obvious that the field was lost, but we were kept from hour to hour under the torture of a sinking poll, till at four o'clock it stood thus—Cowan, 2063; Craig, 1854; Macaulay, 1477 ; Blackburn, 980.

The result of this election was received by the country as a general calamity; but although the Illustrious Rejected could not help feeling the ingratitude of the constituents whom for eight years he had served so faithfully and so well, he retired in the proud satisfaction that he had lost their favour, not by neglecting any duty or forfeiting any pledge, but by firmly retaining his integrity, and discharging what he considered his duty to his country, according to the constitutional principles which he had always maintained.

In his farewell address to the electors of the city of Edinburgh, he says :—

"London, August 2, 1847.
"Gentlemen—You have been pleased to dismiss

me from your service, and I submit to your pleasure without repining. The generous conduct of those who gave me their support, I shall always remember with gratitude. If anything has occurred of which I might justly complain, I have forgiven, and shall soon forget it. The points on which we have differed, I leave with confidence to the judgment of my country. I cannot expect that you will at present admit my views to be correct; but the time will come when you will calmly review the history of my connection with Edinburgh. You will then, I am convinced, acknowledge that if I incurred your displeasure, I incurred it by remaining faithful to the general interests of the empire, and to the fundamental principles of the constitution. I shall always be proud to think that I once enjoyed your favour, but permit me to say, I shall remember not less proudly, how I risked, and how I lost it. With every wish for the peace and prosperity of your city, I have the honour to be, gentlemen, your faithful servant, · "T. B. MACAULAY."

The election of 1847 was to me always a painful subject, and I never liked to refer to it in my future correspondence.

Two years afterwards, Glasgow did itself honour by electing him Lord Rector of its University. The speech he delivered on that occasion, is included in the published volume of his speeches.

In 1852, the retirement of Sir William Gibson-Craig from the representation brought on a new election. By this time the inhabitants of Edinburgh had repented of their folly, and were desirous of rectifying the error they had committed, and atoning for their injustice towards the illustrious statesman whom they had treated with unkindness. But there was a great difficulty in the way; Mr. Macaulay would not offer himself as a candidate, he would not even say he would accept if he were elected; his friends were therefore placed at a great disadvantage during the canvass, as they had to meet two rival candidates, the then Lord Provost (D. M'Laren) and the late member Charles Cowan, who were straining every nerve to attain their object. In the meantime, the secretary of the Protestant Association had written to him with no friendly intention, and received an answer which his opponents perverted for the purpose of preventing his election. He was written to by the chairman of his committee, regretting that he had given them an opportunity of misrepresenting him, which drew from him the following :—

"London, June 30, 1852.

"Dear Sir—I am truly sorry that you should have any cause for anxiety, and I would gladly do my best to save you from any vexation. But what can I do? I despair of being able to use words which malice will not distort. How stands the case? I say that a distinction is so rare, that I lately thought it unattainable, and that even now I hardly venture to expect that I shall attain it;—and I am told that I hold it cheap. I say, that to be elected member for Edinburgh without appearing as a candidate, would be a high and peculiar honour—an honour which would induce me to make a sacrifice such as I would make in no other case; and I am told that this is to treat the electors contemptuously. My language, naturally construed, was respectful, nay, humble. If any person finds an insult in it, the reason must be that he is determined to find an insult in everything that I write. My feeling towards the people of Edinburgh is the very opposite of unkind or contemptuous. I have been much gratified by what I have heard during the last week of their feeling towards me. I give the best proof of my regard for them by consenting to return to public life at their invitation, after repeatedly refusing to do so when invited on the most honourable and liberal terms by others; nor shall I cease to wish well to your fellow-citizens, or to think highly of their general character, even though they should be again estranged from me by misrepresentations, such as you describe. Remember me kindly to Craig when you see him.—Ever yours truly,

"T. B. MACAULAY."

This letter, which expressed the first indication

of his willingness to accept, only arrived a few days before the nomination.

The election took place on the 13th July, and the result of the poll was, Macaulay, 1846; Cowan, 1753; M'Laren, 1561; Bruce, 1068; and Campbell (of Monzie) 625. The triumph of Macaulay was received with one burst of delight, in all quarters of the country, and the following letter shows the feelings with which the tidings were received by himself :—

" TO THE ELECTORS OF EDINBURGH.

"London, July 14, 1852.

"Gentlemen—At a late hour yesterday evening I learned that I was once more your representative. I am truly sorry that it is impossible for me to appear before you to-day in the High Street, and to give utterance to some part of the feelings with which I accept from you a trust, honourable in itself, and made doubly honourable by the peculiar manner in which it has been offered to me.

"On as early a day as my health will permit, I shall have an opportunity of explaining to you the general view which I take of public affairs. But on this day, the day on which my old connection with you is, after an interruption of five years, to be solemnly renewed, I will avoid every subject which can excite dissension: and will only assure you that I am proud of your confidence, that I am grateful for your kindness, and that the peace, the prosperity, and the renown of your noble city, will ever be to me objects of affectionate solicitude.—I have the honour to be, gentlemen, your faithful servant,

"T. B. MACAULAY."

His friends at Edinburgh, after having imposed upon him this public burden, felt anxious about the state of his health, which they feared might hardly be able to sustain the labours of Parliament, and to their anxious inquiry the following answer was received :—

"16 Caledonian Place, Clifton,
"August 13, 1852.

"Dear Sir—I am decidedly better than when I left London. Then, indeed, I could hardly crawl up and down stairs; and I can now walk miles, at a gentle pace, and on tolerably even ground. Still, however, any excitement, or any violent exertion, instantly brings on a derangement of the circulation and an uneasy feeling of the heart. I should, I daresay, have made more rapid progress if the weather had been fine; but since I have been here the rain has been almost incessant. To-day the sun is bright, the western horizon clear, the St. Vincent rocks in full beauty, and the air delicious. I shall not despair of an entire recovery till I have tried what a succession of such days will do for me. I am not however sanguine. Perhaps my complaint depresses my spirits. But I will own to you, that I greatly doubt, judging by my own internal sensations, whether I shall ever be able to go through a session of Parliament in a manner which would satisfy even the most indulgent constituent body.—Ever, dear Sir, yours most truly,   "T. B. MACAULAY."

He was unable to be present with us till the 2d of November, when he met the electors in the Music Hall. The anxiety of the inhabitants to hear him, and their eagerness to greet his return was so great, that the large hall was crammed in every corner; but it was alarmingly evident that although the mind retained all its wonted vigour, a dangerous disease already preyed upon the bodily frame; he was obliged to conclude his admirable address, before he had discussed all the subjects to which he had intended to advert.

The speech is included in the printed volume of speeches, but I cannot refrain from giving the introduction :—

" Gentlemen—I thank you from my heart for this kind reception. In truth, it has almost overcome me. Your good opinion and your good will were always very valuable to me, far more valuable than any vulgar object of ambition; far more valuable than any office, however lucrative or dignified. In truth, no office, however lucrative or dignified, would have tempted me to do what I have done at your summons, to leave again the happiest and most tranquil of all retreats for the bustle of political life. But the honour which you have conferred upon me, an honour of which the greatest men might well be proud, an honour which it is in the power only of a free people to bestow, has laid on me such an obligation that I should have thought it ingratitude, I should have thought it pusillanimity, not to make at least an effort to serve you.

"And here, Gentlemen, we meet again in kindness after a long separation. It is more than five years since I last stood in this very place; a large part of human life. There are few of us on whom those five years have not set their mark, few circles from which those five years have not taken away what can never be replaced. Even in this multitude of friendly faces I look in vain for some which would on this day have been lighted up with joy and kindness. I miss one venerable man, who, before I was born, in evil times, in times of oppression and of corruption, had adhered, with almost solitary fidelity, to the cause of freedom, and whom I knew in advanced age, but still in the full vigour of mind and body, enjoying the respect and gratitude of his fellow-citizens. I should, indeed, be most ungrateful if I could, on this day, forget Sir James Craig, his public spirit, his judicious counsel, his fatherly kindness to myself. And Jeffrey—with what an effusion of generous affection he would, on this day, have

welcomed me back to Edinburgh!   He too is gone;
but the remembrance of him is one of the many ties
which bind me to the city once dear to his heart,
and still inseparably associated with his fame."

The question of education, especially of the paro-
chial schools, had for some time excited considerable
discussion in Scotland. This was a subject in which
he took great interest, and on which he wrote me the
following:—

"Albany, London, January 20, 1854.

" My dear Sir—To whom ought I to write on the
subject of education?   What I should be inclined
to say would be to this effect—I have always thought
it the duty of the state to provide education for the
people of every religious persuasion. My wish would
be to see a national system of secular education
established, and to leave the religious education of
the young to their own parents and pastors. The
state of public feeling in England has hitherto made
such an arrangement impossible. Many persons
whom we should have thought our natural allies,
are violently opposed to all state education. Of
those who are friendly to state education, a majority
will not hear of a purely secular education. In
England, therefore, the system of Privy Council
grants, imperfect as it is, is the best that unfortunate
circumstances permit us to adopt. But if the public
feeling of Scotland be in favour of a system free

from all sectarianism, I should be delighted to see such a system established, and should hope that the success of such a system on one side of the Tweed, would remove the prejudices which now exist on the other. These are my views. I am sorry that the *Scotsman*, an excellent paper as any in the kingdom, blames Lord John for having taken the only course which the unreasonableness both of Churchmen and of Dissenters left open to him.— Very truly yours,   "T. B. MACAULAY."

The fears of his friends in regard to his health were but too surely realized. He was able to give attendance in the House of Commons only on important occasions, and even then he could not remain during late sittings. He repeatedly wrote to his friends lamenting his inability to discharge his parliamentary duties, and requesting to be relieved from his office. They were unwilling for sometime to give up hopes of recovery, and then there was a prospect of an impending dissolution of Parliament —they were therefore anxious that he should retain his seat if possible till then.

The following letters, written twelve months before his resignation, show how earnestly he desired relief from his public labours, and his unwillingness to retain a distinction of which he could not discharge the duties :—

D

"Albany, London, January 25, 1855.

"My dear Sir—I must very earnestly beg you to think about finding some person to succeed me as member for Edinburgh.

"I really can remain titular member no longer; I feel that I am every winter becoming more and more unfit for parliamentary life. It is now the ninth day since I have stirred out of my chambers. Twice this week I have been forced to use blisters, to relieve my chest; and this is likely to be my life till the warm weather returns. Public affairs, meanwhile, are every day looking blacker and blacker. The members for the great cities of the empire ought all to be at their posts; and it is my plain duty to attend the House or to vacate my seat. I must be resolute; the question really troubles my conscience and my reputation. What good reason can I assign to the world, for keeping the title of M.P., while I perform none of the duties of a representative. The unexampled indulgence of my constituents is an additional reason for my doing what I feel to be my duty by them.—Ever yours truly.

"T. B. MACAULAY."

"Albany, London, April 6, 1855.

"My dear Sir—I hope that you will not think me importunate, if I again and very earnestly beg you to consider seriously the state of the representation of the city. I feel every day more and more that my public life is over. I am not, thank God, in intellect or in affections, but in physical power, an older man by some years than I was last Easter. I see no chance of my being able again to take part in debate. By the bye, I hoped till lately that I might be able to go down to Edinburgh in the course of the summer, and give a lecture at the Philosophical Institute.* But the thing is impossible. My voice would not hold out a quarter of an hour. I have been forced to give up reading aloud to my sister; and I seldom pass an evening in animated conversation, without suffering severely afterwards. The little that I can do for mankind must be done at my desk. I try to flatter myself with the hope that a sojourn at Palermo or Malaga may set me up again; and I shall probably try that experiment, as soon as I have brought out the next part of my history. But in the meantime, the feeling that I ought to be in the House of Commons preys upon my mind. I think that I am acting ungenerously and ungratefully to a constituent body, which has been most

* At the opening of the Edinburgh Philosophical Institution in 1846, Mr. Macaulay delivered an admirable speech on the literature of Britain, which is included in the published volume of his speeches. On the death of Professor John Wilson, his predecessor, on the 5th March 1845, he was unanimously elected president, and held that office till his death. It was his desire, had health permitted, to have delivered some lectures during the session; but to show the interest he took in the institution, he made a present of a very valuable collection of books for the library.

indulgent to me.   However I will, as I have said, remain an M.P. till the end of this session.—Ever yours truly.   "T. B. MACAULAY."

His friends were desirous that, if possible, he could be persuaded to retain his seat till the approaching dissolution, to prevent a protracted canvass; but he at length determined on taking the Chiltern Hundreds, and bidding adieu to his constituents, and the following letter was received by them with unfeigned sorrow :—

"TO THE ELECTORS OF EDINBURGH.

"Gentlemen—Very soon after you had done me the high honour of choosing me, without any solicitation on my part, to represent you in the present Parliament, I began to entertain apprehensions that the state of my health would make it impossible for me to repay your kindness by efficient service. During some time I flattered myself with the hope that I might be able to be present at important divisions, and occasionally to take part in important debates.   But the experience of the last two years has convinced me that I cannot reasonably expect to be ever again capable of performing, even in an imperfect manner, those duties which the public has a right to expect from every member of the House of Commons.

"You meanwhile have borne with me in a

manner which entitles you to my warmest gratitude. Had even a small number of my constituents hinted to me a wish that I would vacate my seat, I should have thought it my duty to comply with that wish. But from not one single elector have I ever received a line of reproach or complaint.   If I were disposed to abuse your generosity and delicacy, I might perhaps continue to bear the honourable title of member for Edinburgh till the dissolution of the Parliament; but I feel that by trespassing longer on your indulgence I should prove myself unworthy of it.   I have therefore determined to dissolve our connection, and to put it in your power to choose a better servant than I have been.

" I have applied to the Chancellor of the Exchequer for the Stewardship of the Chiltern Hundreds ; and I have every reason to believe that the new writ will issue on the first day of the approaching session. This notice will, I trust, be long enough to enable you to make a thoroughly satisfactory choice.

"And now, my friends, with sincere thanks for all your kindness, and with fervent wishes for the peace, honour, and prosperity of your noble city, I for the last time bid you farewell.

"T. B. MACAULAY.

"London, January 19, 1856."

On his elevation to the Peerage, I wrote him that the honour so justly conferred upon him, had afforded great gratification to his late constituents, and received the following reply :—

> "Holly Lodge, Kensington,
> September 17, 1857.

"My dear Sir—Thanks for your most kind letter. I am truly glad that my old friends in Edinburgh are not displeased with what I have done. I need hardly assure you that I never, directly or indirectly, solicited the honour which has been conferred on me. The letter in which Palmerston informed me that he had received the Queen's permission to offer me a peerage took me altogether by surprise. I was on the point of starting for the Continent; and I had nobody to consult. I made up my mind very speedily; but I had, I own, serious apprehensions that both Palmerston and myself would be blamed by a large part of the public. It is therefore most gratifying to me to learn that both the offer and the acceptance are generally approved.—Ever, my dear sir, yours most truly.   "MACAULAY."

I did not intend to write a Biography of Lord Macaulay, but cannot conclude these Notes without claiming for Scotland the honour of his being the son of a Scotsman. I find it recorded in Irving's valuable History of Dumbartonshire, that his father, Zachary Macaulay, was the son of the minister of Cardross, a parish on the banks of the Clyde, below

Dumbarton Castle, near the picturesque scenery often visited by tourists. Irving in his list of parish ministers says :—

"John M'Aulay was inducted minister of Cardross parish in 1774. (He had been previously minister of Lismore and Inverary).* Owing to his connection with what was known as the Moderate party, M'Aulay's translation to Cardross met with considerable opposition from the Ultra-Calvinistic section of the Presbytery; but it was ultimately carried in the above year, 1774. He married Margaret, third daughter of Colin Campbell of Inversregan, by whom he had twelve children, the youngest of whom, John, died in infancy. One of them entered the East India Company's service, and rose to the rank of general; another, Zachary, resided for some years as a merchant in Sierra Leone; and on returning to this country became a prominent and useful member of the party then labouring for the abolition of slavery in the British possessions. By his marriage with Miss Mills, daughter of a Bristol merchant, Zachary

---

* Writing under date 25th October 1773, Boswell records:— "Mr. John M'Aulay passed this evening with us at our inn. When Dr. Johnson spoke of people whose principles were good but whose practice was faulty, Mr. M'Aulay said he had "no notion of people being in earnest in their good professions whose practice was not suitable to them." The Doctor grew warm, and said, "Sir, are you so grossly ignorant of human nature as not to know that a man may be very sincere in good principle without having good practice."

had a son, Thomas Babington (now Lord Macaulay of Rothley), the distinguished critic and historian. A sister of Zachary married Thomas Babington, Esq., an English gentleman. John M'Aulay died minister of Cardross in 1789. — *Irving's Dumbartonshire, second edition.*"

Lord Macaulay was born on the 25th October 1800, at Rothely Temple, Leicestershire, and died on Wednesday, 28th December 1859, at his residence, Holly Lodge, Kensington.

A. B.

EDINBURGH, FEBRUARY 1, 1860.

BIOGRAPHIES.

FRANCIS ATTERBURY.

FRANCIS ATTERBURY, a man who holds a conspicuous place in the political, ecclesiastical, and literary history of England, was born in the year 1662, at Middleton in Buckinghamshire, a parish of which his father was rector. Francis was educated at Westminster School, and carried thence to Christ Church a stock of learning which, though really scanty, he through life exhibited with such judicious ostentation that superficial observers believed his attainments to be immense. At Oxford, his parts, his taste, and his bold, contemptuous, and imperious spirit soon made him conspicuous. Here he published, at twenty, his first work, a translation of the noble poem of Absalom and Ahithophel into Latin verse. Neither the style nor the versification of the young scholar was that of the Augustan age. In English composition he succeeded much better. In 1687 he distinguished himself among many able men who wrote in defence of the Church of England, then persecuted by James II., and calumniated by apostates who had for lucre quitted her communion. Among these apostates none was more active or malignant than Obadiah Walker, who was master of University College, and who had set up there, under the royal patronage, a press for printing tracts against the established religion. In one of these tracts, written apparently by Walker himself, many aspersions were thrown on Martin Luther. Atterbury undertook to defend the great Saxon reformer, and performed that task in a manner singularly characteristic. Whoever examines his reply to Walker will be struck by the contrast between the feebleness of those parts which are argumentative and defensive, and the vigour of those parts which are rhetorical and aggressive. The Papists were so much galled by the sarcasms and invectives of the young polemic, that they raised a cry of treason, and accused him of having, by implication, called King James a Judas.

After the Revolution, Atterbury, though bred in the doctrines of non-resistance and passive obedience, readily swore fealty to the new government. In no long time he took holy orders. He occasionally preached in London with an eloquence which raised his reputation, and soon had the honour of being appointed one of the royal chaplains. But he ordinarily resided at Oxford, where he took an active part in academical business, directed the classical studies of the under-graduates of his college, and was the chief adviser and assistant of Dean Aldrich, a divine now chiefly remembered by his catches, but renowned among his contemporaries as a scholar, a Tory, and a high-churchman. It was the practice, not a very judicious practice, of Aldrich, to employ the most promising youths of his college in editing Greek and Latin books. Among the studious and well-disposed lads who were, unfortunately for themselves, induced to become teachers of philology when they should have been content to be learners, was Charles Boyle, son of the Earl of Orrery, and nephew of Robert Boyle, the great experimental philosopher. The task assigned to Charles Boyle was to prepare a new edition of one of the most worthless books in existence. It was a fashion among those Greeks and Romans who cultivated rhetoric as an art, to compose epistles and harangues in the names of eminent men. Some of these counterfeits are fabricated with such exquisite taste and skill, that it is the highest achievement of criticism to distinguish them from originals. Others are so feebly and rudely executed, that they can hardly impose on an intelligent schoolboy. The best specimen which has come down to us is perhaps the oration for Marcellus, such an imitation of Tully's eloquence as Tully would himself have read with wonder and delight. The worst specimen is perhaps a collection of letters purporting to have been written by that Phalaris who governed Agrigentum more than 500 years before the Christian era. The evidence, both internal and external, against the genuineness of these letters is overwhelming. When, in the fifteenth century, they emerged, in company with much that was far more valuable, from their obscurity, they were pronounced spurious by Politian, the greatest scholar of Italy, and by Erasmus, the greatest scholar on our side of the Alps. In truth, it would be as easy to persuade an educated Englishman, that one of Johnson's Ramblers was the work of William Wallace, as to persuade a man like Erasmus, that a pedantic exercise, composed in the trim and artificial Attic of the time of Julian, was a despatch written by a crafty and ferocious Dorian who roasted people alive many years before there existed a volume of prose in the Greek language. But though Christ Church could boast of many good Latinists, of many good English writers, and of a greater number of clever and fashionable men of the world than belonged to any other academic body, there was not then in the college a single man capable of distinguishing between the infancy and the dotage of Greek literature. So superficial indeed was the learning of the rulers of this celebrated society, that they were charmed by an essay which Sir William Temple published in praise of the ancient writers. It now seems strange, that even the eminent public services, the deserved popularity, and the graceful style of Temple, should have saved so silly a performance from universal contempt. Of the books which he most vehemently

eulogized his eulogies proved that he knew nothing.
In fact, he could not read a line of the language in
which they were written. Among many other
foolish things, he said that the letters of Phalaris
were the oldest letters and also the best in the
world. Whatever Temple wrote attracted notice.
People who had never heard of the Epistles of
Phalaris began to inquire about them. Aldrich, who
knew very little Greek, took the word of Temple
who knew none, and desired Boyle to prepare a new
edition of these admirable compositions which,
having long slept in obscurity, had become on a
sudden objects of general interest.

The edition was prepared with the help of Atterbury, who was Boyle's tutor, and of some other
members of the college. It was an edition such as
might be expected from people who would stoop to
edit such a book. The notes were worthy of the
text; the Latin version worthy of the Greek original.
The volume would have been forgotten in a month,
had not a misunderstanding about a manuscript
arisen between the young editor and the greatest
scholar that had appeared in Europe since the revival
of letters, Richard Bentley. The manuscript was in
Bentley's keeping. Boyle wished it to be collated.
A mischief-making bookseller informed him that
Bentley had refused to lend it, which was false, and
also that Bentley had spoken contemptuously of the
letters attributed to Phalaris, and of the critics who

were taken in by such counterfeits, which was perfectly true. Boyle, much provoked, paid, in his preface, a bitterly ironical compliment to Bentley's courtesy. Bentley revenged himself by a short dissertation, in which he proved that the epistles were spurious, and the new edition of them worthless : but he treated Boyle personally with civility as a young gentleman of great hopes, whose love of learning was highly commendable, and who deserved to have had better instructors.

Few things in literary history are more extraordinary than the storm which this little dissertation raised. Bentley had treated Boyle with forbearance ; but he had treated Christ Church with contempt ; and the Christ-Churchmen, wherever dispersed, were as much attached to their college as a Scotchman to his country, or a Jesuit to his order. Their influence was great. They were dominant at Oxford, powerful in the Inns of Court and in the College of Physicians, conspicuous in parliament and in the literary and fashionable circles of London. Their unanimous cry was, that the honour of the college must be vindicated, that the insolent Cambridge pedant must be put down. Poor Boyle was unequal to the task, and disinclined to it. It was, therefore, assigned to his tutor Atterbury.

The answer to Bentley, which bears the name of Boyle, but which was, in truth, no more the work of Boyle than the letters to which the controversy

related were the work of Phalaris, is now read only
by the curious, and will in all probability never be
reprinted again. But it had its day of noisy popularity. It was to be found not only in the studies
of men of letters, but on the tables of the most
brilliant drawing-rooms of Soho Square and Covent
Garden. Even the beaus and coquettes of that age,
the Wildairs and the Lady Lurewells, the Mirabels,
and the Millamants, congratulated each other on
the way in which the gay young gentleman, whose
erudition sate so easily upon him, and who wrote
with so much pleasantry and good breeding about
the Attic dialect and the anapæstic measure, Sicilian
talents and Thericlean cups, had bantered the queer
prig of a doctor. Nor was the applause of the multitude undeserved. The book is, indeed, Atterbury's
masterpiece, and gives a higher notion of his powers
than any of those works to which he put his name.
That he was altogether in the wrong on the main
question, and on all the collateral questions springing
out of it, that his knowledge of the language, the
literature, and the history of Greece, was not equal
to what many freshmen now bring up every year to
Cambridge and Oxford, and that some of his blunders
seem rather to deserve a flogging than a refutation,
is true ; and therefore it is that his performance is,
in the highest degree, interesting and valuable to a
judicious reader. It is good by reason of its exceeding badness. It is the most extraordinary instance

E

that exists of the art of making much show with little substance. There is no difficulty, says the steward of Molière's miser, in giving a fine dinner with plenty of money : the really great cook is he who can set out a banquet with no money at all. That Bentley should have written excellently on ancient chronology and geography, on the development of the Greek language, and the origin of the Greek drama, is not strange. But that Atterbury should, during some years, have been thought to have treated these subjects much better than Bentley, is strange indeed. It is true that the champion of Christ Church had all the help which the most celebrated members of that society could give him. Smalridge contributed some very good wit ; Friend and others some very bad archæology and philology. But the greater part of the volume was entirely Atterbury's: what was not his own was revised and retouched by him ; and the whole bears the mark of his mind, a mind inexhaustibly rich in all the resources of controversy, and familiar with all the artifices which make falsehood look like truth, and ignorance like knowledge. He had little gold ; but he beat that little out to the very thinnest leaf, and spread it over so vast a surface, that to those who judged by a glance, and who did not resort to balances and tests, the glittering heap of worthless matter which he produced seemed to be an inestimable treasure of massy bullion. Such arguments as

he had he placed in the clearest light.   Where he
had no arguments, he resorted to personalities, sometimes serious, generally ludicrous, always clever and
cutting.   But, whether he was grave or merry,
whether he reasoned or sneered, his style was always
pure, polished, and easy.

Party-spirit then ran high ; yet, though Bentley
ranked among Whigs, and Christ Church was a
stronghold of Toryism, Whigs joined with Tories in
applauding Atterbury's volume.   Garth insulted
Bentley, and extolled Boyle in lines which are now
never quoted except to be laughed at.   Swift, in his
Battle of the Books, introduced with much pleasantry
Boyle, clad in armour, the gift of all the gods, and
directed by Apollo in the form of a human friend,
for whose name a blank is left which may easily be
filled up.   The youth, so accoutred and so assisted,
gains an easy victory over his uncourteous and boast-
ful antagonist.   Bentley, meanwhile, was supported
by the consciousness of an immeasurable superiority,
and encouraged by the voices of the few who were
really competent to judge the combat.   "No man,"
he said, justly and nobly, "was ever written down
but by himself."   He spent two years in preparing
a reply, which will never cease to be read and prized
while the literature of ancient Greece is studied in
any part of the world.   This reply proved not only
that the letters ascribed to Phalaris were spurious,
but that Atterbury, with all his wit, his eloquence,

his skill in controversial fence, was the most audacious pretender that ever wrote about what he did not understand. But to Atterbury this exposure was matter of indifference. He was now engaged in a dispute about matters far more important and exciting than the laws of Zaleucus and the laws of Charondas. The rage of religious factions was extreme. High church and low church divided the nation. The great majority of the clergy were on the high church side ; the majority of King William's bishops were inclined to latitudinarianism. A dispute arose between the two parties touching the extent of the powers of the Lower House of Convocation. Atterbury thrust himself eagerly into the front rank of the high-churchmen. Those who take a comprehensive and impartial view of his whole career, will not be disposed to give him credit for religious zeal. But it was his nature to be vehement and pugnacious in the cause of every fraternity of which he was a member. He had defended the genuineness of a spurious book simply because Christ Church had put forth an edition of that book ; he now stood up for the clergy against the civil power simply because he was a clergyman, and for the priests against the episcopal order, simply because he was as yet only a priest. He asserted the pretensions of the class to which he belonged in several treatises written with much wit, ingenuity, audacity, and acrimony. In this, as in his first controversy, he was opposed to antagonists whose knowledge of the subject in dispute was far superior to his; but in this, as in his first controversy, he imposed on the multitude by bold assertion, by sarcasm, by declamation, and, above all, by his peculiar knack of exhibiting a little erudition in such a manner as to make it look like a great deal. Having passed himself off on the world as a greater master of classical learning than Bentley, he now passed himself off as a greater master of ecclesiastical learning than Wake or Gibson. By the great body of the clergy he was regarded as the ablest and most intrepid tribune that had ever defended their rights against the oligarchy of prelates. The Lower House of Convocation voted him thanks for his services; the University of Oxford created him a doctor of divinity; and soon after the accession of Anne, while the Tories still had the chief weight in the government, he was promoted to the deanery of Carlisle.

Soon after he had obtained this preferment, the Whig party rose to ascendancy in the state. From that party he could expect no favour. Six years elapsed before a change of fortune took place. At length, in the year 1710, the prosecution of Sacheverell produced a formidable explosion of high-church fanaticism. At such a moment Atterbury could not fail to be conspicuous. His inordinate zeal for the body to which he belonged, his turbulent and aspiring temper, his rare talents for agitation and for

controversy were again signally displayed. He bore
a chief part in framing that artful and eloquent
speech which the accused divine pronounced at the
bar of the Lords, and which presents a singular contrast to the absurd and scurrilous sermon which had
very unwisely been honoured with impeachment.
During the troubled and anxious months which
followed the trial, Atterbury was among the most
active of those pamphleteers who inflamed the nation
against the Whig ministry and the Whig parliament.
When the ministry had been changed and the
parliament dissolved, rewards were showered upon
him. The Lower House of Convocation elected
him prolocutor. The Queen appointed him Dean
of Christ Church on the death of his old friend and
patron Aldrich. The college would have preferred
a gentler ruler. Nevertheless, the new head was
received with every mark of honour. A congratula-
tory oration in Latin was addressed to him in the
magnificent vestibule of the hall; and he in reply
professed the warmest attachment to the venerable
house in which he had been educated, and paid
many gracious compliments to those over whom he
was to preside. But it was not in his nature to be
a mild or an equitable governor. He had left the
chapter of Carlisle distracted by quarrels. He found
Christ Church at peace; but in three months his
despotic and contentious temper did at Christ Church
what it had done at Carlisle. He was succeeded in

both his deaneries by the humane and accomplished Smalridge, who gently complained of the state in which both had been left. "Atterbury goes before, and sets everything on fire. I come after him with a bucket of water." It was said by Atterbury's enemies that he was made a bishop because he was so bad a dean. Under his administration Christ Church was in confusion, scandalous altercations took place, opprobrious words were exchanged; and there was reason to fear that the great Tory college would be ruined by the tyranny of the great Tory doctor. He was soon removed to the bishopric of Rochester, which was then always united with the deanery of Westminster. Still higher dignities seemed to be before him. For, though there were many able men on the episcopal bench, there was none who equalled or approached him in parliamentary talents. Had his party continued in power, it is not improbable that he would have been raised to the archbishopric of Canterbury. The more splendid his prospects, the more reason he had to dread the accession of a family which was well known to be partial to the Whigs. There is every reason to believe that he was one of those politicians who hoped that they might be able, during the life of Anne, to prepare matters in such a way that at her decease there might be little difficulty in setting aside the Act of Settlement and placing the Pretender on the throne. Her sudden death confounded the projects of these conspirators. Atterbury, who wanted no kind of courage, implored his confederates to proclaim James III., and offered to accompany the heralds in lawn sleeves. But he found even the bravest soldiers of his party irresolute, and exclaimed, not, it is said, without interjections which ill became the mouth of a father of the church, that the best of all causes and the most precious of all moments had been pusillanimously thrown away. He acquiesced in what he could not prevent, took the oaths to the House of Hanover, and at the coronation officiated with the outward show of zeal, and did his best to ingratiate himself with the royal family. But his servility was requited with cold contempt. No creature is so revengeful as a proud man who has humbled himself in vain. Atterbury became the most factious and pertinacious of all the opponents of the government. In the House of Lords his oratory, lucid, pointed, lively, and set off with every grace of pronunciation and of gesture, extorted the attention and admiration even of a hostile majority. Some of the most remarkable protests which appear in the journals of the peers were drawn up by him; and, in some of the bitterest of those pamphlets which called on the English to stand up for their country against the aliens who had come from beyond the seas to oppress and plunder her, critics easily detected his style. When the rebellion of 1715 broke out, he refused to sign the paper in which the bishops of the province of Canterbury declared their attachment to the Protestant succession. He busied himself in electioneering, especially at Westminster, where as dean he possessed great influence; and was, indeed, strongly suspected of having once set on a riotous mob to prevent his Whig fellow-citizens from polling.

After having been long in indirect communication with the exiled family, he, in 1717, began to correspond directly with the Pretender. The first letter of the correspondence is extant. In that letter Atterbury boasts of having, during many years past, neglected no opportunity of serving the Jacobite cause. "My daily prayer," he says, "is that you may have success. May I live to see that day, and live no longer than I do what is in my power to forward it." It is to be remembered that he who wrote thus was a man bound to set to the church of which he was overseer an example of strict probity; that he had repeatedly sworn allegiance to the House of Brunswick; that he had assisted in placing the crown on the head of George I., and that he had abjured James III., "without equivocation or mental reservation, on the true faith of a Christian."

It is agreeable to turn from his public to his private life. His turbulent spirit, wearied with faction and treason, now and then required repose, and found it in domestic endearments, and in the society of the most illustrious of the living and of the dead. Of his wife little is known: but between him and his daughter there was an affection singularly close and tender. The gentleness of his manners when he was in the company of a few friends was such as seemed hardly credible to those who knew him only by his writings and speeches. The charm of his "softer hour" has been commemorated by one of those friends in imperishable verse. Though Atterbury's classical attainments were not great, his taste in English literature was excellent; and his admiration of genius was so strong that it overpowered even his political and religious antipathies. His fondness for Milton, the mortal enemy of the Stuarts and of the church, was such as to many Tories seemed a crime. On the sad night on which Addison was laid in the chapel of Henry VII., the Westminster boys remarked that Atterbury read the funeral service with a peculiar tenderness and solemnity. The favourite companions, however, of the great Tory prelate were, as might have been expected, men whose politics had at least a tinge of Toryism. He lived on friendly terms with Swift, Arbuthnot, and Gay. With Prior he had a close intimacy, which some misunderstanding about public affairs at last dissolved. Pope found in Atterbury not only a warm admirer, but a most faithful, fearless, and judicious adviser. The poet was a frequent guest at the episcopal palace among the elms of Bromley, and entertained not the slightest suspicion that his host, now declining in years, confined to an easy chair by gout, and apparently devoted to literature, was deeply concerned in criminal and perilous designs against the government.

The spirit of the Jacobites had been cowed by the events of 1715. It revived in 1721. The failure of the South Sea project, the panic in the money market, the downfall of great commercial houses, the distress from which no part of the kingdom was exempt, had produced general discontent. It seemed not improbable that at such a moment an insurrection might be successful. An insurrection was planned. The streets of London were to be barricaded; the Tower and the Bank were to be surprised; King George, his family, and his chief captains and councillors were to be arrested, and King James was to be proclaimed. The design became known to the duke of Orleans, regent of France, who was on terms of friendship with the House of Hanover. He put the English government on its guard. Some of the chief malcontents were committed to prison; and among them was Atterbury. No bishop of the Church of England had been taken into custody since that memorable day when the applauses and prayers of all London had followed the seven bishops to the gate of the Tower. The Opposition entertained some hope that it might be possible to excite among the people an enthusiasm resembling that of their fathers, who rushed into

the waters of the Thames to implore the blessing of
Sancroft. Pictures of the heroic confessor in his
cell were exhibited at the shop windows. Verses
in his praise were sung about the streets. The
restraints by which he was prevented from communi-
cating with his accomplices were represented as
cruelties worthy of the dungeons of the Inquisition.
Strong appeals were made to the priesthood. Would
they tamely permit so gross an insult to be offered
to their cloth? Would they suffer the ablest, the
most eloquent member of their profession, the man
who had so often stood up for their rights against
the civil power, to be treated like the vilest of mankind? There was considerable excitement; but it
was allayed by a temperate and artful letter to the
clergy, the work, in all probability, of Bishop Gibson,
who stood high in the favour of Walpole, and shortly
after became minister for ecclesiastical affairs.

Atterbury remained in close confinement during
some months. He had carried on his correspondence
with the exiled family so cautiously that the circum-
stantial proofs of his guilt, though sufficient to
produce entire moral conviction, were not sufficient
to justify legal conviction. He could be reached
only by a bill of pains and penalties. Such a bill
the Whig party, then decidedly predominant in
both houses, was quite prepared to support. Many
hot-headed members of that party were eager to follow
the precedent which had been set in the case of Sir

John Fenwick, and to pass an act for cutting off the
bishop's head. Cadogan, who commanded the army,
a brave soldier, but a headstrong politician, is said
to have exclaimed with great vehemence : " Fling
him to the lions in the Tower." But the wiser and
more humane Walpole was always unwilling to shed
blood ; and his influence prevailed. When parliament met, the evidence against the bishop was laid
before committees of both houses. Those committees
reported that his guilt was proved. In the Commons
a resolution, pronouncing him a traitor, was carried
by nearly two to one. A bill was then introduced
which provided that he should be deprived of his
spiritual dignities, that he should be banished for
life, and that no British subject should hold any
intercourse with him except by the royal permission.

This bill passed the Commons with little difficulty.
For the bishop, though invited to defend himself,
chose to reserve his defence for the assembly of
which he was a member. In the Lords the contest
was sharp. The young Duke of Wharton, distinguished by his parts, his dissoluteness, and his
versatility, spoke for Atterbury with great effect ;
and Atterbury's own voice was heard for the last
time by that unfriendly audience which had so often
listened to him with mingled aversion and delight.
He produced few witnesses, nor did those witnesses
say much that could be of service to him. Among
them was Pope. He was called to prove that, while

he was an inmate of the palace at Bromley, the bishop's time was completely occupied by literary and domestic matters, and that no leisure was left for plotting. But Pope, who was quite unaccustomed to speak in public, lost his head, and, as he afterwards owned, though he had only ten words to say, made two or three blunders.

The bill finally passed the Lords by eighty-three votes to forty-three. The bishops, with a single exception, were in the majority. Their conduct drew on them a sharp taunt from Lord Bathurst, a warm friend of Atterbury and a zealous Tory. "The wild Indians," he said, "give no quarter, because they believe that they shall inherit the skill and prowess of every adversary whom they destroy. Perhaps the animosity of the right reverend prelates to their brother may be explained in the same way."

Atterbury took leave of those whom he loved with a dignity and tenderness worthy of a better man. Three fine lines of his favourite poet were often in his mouth:—

"Some natural tears he dropped, but wiped them soon :
The world was all before him, where to chuse
His place of rest, and providence his guide."

At parting he presented Pope with a Bible, and said with a disingenuousness of which no man who had studied the Bible to much purpose would have been guilty: "If ever you learn that I have any dealings with the Pretender, I give you leave to say that my punishment is just." Pope at this time really believed the bishop to be an injured man. Arbuthnot seems to have been of the same opinion. Swift, a few months later, ridiculed with great bitterness, in the Voyage to Laputa, the evidence which had satisfied the two houses of parliament. Soon, however, the most partial friends of the banished prelate ceased to assert his innocence, and contented themselves with lamenting and excusing what they could not defend. After a short stay at Brussels, he had taken up his abode at Paris, and had become the leading man among the Jacobite refugees who were assembled there. He was invited to Rome by the Pretender, who then held his mock court under the immediate protection of the Pope. But Atterbury felt that a bishop of the Church of England would be strangely out of place at the Vatican, and declined the invitation. During some months, however, he might flatter himself that he stood high in the good graces of James. The correspondence between the master and the servant was constant, Atterbury's merits were warmly acknowledged, his advice was respectfully received, and he was, as Bolingbroke had been before him, the prime minister of a king without a kingdom. But the new favourite found, as Bolingbroke had found before him, that it was quite as hard to keep the shadow of power under a vagrant and mendicant prince as to keep the reality of power at Westminster. Though

James had neither territories nor revenues, neither army nor navy, there was more faction and more intrigue among his courtiers than among those of his successful rival. Atterbury·soon perceived that his counsels were disregarded if not distrusted. His proud spirit was deeply wounded. He quitted Paris, fixed his residence at Montpelier, gave up politics, and devoted himself entirely to letters. In the sixth year of his exile he had so severe an illness that his daughter, herself in very delicate health, determined to run all risks that she might see him once more. Having obtained a license from the English Government, she went by sea to Bordeaux, but landed there in such a state that she could travel only by boat or in a litter. Her father, in spite of his infirmities, set out from Montpelier to meet her; and she, with the impatience which is often the sign of approaching death, hastened towards him. Those who were about her in vain implored her to travel slowly. She said that every hour was precious, that she only wished to see her papa and to die. She met him at Toulouse, embraced him, received from his hand the sacred bread and wine, and thanked God that they had passed one day in each other's society before they parted for ever. She died that night.

It was some time before even the strong mind of Atterbury recovered from this cruel blow. As soon as he was himself again he became eager for action and conflict: for grief, which disposes gentle natures to retirement, to inaction, and to meditation, only makes restless spirits more restless. The Pretender, dull and bigoted as he was, had found out that he had not acted wisely in parting with one who, though a heretic, was, in abilities and accomplishments, the foremost man of the Jacobite party. The bishop was courted back, and was without much difficulty induced to return to Paris and to become once more the phantom minister of a phantom monarchy. But his long and troubled life was drawing to a close. To the last, however, his intellect retained all its keenness and vigour. He learned, in the ninth year of his banishment, that he had been accused by Oldmixon, as dishonest and malignant a scribbler as any that has been saved from oblivion by the Dunciad, of having, in concert with other Christ Churchmen, garbled Clarendon's History of the Rebellion. The charge, as respected Atterbury, had not the slightest foundation: for he was not one of the editors of the History, and never saw it till it was printed. He published a short vindication of himself, which is a model in its kind, luminous, temperate, and dignified. A copy of this little work he sent to the Pretender, with a letter singularly eloquent and graceful. It was impossible, the old man said, that he should write anything on such a subject without being reminded of the resemblance between his own fate and that of Clarendon. They were the only two English subjects that had ever

been banished from their country and debarred from
all communication with their friends by act of parliament.   But here the resemblance ended.   One of
the exiles had been so happy to bear a chief part in
the restoration of the Royal house.   All that the
other could now do was to die asserting the rights
of that house to the last.   A few weeks after this
letter was written Atterbury died.   He had just
completed his seventieth year.

His body was brought to England, and laid, with
great privacy, under the nave of Westminster Abbey.
Only three mourners followed the coffin.   No inscription marks the grave.   That the epitaph with which
Pope honoured the memory of his friend does not
appear on the walls of the great national cemetery
is no subject of regret: for nothing worse was ever
written by Colley Cibber.

Those who wish for more complete information
about Atterbury may easily collect it from his
sermons and his controversial writings, from the
report of the parliamentary proceedings against him,
which will be found in the State Trials; from the
five volumes of his correspondence, edited by Mr.
Nichols, and from the first volume of the Stuart
papers, edited by Mr. Glover.   A very indulgent
but a very interesting account of the Bishop's
political career will be found in Lord Mahon's
valuable History of England.

JOHN BUNYAN, the most popular religious writer in the English language, was born at Elstow, about a mile from Bedford, in the year 1628. He may be said to have been born a tinker. The tinkers then formed a hereditary caste, which was held in no high estimation. They were generally vagrants and pilferers, and were often confounded with the gipsies, whom in truth they nearly resembled. Bunyan's father was more respectable than most of the tribe. He had a fixed residence, and was able to send his son to a village school where reading and writing were taught.

The years of John's boyhood were those during which the puritan spirit was in the highest vigour all over England; and nowhere had that spirit more influence than in Bedfordshire. It is not wonderful, therefore, that a lad to whom nature had given a powerful imagination and sensibility which amounted to a disease, should have been early haunted by religious terrors. Before he was ten, his sports were

interrupted by fits of remorse and despair; and his
sleep was disturbed by dreams of fiends trying to fly
away with him.   As he grew older, his mental conflicts became still more violent.   The strong language
in which he described them has strangely misled all
his biographers except Mr. Southey.   It has long
been an ordinary practice with pious writers to cite
Bunyan as an instance of the supernatural power of
divine grace to rescue the human soul from the
lowest depths of wickedness.   He is called in one
book the most notorious of profligates; in another,
the brand plucked from the burning.   He is designated in Mr. Ivimey's History of the Baptists as the
depraved Bunyan, the wicked tinker of Elstow.
Mr. Ryland, a man once of great note among the
Dissenters, breaks out into the following rhapsody:—
"No man of common sense and common integrity
can deny that Bunyan was a practical atheist, a
worthless contemptible infidel, a vile rebel to God
and goodness, a common profligate, a soul-despising,
a soul-murdering, a soul-damning, thoughtless wretch
as could exist on the face of the earth.   Now be
astonished, O heavens, to eternity! and wonder, O
earth and hell! while time endures.   Behold this
very man become a miracle of mercy, a mirror of
wisdom, goodness, holiness, truth, and love."   But
whoever takes the trouble to examine the evidence
will find that the good men who wrote this had
been deceived by a phraseology which, as they had

been hearing it and using it all their lives, they ought to have understood better. There cannot be a greater mistake than to infer from the strong expressions in which a devout man bemoans his exceeding sinfulness, that he has led a worse life than his neighbours. Many excellent persons, whose moral character from boyhood to old age has been free from any stain discernible to their fellow creatures, have, in their autobiographies and diaries, applied to themselves, and doubtless with sincerity, epithets as severe as could be applied to Titus Oates or Mrs. Brownrigg. It is quite certain that Bunyan was, at eighteen, what, in any but the most austerely puritanical circles, would have been considered as a young man of singular gravity and innocence. Indeed, it may be remarked that he, like many other penitents who, in general terms, acknowledge themselves to have been the worst of mankind, fired up, and stood vigorously on his defence, whenever any particular charge was brought against him by others. He declares, it is true, that he had let loose the reins on the neck of his lusts, that he had delighted in all transgressions against the divine law, and that he had been the ringleader of the youth of Elstow in all manner of vice. But when those who wished him ill accused him of licentious amours, he called on God and the angels to attest his purity. No woman, he said, in heaven, earth, or hell, could charge him with having ever made any improper advances to her. Not only had he been strictly faithful to his wife; but he had, even before his marriage, been perfectly spotless. It does not appear from his own confessions, or from the railings of his enemies, that he ever was drunk in his life. One bad habit he contracted, that of using profane language; but he tells us that a single reproof cured him so effectually that he never offended again. The worst that can be laid to the charge of this poor youth, whom it has been the fashion to represent as the most desperate of reprobates, as a village Rochester, is, that he had a great liking for some diversions, quite harmless in themselves, but condemned by the rigid precisians among whom he lived, and for whose opinion he had a great respect. The four chief sins of which he was guilty were dancing, ringing the bells of the parish church, playing at tipcat, and reading the History of Sir Bevis of Southampton. A Rector of the school of Laud would have held such a young man up to the whole parish as a model. But Bunyan's notions of good and evil had been learned in a very different school; and he was made miserable by the conflict between his tastes and his scruples.

When he was about seventeen, the ordinary course of his life was interrupted by an event which gave a lasting colour to his thoughts. He enlisted in the parliamentary army, and served during the decisive campaign of 1645. All that we know of his military career is, that, at the siege of Leicester, one of his comrades, who had taken his post, was killed by a shot from the town. Bunyan ever after considered himself as having been saved from death by the special interference of Providence. It may be observed, that his imagination was strongly impressed by the glimpse which he had caught of the pomp of war. To the last he loved to draw his illustrations of sacred things from camps and fortresses, from guns, drums, trumpets, flags of truce, and regiments arrayed, each under its own banner. His Greatheart, his Captain Boanerges, and his Captain Credence, are evidently portraits, of which the originals were among those martial saints who fought and expounded in Fairfax's army.

In a few months Bunyan returned home, and married. His wife had some pious relations, and brought him as her only portion some pious books. And now his mind, excitable by nature, very imperfectly disciplined by education, and exposed, without any protection, to the infectious virulence of the enthusiasm which was then epidemic in England, began to be fearfully disordered. In outward things he soon became a strict Pharisee. He was constant in attendance at prayers and sermons. His favourite amusements were, one after another, relinquished, though not without many painful struggles. In the middle of a game at tipcat he paused, and stood staring wildly upwards with his stick in his hand.

He had heard a voice asking him whether he would
leave his sins and go to heaven, or keep his sins and
go to hell; and he had seen an awful countenance
frowning on him from the sky.   The odious vice of
bell-ringing he renounced; but he still for a time
ventured to go to the church tower and look on
while others pulled the ropes.   But soon the thought
struck him that, if he persisted in such wickedness,
the steeple would fall on his head; and he fled in
terror from the accursed place.   To give up dancing
on the village green was still harder; and some
months elapsed before he had the fortitude to part
with his darling sin.   When this last sacrifice had
been made, he was, even when tried by the maxims
of that austere time, faultless.   All Elstow talked of
him as an eminently pious youth.   But his own
mind was more unquiet than ever.   Having nothing
more to do in the way of visible reformation, yet
finding in religion no pleasures to supply the place of
the juvenile amusements which he had relinquished,
he began to apprehend that he lay under some special
malediction; and he was tormented by a succession
of fantasies which seemed likely to drive him to
suicide or to Bedlam.

At one time he took it into his head that all persons
of Israelite blood would be saved, and tried to make
out that he partook of that blood; but his hopes
were speedily destroyed by his father, who seems
to have had no ambition to be regarded as a Jew.

At another time Bunyan was disturbed by a strange dilemma: "If I have not faith, I am lost; if I have faith, I can work miracles." He was tempted to cry to the puddles between Elstow and Bedford, "Be ye dry," and to stake his eternal hopes on the event.

Then he took up a notion that the day of grace for Bedford and the neighbouring villages was passed; that all who were to be saved in that part of England were already converted; and that he had begun to pray and strive some months too late.

Then he was harassed by doubts whether the Turks were not in the right, and the Christians in the wrong. Then he was troubled by a maniacal impulse which prompted him to pray to the trees, to a broomstick, to the parish bull. As yet, however, he was only entering the Valley of the Shadow of Death. Soon the darkness grew thicker. Hideous forms floated before him. Sounds of cursing and wailing were in his ears. His way ran through stench and fire, close to the mouth of the bottomless pit. He began to be haunted by a strange curiosity about the unpardonable sin, and by a morbid longing to commit it. But the most frightful of all the forms which his disease took was a propensity to utter blasphemy, and especially to renounce his share in the benefits of the redemption. Night and day, in bed, at table, at work, evil spirits, as he imagined, were repeating close to his ear the words,

"Sell him, sell him." He struck at the hobgoblins; he pushed them from him; but still they were ever at his side. He cried out in answer to them, hour after hour, "Never, never; not for thousands of worlds; not for thousands." At length, worn out by this long agony, he suffered the fatal words to escape him, "Let him go if he will." Then his misery became more fearful than ever. He had done what could not be forgiven. He had forfeited his part of the great sacrifice. Like Esau, he had sold his birthright; and there was no longer any place for repentance. "None," he afterwards wrote, "knows the terrors of those days but myself." He has described his sufferings with singular energy, simplicity, and pathos. He envied the brutes; he envied the very stones on the street, and the tiles on the houses. The sun seemed to withhold its light and warmth from him. His body, though cast in a sturdy mould, and though still in the highest vigour of youth, trembled whole days together with the fear of death and judgment. He fancied that this trembling was the sign set on the worst reprobates, the sign which God had put on Cain. The unhappy man's emotion destroyed his power of digestion. He had such pains that he expected to burst asunder like Judas, whom he regarded as his prototype.

Neither the books which Bunyan read, nor the advisers whom he consulted, were likely to do much good in a case like his. His small library had received a most unseasonable addition, the account of the lamentable end of Francis Spira. One ancient man of high repute for piety, whom the sufferer consulted, gave an opinion which might well have produced fatal consequences. "I am afraid," said Bunyan, "that I have committed the sin against the Holy Ghost." "Indeed," said the old fanatic, "I am afraid that you have."

At length the clouds broke; the light became clearer and clearer; and the enthusiast, who had imagined that he was branded with the mark of the first murderer, and destined to the end of the arch traitor, enjoyed peace and a cheerful confidence in the mercy of God. Years elapsed, however, before his nerves, which had been so perilously overstrained, recovered their tone. When he had joined a Baptist society at Bedford, and was for the first time admitted to partake of the Eucharist, it was with difficulty that he could refrain from imprecating destruction on his brethren while the cup was passing from hand to hand. After he had been some time a member of the congregation, he began to preach; and his sermons produced a powerful effect. He was indeed illiterate; but he spoke to illiterate men. The severe training through which he had passed had given him such an experimental knowledge of all the modes of religious melancholy as he could never have gathered from books; and his vigorous genius, animated by a fervent spirit of devotion, enabled him not only to exercise a great influence over the vulgar, but even to extort the half contemptuous admiration of scholars. Yet it was long before he ceased to be tormented by an impulse which urged him to utter words of horrible impiety in the pulpit.

Counter-irritants are of as great use in moral as in physical diseases. It should seem that Bunyan was finally relieved from the internal sufferings which had embittered his life by sharp persecution from without. He had been five years a preacher, when the Restoration put it in the power of the Cavalier gentlemen and clergymen all over the country to oppress the Dissenters; and, of all the Dissenters whose history is known to us, he was perhaps the most hardly treated. In November 1660 he was flung into Bedford gaol; and there he remained, with some intervals of partial and precarious liberty, during twelve years. His persecutors tried to extort from him a promise that he would abstain from preaching; but he was convinced that he was divinely set apart and commissioned to be a teacher of righteousness, and he was fully determined to obey God rather than man. He was brought before several tribunals, laughed at, caressed, reviled, menaced, but in vain. He was facetiously told that he was quite right in thinking that he ought not to hide his gift; but that his real gift was skill in repairing old kettles. He was compared to Alexander the coppersmith. He was told that, if he would give up preaching he should be instantly liberated. He was warned that, if he persisted in disobeying the law, he would be liable to banishment, and that, if he were found in England after a certain time, his neck would be stretched. His answer was, "If you let me out to-day, I will preach again to-morrow." Year after year he lay patiently in a dungeon, compared with which the worst prison now to be found in the island is a palace. His fortitude is the more extraordinary, because his domestic feelings were unusually strong. Indeed, he was considered by his stern brethren as somewhat too fond and indulgent a parent. He had several small children, and among them a daughter who was blind, and whom he loved with peculiar tenderness. He could not, he said, bear even to let the wind blow on her; and now she must suffer cold and hunger; she must beg; she must be beaten; "yet," he added, "I must, I must do it." While he lay in prison he could do nothing in the way of his old trade for the support of his family. He determined, therefore to take up a new trade. He learned to make long tagged thread laces; and many thousands of these articles were furnished by him to the hawkers. While his hands were thus busied, he had other employment for his mind and his lips. He gave religious instruction to his fellow-captives, and formed from among them a little flock, of which he

was himself the pastor. He studied indefatigably
the few books which he possessed. His two chief
companions were the Bible and Fox's Book of
Martyrs. His knowledge of the Bible was such that
he might have been called a living concordance; and
on the margin of his copy of the Book of Martyrs
are still legible the ill spelt lines of doggrel in which
he expressed his reverence for the brave sufferers,
and his implacable enmity to the mystical Babylon.

At length he began to write, and, though it was
some time before he discovered where his strength
lay, his writings were not unsuccessful. They were
coarse, indeed, but they showed a keen mother wit,
a great command of the homely mother tongue, an
intimate knowledge of the English Bible, and a vast
and dearly bought spiritual experience. They therefore, when the corrector of the press had improved
the syntax and the spelling, were well received by
the humbler class of Dissenters.

Much of Bunyan's time was spent in controversy.
He wrote sharply against the Quakers, whom he
seems always to have held in utter abhorrence. It
is, however, a remarkable fact that he adopted one
of their peculiar fashions : his practice was to write,
not November or December, but eleventh month and
twelfth month.

He wrote against the liturgy of the Church of
England. No two things, according to him, had less
affinity than the form of prayer and the spirit of

prayer. Those, he said with much point, who have
most of the spirit of prayer are all to be found in
gaol ; and those who have most zeal for the form of
prayer are all to be found at the alehouse. The
doctrinal articles, on the other hand, he warmly
praised, and defended against some Arminian clergymen who had signed them. The most acrimonious
of all his works is his answer to Edward Fowler,
afterwards bishop of Gloucester, an excellent man.
but not free from the taint of Pelagianism.

Bunyan had also a dispute with some of the chiefs
of the sect to which he belonged. He doubtless
held with perfect sincerity the distinguishing tenet
of that sect, but he did not consider that tenet as
one of high importance, and willingly joined in communion with pious Presbyterians and Independents.
The sterner Baptists, therefore, loudly pronounced
him a false brother. A controversy arose which
long survived the original combatants. In our own
time the cause which Bunyan had defended with
rude logic and rhetoric against Kiffin and Danvers
was pleaded by Robert Hall with an ingenuity and
eloquence such as no polemical writer has ever
surpassed.

During the years which immediately followed
the Restoration, Bunyan's confinement seems to have
been strict. But as the passions of 1660 cooled, as
the hatred with which the Puritans had been regarded
while their reign was recent gave place to pity, he

. was less and less harshly treated. The distress of
his family, and his own patience, courage, and piety,
softened the hearts of his persecutors. Like his
own Christian in the cage, he found protectors even
among the crowd of Vanity Fair. The Bishop of
the diocese, Dr. Barlow, is said to have interceded
for him. At length the prisoner was suffered to
pass most of his time beyond the walls of the gaol,
on condition, as it should seem, that he remained
within the town of Bedford.

He owed his complete liberation to one of the
worst acts of one of the worst governments that
England has ever seen. In 1671 the Cabal was in
power. Charles II. had concluded the treaty by
which he bound himself to set up the Roman Catholic
religion in England. The first step which he took
towards that end was to annul, by an unconstitutional
exercise of his prerogative, all the penal statutes
against the Roman Catholics; and, in order to disguise his real design, he annulled at the same time
the penal statutes against Protestant nonconformists.
Bunyan was consequently set at large. In the first
warmth of his gratitude he published a tract in
which he compared Charles to that humane and
generous Persian king who, though not himself
blessed with the light of the true religion, favoured
the chosen people, and permitted them, after years
of captivity, to rebuild their beloved temple. To
candid men, who consider how much Bunyan had

suffered, and how little he could guess the secret designs of the court, the unsuspicious thankfulness with which he accepted the precious boon of freedom will not appear to require any apology.

Before he left his prison he had begun the book which has made his name immortal. The history of that book is remarkable. The author was, as he tells us, writing a treatise, in which he had occasion to speak of the stages of the Christian progress. He compared that progress, as many others had compared it, to a pilgrimage. Soon his quick wit discovered innumerable points of similarity which had escaped his predecessors. Images came crowding on his mind faster than he could put them into words, quagmires and pits, steep hills, dark and horrible glens, soft vales, sunny pastures, a gloomy castle of which the courtyard was strewn with the skulls and bones of murdered prisoners, a town all bustle and splendour, like London on the Lord Mayor's Day, and the narrow path, straight as a rule could make it, running on up hill and down hill, through city and through wilderness, to the Black River and the Shining Gate. He had found out, as most people would have said, by accident, as he would doubtless have said, by the guidance of Providence, where his powers lay. He had no suspicion, indeed, that he was producing a masterpiece. He could not guess what place his allegory would occupy in English literature; for of English litera-

ture he knew nothing. Those who suppose him to
have studied the Fairy Queen might easily be con-
futed, if this were the proper place for a detailed
examination of the passages in which the two allego-
ries have been thought to resemble each other. The
only work of fiction, in all probability, with which
he could compare his Pilgrim, was his old favourite,
the legend of Sir Bevis of Southampton. He would
have thought it a sin to borrow any time from the
serious business of his life, from his expositions, his
controversies, and his lace tags, for the purpose of
amusing himself with what he considered merely as
a trifle. It was only, he assures us, at spare moments that he returned to the House Beautiful,
the Delectable Mountains, and the Enchanted
Ground. He had no assistance. Nobody but himself saw a line till the whole was complete. He
then consulted his pious friends. Some were pleased.
Others were much scandalized. It was a vain story,
a mere romance, about giants, and lions, and goblins,
and warriors, sometimes fighting with monsters, and
sometimes regaled by fair ladies in stately palaces.
The loose atheistical wits at Will's might write such
stuff to divert the painted Jezebels of the court : but
did it become a minister of the gospel to copy the
evil fashions of the world ? There had been a time
when the cant of such fools would have made
Bunyan miserable. But that time was passed ; and
his mind was now in a firm and healthy state. He

saw that, in employing fiction to make truth clear
and goodness attractive, he was only following the
example which every Christian ought to propose to
himself; and he determined to print.

The *Pilgrim's Progress* stole silently into the
world. Not a single copy of the first edition is
known to be in existence. The year of publication
has not been ascertained. It is probable that, during some months, the little volume circulated only
among poor and obscure sectaries. But soon the
irresistible charm of a book which gratified the imagination of the reader with all the action and scenery
of a fairy tale, which exercised his ingenuity by
setting him to discover a multitude of curious analo-
gies, which interested his feelings for human beings,
frail like himself, and struggling with temptations
from within and from without, which every moment
drew a smile from him by some stroke of quaint yet
simple pleasantry, and nevertheless left on his mind
a sentiment of reverence for God and of sympathy
for man, began to produce its effect. In puritanical
circles, from which plays and novels were strictly
excluded, that effect was such as no work of genius,
though it were superior to the Iliad, to Don Quixote,
or to Othello, can ever produce on a mind accustomed to indulge in literary luxury. In 1678 came
forth a second edition with additions; and then the
demand became immense. In the four following
years the book was reprinted six times. The eighth

edition, which contains the last improvements made
by the author, was published in 1682, the ninth in
1684, the tenth in 1685. The help of the engraver
had early been called in ; and tens of thousands of
children looked with terror and delight on execrable
copperplates, which represented Christian thrusting
his sword into Apollyon, or writhing in the grasp of
Giant Despair. In Scotland, and in some of the
colonies, the Pilgrim was even more popular than in
his native country. Bunyan has told us, with very
pardonable vanity, that in New England his dream
was the daily subject of the conversation of thousands, and was thought worthy to appear in the
most superb binding. He had numerous admirers
in Holland, and among the Huguenots of France.
With the pleasures, however, he experienced some
of the pains of eminence. Knavish booksellers put
forth volumes of trash under his name, and envious
scribblers maintained it to be impossible that the
poor ignorant tinker should really be the author of
the book which was called his.

He took the best way to confound both those
who counterfeited him and those who slandered him.
He continued to work the Gold-field which he had
discovered, and to draw from it new treasures, not
indeed with quite such ease and in quite such abun-
dance as when the precious soil was still virgin, but
yet with success which left all competition far behind. In 1684 appeared the second part of the

Pilgrim's Progress. It was soon followed by the *Holy War*, which, if the *Pilgrim's Progress* did not exist, would be the best allegory that ever was written.

Bunyan's place in society was now very different from what it had been. There had been a time when many Dissenting ministers, who could talk Latin and read Greek, had affected to treat him with scorn. But his fame and influence now far exceeded theirs. He had so great an authority among the Baptists that he was popularly called Bishop Bunyan. His episcopal visitations were annual. From Bedford he rode every year to London, and preached there to large and attentive congregations. From London he went his circuit through the country, animating the zeal of his brethren, collecting and distributing alms, and making up quarrels. The magistrates seem in general to have given him little trouble, . But there is reason to believe that, in the year 1685, he was in some danger of again occupying his old quarters in Bedford gaol. In that year the rash and wicked enterprise of Monmouth gave the Government a pretext for prosecuting the nonconformists ; and scarcely one eminent divine of the Presbyterian, Independent, or Baptist persuasion remained unmolested. Baxter was in prison : Howe was driven into exile : Henry was arrested. Two eminent Baptists, with whom Bunyan had been engaged in controversy, were in great peril and distress. Danvers was in danger of being hanged ; and Kiffin's grandsons were actually hanged. The tradition is that, during those evil days, Bunyan was forced to disguise himself as a waggoner, and that he preached to his congregation at Bedford in a smock-frock, with a cart-whip in his hand. But soon a great change took place. James the Second was at open war with the church, and found it necessary to court the Dissenters. Some of the creatures of the government tried to secure the aid of Bunyan. They probably knew that he had written in praise of the indulgence of 1672, and therefore hoped that he might be equally pleased with the indulgence of 1687. But fifteen years of thought, observation, and commerce with the world had made him wiser. Nor were the cases exactly parallel. Charles was a professed Protestant : James was a professed Papist. The object of Charles's indulgence was disguised : the object of James's indulgence was patent. Bunyan was not deceived. He exhorted his hearers to prepare themselves by fasting and prayer for the danger which menaced their civil and religious liberties, and refused even to speak to the courtier who came down to remodel the corporation of Bedford, and who, as was supposed, had it in charge to offer some municipal dignity to the Bishop of the Baptists.

Bunyan did not live to see the Revolution. In the summer of 1688 he undertook to plead the cause of a son with an angry father, and at length prevailed on the old man not to disinherit the young one. This good work cost the benevolent inter-cessor his life. He had to ride through heavy rain. He came drenched to his lodgings on Snow Hill, was seized with a violent fever, and died in a few days. He was buried in Bunhill Fields ; and the spot where he lies is still regarded by the noncon-formists with a feeling which seems scarcely in harmony with the stern spirit of their theology. Many puritans to whom the respect paid by Roman Catholics to the reliques and tombs of saints seemed childish or sinful, are said to have begged with their dying breath that their coffins might be placed as near as possible to the coffin of the author of the *Pilgrim's Progress.*

The fame of Bunyan during his life, and during the century which followed his death, was indeed great, but was almost entirely confined to religious families of the middle and lower classes. Very seldom was he during that time mentioned with respect by any writer of great literary eminence. Young coupled his prose with the poetry of the wretched D'Urfey. In the Spiritual Quixote, the adventures of Christian are ranked with those of Jack the Giant-Killer and John Hickathrift. Cow-per ventured to praise the great allegorist, but did not venture to name him. It is a significant cir-cumstance that, till a recent period, all the numerous

editions of the *Pilgrim's Progress* were evidently
meant for the cottage and the servant's hall. The
paper, the printing, the plates, were all of the
meanest description. In general, when the educated
minority and the common people differ about the
merit of a book, the opinion of the educated minority finally prevails. The *Pilgrim's Progress* is
perhaps the only book about which, after the
lapse of a hundred years, the educated minority has
come over to the opinion of the common people.

The attempts which have been made to improve
and to imitate this book are not to be numbered.
It has been done into verse : it has been done
into modern English. The Pilgrimage of Tender
Conscience, the Pilgrimage of Good Intent, the
.Pilgrimage of Seek Truth, the Pilgrimage of Theo-
philus, the Infant Pilgrim, the Hindoo Pilgrim, are
among the many feeble copies of the great original.
But the peculiar glory of Bunyan is that those who
most hated his doctrines have tried to borrow the
help of his genius. A Catholic version of his par-
able may be seen with the head of the Virgin in the
title page. On the other hand, those Antinomians
for whom his Calvinism is not strong enough, may
study the pilgrimage of Hephzibah, in which nothing
will be found which can be construed into an admission of free agency and universal redemption.
But the most extraordinary of all the acts of Van-
· dalism by which a fine work of art was ever defaced

was committed so late as the year 1853. It was determined to transform the *Pilgrim's Progress* into a Tractarian book. The task was not easy : for it was necessary to make the two sacraments the most prominent objects in the allegory ; and of all Christian theologians, avowed Quakers excepted, Bunyan was the one in whose system the sacraments held the least prominent place. However, the Wicket Gate became a type of baptism, and the House Beautiful of the Eucharist. The effect of this change is such as assuredly the ingenious person who made it never contemplated. For, as not a single pilgrim passes through the Wicket Gate in infancy, and as Faithful hurries past the House Beautiful without stopping, the lesson which the fable in its altered shape teaches, is that none but adults ought to be baptized, and that the Eucharist may safely be neglected. Nobody would have discovered from the original *Pilgrim's Progress* that the author was not a Pædobaptist. To turn his book into a book against Pædobaptism was an achievement reserved for an Anglo-Catholic divine. Such blunders must necessarily be committed by every man who mutilates parts of a great work, without taking a comprehensive view of the whole.

OLIVER GOLDSMITH.

———◆———

OLIVER GOLDSMITH, one of the most pleasing English writers of the eighteenth century.   He was of a Protestant and Saxon family which had been long settled in Ireland, and which had, like most other Protestant and Saxon families, been, in troubled times, harassed and put in fear by the native population.   His father, Charles Goldsmith, studied in the reign of Queen Anne at the diocesan school of Elphin, became attached to the daughter of the schoolmaster, married her, took orders, and settled at a place called Pallas in the county of Longford. There he with difficulty supported his wife and children on what he could earn, partly as a curate and partly as a farmer.

At Pallas Oliver Goldsmith was born in November 1728.   That spot was then, for all practical purposes, almost as remote from the busy and splendid capital in which his later years were passed, as any clearing in Upper Canada or any sheep-walk in Australasia now is.   Even at this day those enthusiasts who

venture to make a pilgrimage to the birthplace of
the poet are forced to perform the latter part of their
journey on foot.   The hamlet lies far from any high
road, on a dreary plain which, in wet weather, is
often a lake.   The lanes would break any jaunting
car to pieces; and there are ruts and sloughs through
which the most strongly built wheels cannot be
dragged.   .

While Oliver was still a child his father was
presented to a living worth about £200 a year, in
the county of Westmeath.   The family accordingly
quitted their cottage in the wilderness for a spacious
house on a frequented road, near the village of
Lissoy.   Here the boy was taught his letters by a
maid-servant, and was sent in his seventh year to a
village school kept by an old quartermaster on half-
pay, who professed to teach nothing but reading,
writing and arithmetic, but who had an inexhaustible
fund of stories about ghosts, banshees, and fairies,
about the great Rapparee chiefs, Baldearg O'Donnell
and galloping Hogan, and about the exploits of
Peterborough and Stanhope, the surprise of Monjuich,
and the glorious disaster of Brihuega.   This man
must have been of the Protestant religion; but he
was of the aboriginal race, and not only spoke the
Irish language, but could pour forth unpremeditated
Irish verses.   Oliver early became, and through life
continued to be, a passionate admirer of the Irish
music, and especially of the compositions of Carolan,

some of the last notes of whose harp he heard. It ought to be added that Oliver, though by birth one of the Englishry, and though connected by numerous ties with the Established Church, never showed the least sign of that contemptuous antipathy with which, in his days, the ruling minority in Ireland too generally regarded the subject majority. So far indeed was he from sharing in the opinions and feelings of the caste to which he belonged, that he conceived an aversion to the Glorious and Immortal Memory, and, even when George the Third was on the throne, maintained that nothing but the restoration of the banished dynasty could save the country.

From the humble academy kept by the old soldier Goldsmith was removed in his ninth year. He went to several grammar-schools and acquired some knowledge of the ancient languages. His life at this time seems to have been far from happy. He had, as appears from the admirable portrait of him at Knowle, features harsh even to ugliness. The small-pox had set its mark on him with more than usual severity. His stature was small, and his limbs ill put together. Among boys little tenderness is shown to personal defects; and the ridicule excited by poor Oliver's appearance was heightened by a peculiar simplicity and a disposition to blunder which he retained to the last. He became the common butt of boys and masters, was pointed at as a fright in the play-ground, and flogged as a dunce in the school-room. When he had risen to eminence, those who had once derided him ransacked their memory for the events of his early years, and recited repartees and couplets which had dropped from him, and which, though little noticed at the time, were supposed, a quarter of a century later, to indicate the powers which produced the *Vicar of Wakefield* and the *Deserted Village.*

In his seventeenth year Oliver went up to Trinity College, Dublin, as a sizar. The sizars paid nothing for food and tuition, and very little for lodging; but they had to perform some menial services from which they have long been relieved. They swept the court : they carried up the dinner to the fellows' table, and changed the plates and poured out the ale of the rulers of the society. Goldsmith was quartered, not alone, in a garret, on the window of which his name, scrawled by himself, is still read with interest. From such garrets many men of less parts than his have made their way to the woolsack or to the episcopal bench. But Goldsmith, while he suffered all the humiliations, threw away all the advantages of his situation. He neglected the studies of the place, stood low at the examinations, was turned down to the bottom of his class for playing the buffoon in the lecture room, was severely reprimanded for pumping on a constable, and was caned by a brutal tutor for giving a ball in the attic story of the college to some gay youths and damsels from the city.

While Oliver was leading at Dublin a life divided between squalid distress and squalid dissipation, his father died, leaving a mere pittance. The youth obtained his bachelor's degree, and left the university. During some time the humble dwelling to which his widowed mother had retired was his home. He was now in his twenty-first year; it was necessary that he should do something; and his education seemed to have fitted him to do nothing but to dress himself in gaudy colours, of which he was as fond as a magpie, to take a hand at cards, to sing Irish airs, to play the flute, to angle in summer, and to tell ghost stories by the fire in winter. He tried five or six professions in turn without success. He applied for ordination; but, as he applied in scarlet clothes, he was speedily turned out of the episcopal palace. He then became tutor in an opulent family, but soon quitted his situation in consequence of a dispute about play. Then he determined to emigrate to America. His relations, with much satisfaction, saw him set out for Cork on a good horse, with thirty pounds in his pocket. But in six weeks he came back on a miserable hack, without a penny, and informed his mother that the ship in which he had taken his passage, having got a fair wind while he was at a party of pleasure, had sailed without him. Then he resolved to study the law. A generous kinsman advanced fifty pounds. With this sum Goldsmith went to Dublin, was enticed into a gaming house, and lost every shilling. He then thought of medicine. A small purse was made up; and in his twenty-fourth year he was sent to Edinburgh. At Edinburgh he passed eighteen months in nominal attendance on lectures, and picked up some superficial information about chemistry and natural history. Thence he went to Leyden, still pretending to study physic. He left that celebrated university, the third university at which he had resided, in his twenty-seventh year, without a degree, with the merest smattering of medical knowledge, and with no property but his clothes and his flute. His flute, however, proved a useful friend. He rambled on foot through Flanders, France, and Switzerland, playing tunes which everywhere set the peasantry dancing, and which often procured for him a supper and a bed. He wandered as far as Italy. His musical performances, indeed, were not to the taste of the Italians; but he contrived to live on the alms which he obtained at the gates of convents. It should, however, be observed, that the stories which he told about this part of his life ought to be received with great caution; for strict veracity was never one of his virtues; and a man who is ordinarily inaccurate in narration is likely to be more than ordinarily inaccurate when he talks about his own travels. Goldsmith, indeed, was so regardless of truth as to assert in print that he was present at a most interesting conversation between Voltaire and Fontenelle, and that this conversation took place at Paris. Now it is certain that Voltaire never was within a hundred leagues of Paris during the whole time which Goldsmith passed on the continent.

In 1756 the wanderer landed at Dover, without a shilling, without a friend, and without a calling. He had, indeed, if his own unsupported evidence may be trusted, obtained from the University of Padua a doctor's degree; but this dignity proved utterly useless to him. In England his flute was not in request: there were no convents; and he was forced to have recourse to a series of desperate expedients. He turned strolling player; but his face and figure were ill suited to the boards even of the humblest theatre. He pounded drugs and ran about London with phials for charitable chemists. He joined a swarm of beggars, which made its nest in Axe Yard. He was for a time usher of a school, and felt the miseries and humiliations of this situation so keenly, that he thought it a promotion to be permitted to earn his bread as a bookseller's hack; but he soon found the new yoke more galling than the old one, and was glad to become an usher again. He obtained a medical appointment in the service of the East India Company; but the appointment was speedily revoked. Why it was revoked we are not told. The subject was one on which he never liked to talk. It is probable that he was incompetent to perform the duties of the place. Then he presented

himself at Surgeons' Hall for examination, as mate
to a naval hospital.   Even to so humble a post he
was found unequal.   By this time the schoolmaster
whom he had served for a morsel of food and
the third part of a bed was no more.   Nothing
remained but to return to the lowest drudgery of
literature.   Goldsmith took a garret in a miserable
court, to which he had to climb from the brink of
Fleet Ditch by a dizzy ladder of flagstones called
Breakneck Steps.   The court and the ascent have
long disappeared; but old Londoners well remember
both.   Here, at thirty, the unlucky adventurer sat
down to toil like a galley slave.

In the succeeding six years he sent to the press
some things which have survived, and many which
have perished.   He produced articles for reviews,
magazines, and newspapers; children's books, which,
bound in gilt paper and adorned with hideous wood-
cuts, appeared in the window of the once far-famed
shop at the corner of Saint Paul's Churchyard; *An
Inquiry into the State of Polite Learning in Europe,*
which, though of little or no value, is still reprinted
among his works; a *Life of Beau Nash,* which is
not reprinted, though it well deserves to be so; a
superficial and incorrect, but very readable, *History
of England,* in a series of letters purporting to be
addressed by a nobleman to his son; and some very
lively and amusing *Sketches of London Society,* in a
series of letters purporting to be addressed by a

Chinese traveller to his friends. All these works were anonymous; but some of them were well known to be Goldsmith's; and he gradually rose in the estimation of the booksellers for whom he drudged. He was, indeed, emphatically a popular writer. For accurate research or grave disquisition he was not well qualified by nature or by education. He knew nothing accurately: his reading had been desultory; nor had he meditated deeply on what he had read. He had seen much of the world; but he had noticed and retained little more of what he had seen than some grotesque incidents and characters which had happened to strike his fancy. But, though his mind was very scantily stored with materials, he used what materials he had in such a way as to produce a wonderful effect. There have been many greater writers; but perhaps no writer was ever more uniformly agreeable. His style was always pure and easy, and, on proper occasions, pointed and energetic. His narratives were always amusing, his descriptions always picturesque, his humour rich and joyous, yet not without an occasional tinge of amiable sadness. About everything that he wrote, serious or sportive, there was a certain natural grace and decorum, hardly to be expected from a man a great part of whose life had been passed among thieves and beggars, street-walkers and merry-andrews, in those squalid dens which are the reproach of great capitals.

As his name gradually became known, the circle of his acquaintance widened. He was introduced to Johnson, who was then considered as the first of living English writers; to Reynolds, the first of English painters; and to Burke, who had not yet entered parliament, but had distinguished himself greatly by his writings and by the eloquence of his conversation. With these eminent men Goldsmith became intimate. In 1763 he was one of the nine original members of that celebrated fraternity which has sometimes been called the Literary Club, but which has always disclaimed that epithet, and still glories in the simple name of The Club.

By this time Goldsmith had quitted his miserable dwelling at the top of Breakneck Steps, and had taken chambers in the more civilized region of the Inns of Court. But he was still often reduced to pitiable shifts. Towards the close of 1764 his rent was so long in arrear that his landlady one morning called in the help of a sheriff's officer. The debtor, in great perplexity, despatched a messenger to Johnson; and Johnson, always friendly, though often surly, sent back the messenger with a guinea, and promised to follow speedily. He came, and found that Goldsmith had changed the guinea, and was railing at the landlady over a bottle of Madeira. Johnson put the cork into the bottle, and entreated his friend to consider calmly how money was to be procured. Goldsmith said that he had a novel

ready for the press. Johnson glanced at the manuscript, saw that there were good things in it, took
it to a bookseller, sold it for £60, and soon returned
with the money. The rent was paid; and the
sheriff's officer withdrew. According to one story,
Goldsmith gave his landlady a sharp reprimand for
her treatment of him; according to another, he
insisted on her joining him in a bowl of punch.
Both stories are probably true. The novel which
was thus ushered into the world was the *Vicar of
Wakefield*.

But before the *Vicar of Wakefield* appeared in
print, came the great crisis of Goldsmith's literary
life. In Christmas week 1764, he published a poem,
entitled the *Traveller*. It was the first work to
which he had put his name; and it at once raised
him to the rank of a legitimate English classic. The
opinion of the most skilful critics was, that nothing
finer had appeared in verse since the fourth book of
the *Dunciad*. In one respect the *Traveller* differs
from all Goldsmith's other writings. In general his
designs were bad, and his execution good. In the
Traveller, the execution, though deserving of much
praise, is far inferior to the design. No philosophical
poem, ancient or modern, has a plan so noble, and
at the same time so simple. An English wanderer,
seated on a crag among the Alps, near the point
where three great countries meet, looks down on the
boundless prospect, reviews his long pilgrimage,

recalls the varieties of scenery, of climate, of government, of religion, of national character, which he has
observed, and comes to the conclusion, just or unjust,
that our happiness depends little on political institutions, and much on the temper and regulation of our
own minds.

While the fourth edition of the *Traveller* was on
the counters of the booksellers, the *Vicar of Wakefield* appeared, and rapidly obtained a popularity
which has lasted down to our own time, and which
is likely to last as long as our language. The fable
is indeed one of the worst that ever was constructed.
It wants, not merely that probability which ought
to be found in a tale of common English life, but
that consistency which ought to be found even in
the wildest fiction about witches, giants, and fairies.
But the earlier chapters have all the sweetness of
pastoral poetry, together with all the vivacity of
comedy. Moses and his spectacles, the vicar and his
monogamy, the sharper and his cosmogony, the squire
proving from Aristotle that relatives are related,
Olivia preparing herself for the arduous task of converting a rakish lover by studying the controversy
between Robinson Crusoe and Friday, the great ladies
with their scandal about Sir Tomkyn's amours and
Dr. Burdock's verses, and Mr. Burchell with his
"Fudge," have caused as much harmless mirth as
has ever been caused by matter packed into so small
a number of pages. The latter part of the tale is

unworthy of the beginning. As we approach the catastrophe, the absurdities lie thicker and thicker; and the gleams of pleasantry become rarer and rarer.

The success which had attended Goldsmith as a novelist emboldened him to try his fortune as a dramatist. He wrote the *Goodnatured Man*, a piece which had a worse fate than it deserved. Garrick refused to produce it at Drury Lane. It was acted at Covent Garden in 1768, but was coldly received. The author, however, cleared by his benefit nights, and by the sale of the copyright no less than £500, five times as much as he had made by the *Traveller* and the *Vicar of Wakefield* together. The plot of the *Goodnatured Man* is, like almost all Goldsmith's plots, very ill constructed. But some passages are exquisitely ludicrous; much more ludicrous, indeed, than suited the taste of the town at that time. A canting, mawkish play, entitled *False Delicacy*, had just had an immense run. Sentimentality was all the mode. During some years, more tears were shed at comedies than at tragedies; and a pleasantry which moved the audience to anything more than a grave smile was reprobated as low. It is not strange, therefore, that the very best scene in the *Goodnatured Man*, that in which Miss Richland finds her lover attended by the bailiff and the bailiff's follower in full court dresses, should have been mercilessly hissed, and should have been omitted after the first night.

In 1770 appeared the *Deserted Village*. In mere diction and versification this celebrated poem is fully equal, perhaps superior to the *Traveller;* and it is generally preferred to the *Traveller* by that large class of readers who think, with Bayes in the *Rehearsal*, that the only use of a plan is to bring in fine things. More discerning judges, however, while they admire the beauty of the details, are shocked by one unpardonable fault which pervades the whole. The fault which we mean is not that theory about wealth and luxury which has so often been censured by political economists. The theory is indeed false : but the poem, considered merely as a poem, is not necessarily the worse on that account. The finest poem in the Latin language, indeed the finest didactic poem in any language, was written in defence of the silliest and meanest of all systems of natural and moral philosophy. A poet may easily be pardoned for reasoning ill ; but he cannot be pardoned for describing ill, for observing the world in which he lives so carelessly that his portraits bear no resemblance to the originals, for exhibiting as copies from real life monstrous combinations of things which never were and never could be found together. What would be thought of a painter who should mix August and January in one landscape, who should introduce a frozen river into a harvest scene ? Would it be a sufficient defence of such a picture to say that every part was exquisitely coloured, that the green hedges, the apple-trees loaded with fruit, the waggons reeling under the yellow sheaves, and the sun-burned reapers wiping their foreheads were very fine, and that the ice and the boys sliding were also very fine? To such a picture the *Deserted Village* bears a great resemblance. It is made up of incongruous parts. The village in its happy days is a true English village. The village in its decay is an Irish village. The felicity and the misery which Goldsmith has brought close together belong to two different countries, and to two different stages in the progress of society. He had assuredly never seen in his native island such a rural paradise, such a seat of plenty, content, and tranquillity, as his *Auburn.* He had assuredly never seen in England all the inhabitants of such a paradise turned out of their homes in one day and forced to emigrate in a body to America. The hamlet he had probably seen in Kent : the ejectment he had probably seen in Munster ; but by joining the two, he has produced something which never was and never will be seen in any part of the world.

In 1773 Goldsmith tried his chance at Covent Garden with a second play, *She Stoops to Conquer.* The manager was not without great difficulty induced to bring this piece out. The sentimental comedy still reigned, and Goldsmith's comedies were not sentimental. The *Goodnatured Man* had been too funny to succeed ; yet the mirth of the

Goodnatured Man was sober when compared with
the rich drollery of *She Stoops to Conquer*, which
is, in truth, an incomparable farce in five acts. On
this occasion, however, genius triumphed. Pit,
boxes, and galleries, were in a constant roar of
laughter. If any bigoted admirer of Kelly and
Cumberland ventured to hiss or groan, he was
speedily silenced by a general cry of "turn him
out," or "throw him over." Two generations have
since confirmed the verdict which was pronounced
on that night.

While Goldsmith was writing the *Deserted Vil
lage* and *She Stoops to Conquer*, he was employed
on works of a very different kind, works from
which he derived little reputation but much profit.
He compiled for the use of schools a *History of Rome*
by which he made £300, a *History of England* by
which he made £600, a *History of Greece* for which
he received £250, a *Natural History*, for which
the booksellers covenanted to pay him 800 guineas.
These works he produced without any elaborate
research, by merely selecting, abridging, and translat-
ing into his own clear, pure, and flowing language,
what he found in books well known to the world,
but too bulky or too dry for boys and girls. He
committed some strange blunders : for he knew
nothing with accuracy. Thus in his *History of
England* he tells us that Naseby is in Yorkshire ;
nor did he correct this mistake when the book was

reprinted. He was very nearly hoaxed into putting into the *History of Greece* an account of a battle between Alexander the Great and Montezuma. In his *Animated Nature* he relates, with faith and with perfect gravity, all the most absurd lies which he could find in books of travels about gigantic Patagonians, monkeys that preach sermons, nightingales that repeat long conversations. "If he can tell a horse from a cow," said Johnson, "that is the extent of his knowledge of zoology." How little Goldsmith was qualified to write about the physical sciences is sufficiently proved by two anecdotes. He on one occasion denied that the sun is longer in the northern than in the southern signs. It was vain to cite the authority of Maupertuis. "Maupertuis!" he cried, "I understand those matters better than Maupertuis." On another occasion he, in defiance of the evidence of his own senses, maintained obstinately, and even angrily, that he chewed his dinner by moving his upper jaw.

Yet, ignorant as Goldsmith was, few writers have done more to make the first steps in the laborious road to knowledge easy and pleasant. His compilations are widely distinguished from the compilations of ordinary bookmakers. He was a great, perhaps an unequalled, master of the arts of selection and condensation. In these respects his histories of Rome and of England, and still more his own abridgments of these histories, well deserve to be studied. In general nothing is less attractive than an epitome : but the epitomes of Goldsmith, even when most concise, are always amusing; and to read them is considered by intelligent children not as a task, but as a pleasure.

Goldsmith might now be considered as a prosperous man.   He had the means of living in comfort, and even in what to one who had so often slept in barns and on bulks must have been luxury.   His fame was great and was constantly rising.   He lived in what was intellectually far the best society of the kingdom, in a society in which no talent or accomplishment was wanting, and in which the art of conversation was cultivated with splendid success. There probably were never four talkers, more admirable in four different ways than Johnson, Burke, Beauclerk, and Garrick ; and Goldsmith was on terms of intimacy with all the four.   He aspired to share in their colloquial renown ; but never was ambition more unfortunate.   It may seem strange that a man who wrote with so much perspicuity, vivacity, and grace, should have been, whenever he took a part in conversation, an empty, noisy, blundering, rattle.   But on this point the evidence is overwhelming.   So extraordinary was the contrast between Goldsmith's published works and the silly things which he said, that Horace Walpole described him as an inspired idiot.   "Noll," said Garrick, " wrote like an angel, and talked like poor Pol," Chamier declared that it was a hard exercise of faith to believe that so foolish a chatterer could have really written the *Traveller*. Even Boswell could say, with contemptuous compassion, that he liked very well to hear honest Goldsmith run on. " Yes, sir," said Johnson, "but he should not like to hear himself." Minds differ as rivers differ. There are transparent and sparkling rivers from which it is delightful to drink as they flow ; to such rivers the minds of such men as Burke and Johnson may be compared. But there are rivers of which the water when first drawn is turbid and noisome, but becomes pellucid as crystal and delicious to the taste if it be suffered to stand till it has deposited a sediment ; and such a river is a type of the mind of Goldsmith. His first thoughts on every subject were confused even to absurdity, but they required only a little time to work themselves clear. When he wrote they had that time ; and therefore his readers pronounced him a man of genius : but when he talked he talked nonsense, and made himself the laughing-stock of his hearers. He was painfully sensible of his inferiority in conversation ; he felt every failure keenly ; yet he had not sufficient judgment and self-command to hold his tongue. His animal spirits and vanity were always impelling him to try to do the one thing which he could not do. After every attempt he felt that he had exposed himself, and writhed with shame and vexation ; yet the next moment he began again.

His associates seem to have regarded him with kindness, which, in spite of their admiration of his writings, was not unmixed with contempt. In truth, there was in his character much to love, but very little to respect. His heart was soft even to weakness : he was so generous, that he quite forgot to be just ; he forgave injuries so readily, that he might be said to invite them, and was so liberal to beggars, that he had nothing left for his tailor and his butcher. He was vain, sensual, frivolous, profuse, improvident. One vice of a darker shade was imputed to him, envy. But there is not the least reason to believe that this bad passion, though it sometimes made him wince and utter fretful exclamations, ever impelled him to injure by wicked arts the reputation of any of his rivals. The truth probably is, that he was not more envious, but merely less prudent than his neighbours. His heart was on his lips. All those small jealousies, which are but too common among men of letters, but which a man of letters who is also a man of the world does his best to conceal, Goldsmith avowed with the simplicity of a child. When he was envious, instead of affecting indifference, instead of damning with faint praise, instead of doing injuries slily and in the dark, he told everybody that he was envious. "Do not, pray, do not, talk of Johnson in such terms," he said to Boswell ; "you harrow up my very soul." George Steevens and Cumberland were men far too cunning to say such a thing. They would have echoed the praises of the man whom they envied, and then have sent to the newspapers anonymous libels upon him. Both what was good and what was bad in Goldsmith's character was to his associates a perfect security that he would never commit such villany. He was neither ill-natured enough, nor long-headed enough, to be guilty of any malicious act which required contrivance and disguise.

Goldsmith has sometimes been represented as a man of genius, cruelly treated by the world, and doomed to struggle with difficulties, which at last broke his heart. But no representation can be more remote from the truth. He did, indeed, go through much sharp misery before he had done anything considerable in literature. But after his name had appeared on the title-page of the *Traveller*, he had none but himself to blame for his distresses. His average income, during the last seven years of his life, certainly exceeded £400 a year, and £400 a year ranked, among the incomes of that day, at least as high as £800 a year would rank at present. A single man living in the Temple, with £400 a year, might then be called opulent. Not one in ten of the young gentlemen of good families who were studying the law there had so much. But all the wealth which Lord Clive had brought from Bengal, and Sir Lawrence Dundas from Germany, joined together, would not have sufficed for Goldsmith.

He spent twice as much as he had. He wore fine
clothes, gave dinners of several courses, paid court
to venal beauties. He had also, it should be remembered, to the honour of his heart, though not
of his head, a guinea, or five, or ten, according
to the state of his purse, ready for any tale of distress, true or false. But it was not in dress or feast-
ing, in promiscuous amours or promiscuous charities,
that his chief expense lay. He had been from boyhood a gambler, and at once the most sanguine and
the most unskilful of gamblers. For a time he put
off the day of inevitable ruin by temporary expedients. He obtained advances from booksellers, by
promising to execute works which he never began.
But at length this source of supply failed. He owed
more than £2000 ; and he saw no hope of extrica-
tion from his embarrassments. His spirits and
health gave way. He was attacked by a nervous
fever, which he thought himself competent to treat.
It would have been happy for him if his medical
skill had been appreciated as justly by himself as by
others. Notwithstanding the degree which he pre-
tended to have received at Padua, he could procure
no patients. " I do not practise," he once said ; " I
make it a rule to prescribe only for my friends."
" Pray, dear Doctor," said Beauclerk, " alter your
rule ; and prescribe only for your enemies." Goldsmith now, in spite of this excellent advice, prescribed for himself. The remedy aggravated the

malady. The sick man was induced to call in real physicians; and they at one time imagined that they had cured the disease. Still his weakness and restlessness continued. He could get no sleep. He could take no food. "You are worse," said one of his medical attendants, "than you should be from the degree of fever which you have. Is your mind at ease?" "No; it is not," were the last recorded words of Oliver Goldsmith. He died on the 3d of April 1774, in his forty-sixth year. He was laid in the churchyard of the Temple; but the spot was not marked by any inscription, and is now forgotten. The coffin was followed by Burke and Reynolds. Both these great men were sincere mourners. Burke, when he heard of Goldsmith's death, had burst into a flood of tears. Reynolds had been so much moved by the news, that he had flung aside his brush and palette for the day.

A short time after Goldsmith's death, a little poem appeared, which will, as long as our language lasts, associate the names of his two illustrious friends with his own. It has already been mentioned that he sometimes felt keenly the sarcasm which his wild blundering talk brought upon him. He was, not long before his last illness, provoked into retaliating. He wisely betook himself to his pen; and at that weapon he proved himself a match for all his assailants together. Within a small compass he drew with a singularly easy and vigorous pencil the characters of

I

nine or ten of his intimate associates. Though this little work did not receive his last touches, it must always be regarded as a masterpiece. It is impossible, however, not to wish that four or five likenesses which have no interest for posterity were wanting to that noble gallery, and that their places were supplied by sketches of Johnson and Gibbon, as happy and vivid as the sketches of Burke and Garrick.

Some of Goldsmith's friends and admirers honoured him with a cenotaph in Westminster Abbey. Nollekens was the sculptor; and Johnson wrote the inscription. It is much to be lamented that Johnson did not leave to posterity a more durable and a more valuable memorial of his friend. A life of Goldsmith would have been an inestimable addition to the Lives of the Poets. No man appreciated Goldsmith's writings more justly than Johnson: no man was better acquainted with Goldsmith's character and habits; and no man was more competent to delineate with truth and spirit the peculiarities of a mind in which great powers were found in company with great weaknesses. But the list of poets to whose works Johnson was requested by the booksellers to furnish prefaces ended with Lyttelton, who died in 1773. The line seems to have been drawn expressly for the purpose of excluding the person whose portrait would have most fitly closed the series. Goldsmith, however, has been fortunate in his biographers. Within a few years his life has been written by Mr. Prior, by Mr. Washington Irving, and by Mr. Forster. The diligence of Mr. Prior deserves great praise; the style of Mr. Washington Irving is always pleasing; but the highest place must, in justice, be assigned to the eminently interesting work of Mr. Forster.

SAMUEL JOHNSON.

SAMUEL JOHNSON, one of the most eminent English writers of the eighteenth century, was the son of Michael Johnson, who was, at the beginning of that century, a magistrate of Lichfield, and a bookseller of great note in the midland counties. Michael's abilities and attainments seem to have been considerable. He was so well acquainted with the contents of the volumes which he exposed to sale, that the country rectors of Staffordshire and Worcestershire thought him an oracle on points of learning. Between him and the clergy, indeed, there was a strong religious and political sympathy. He was a zealous churchman, and, though he had qualified himself for municipal office by taking the oaths to the sovereigns in possession, was to the last a Jacobite in heart. At his house, a house which is still pointed out to every traveller who visits Lichfield, Samuel was born on the 18th of September 1709. In the child the physical, intellectual, and moral peculiarities which afterwards distinguished the man were plainly discernible; great muscular strength accompanied by much awkwardness and many infirmities; great quickness of parts, with a morbid propensity to sloth and procrastination; a kind and generous heart, with a gloomy and irritable temper. He had inherited from his ancestors a scrofulous taint, which it was beyond the power of medicine to remove. His parents were weak enough to believe that the royal touch was a specific for this malady. In his third year he was taken up to London, inspected by the court surgeon, prayed over by the court chaplains, and stroked and presented with a piece of gold by Queen Anne. One of his earliest recollections was that of a stately lady in a diamond stomacher and a long black hood. Her hand was applied in vain. The boy's features, which were originally noble and not irregular, were distorted by his malady. His cheeks were deeply scarred. He lost for a time the sight of one eye; and he saw but very imperfectly with the other. But the force of his mind overcame every impediment. Indolent as he was, he acquired knowledge with such ease and rapidity, that at every school to which he was sent he was soon the best scholar. From sixteen to eighteen he resided at home, and was left to his own devices. He learned much at this time, though his studies were without guidance and without plan. He ransacked his father's shelves, dipped into a multitude of books, read what was interesting, and passed over what was dull. An ordinary lad would have acquired little or no useful knowledge in such a way: but much that was dull to ordinary lads was interesting to Samuel. He read little Greek; for his proficiency in that language was not such that he could take much pleasure in the masters of Attic poetry and eloquence. But he had left school a good Latinist, and he soon acquired, in the large and miscellaneous library of which he now had the command, an extensive knowledge of Latin literature. That Augustan delicacy of taste, which is the boast of the great public schools of England, he never possessed. But he was early familiar with some classical writers, who were quite unknown to the best scholars in the sixth form at Eton. He was peculiarly attracted by the works of the great restorers of learning. Once, while searching for some apples, he found a huge folio volume of Petrarch's works. The name excited his curiosity, and he eagerly devoured hundreds of pages. Indeed, the diction and versification of his own Latin compositions show that he had paid at least as much attention to modern copies from the antique as to the original models.

While he was thus irregularly educating himself, his family was sinking into hopeless poverty. Old Michael Johnson was much better qualified to pore upon books, and to talk about them, than to trade in them. His business declined: his debts increased: it was with difficulty that the daily expenses of his household were defrayed. It was out of his power to support his son at either university; but a wealthy neighbour offered assistance; and, in reliance on promises which proved to be of very little value, Samuel was entered at Pembroke College, Oxford. When the young scholar presented himself to the rulers of that society, they were amazed not more by his ungainly figure and eccentric manners than by the quantity of extensive and curious information which he had picked up during many months of desultory, but not unprofitable study. On the first day of his residence he surprised his teachers by quoting Macrobius; and one of the most learned among them declared, that he had never known a freshman of equal attainments.

At Oxford, Johnson resided during about three years. He was poor, even to raggedness; and his appearance excited a mirth and a pity, which were equally intolerable to his haughty spirit. He was driven from the quadrangle of Christ Church by the sneering looks which the members of that aristocratical society cast at the holes in his shoes. Some charitable person placed a new pair at his door; but he spurned them away in a fury. Distress made him, not servile, but reckless and ungovernable. No opulent gentleman commoner, panting for one-and-twenty, could have treated the academical authorities with more gross disrespect. The needy scholar was generally to be seen under the gate of Pembroke, a gate now adorned with his effigy, haranguing a circle of lads, over whom, in spite of his tattered gown and dirty linen, his wit and audacity gave him an undisputed ascendency. In every mutiny against the discipline of the college he was the ringleader. Much was pardoned, however, to a youth so highly distinguished by abilities and acquirements. He had early made himself known by turning Pope's Messiah into Latin verse. The style and rhythm, indeed, were not exactly Virgilian; but the translation found many admirers, and was read with pleasure by Pope himself.

The time drew near at which Johnson would, in the ordinary course of things, have become a Bachelor of Arts: but he was at the end of his resources. Those promises of support on which he had relied had not been kept. His family could do nothing for him. His debts to Oxford tradesmen were small indeed, yet larger than he could pay. In the autumn of 1731, he was under the necessity of quitting the university without a degree. In the following winter his father died. The old man left but a pittance; and of that pittance almost the whole was appropriated to the support of his widow. The property to which Samuel succeeded amounted to no more than twenty pounds.

His life, during the thirty years which followed, was one hard struggle with poverty. The misery of that struggle needed no aggravation, but was aggra-

vated by the sufferings of an unsound body and an
unsound mind. Before the young man left the
university, his hereditary malady had broken forth
in a singularly cruel form. He had become an
incurable hypochondriac. He said long after that
he had been mad all his life, or at least not perfectly
sane ; and, in truth, eccentricities less strange than
his have often been thought grounds sufficient for
absolving felons, and for setting aside wills. His
grimaces, his gestures, his mutterings, sometimes
diverted and sometimes terrified people who did not
know him. At a dinner table he would, in a fit of
absence, stoop down and twitch off a lady's shoe.
He would amaze a drawing room by suddenly
ejaculating a clause of the Lord's Prayer. He would
conceive an unintelligible aversion to a particular
alley, and perform a great circuit rather than see the
hateful place. He would set his heart on touching
every post in the streets through which he walked.
If by any chance he missed a post, he would go back
a hundred yards and repair the omission. Under
the influence of his disease, his senses became morbidly torpid, and his imagination morbidly active.
At one time he would stand poring on the town
clock without being able to tell the hour. At another,
he would distinctly hear his mother, who was many
miles off, calling him by his name. But this was
not the worst. A deep melancholy took possession
of him, and gave a dark tinge to all his views of

human nature and of human destiny. Such wretchedness as he endured has driven many men to shoot themselves or drown themselves. But he was under no temptation to commit suicide. He was sick of life ; but he was afraid of death ; and he shuddered at every sight or sound which reminded him of the inevitable hour. In religion he found but little comfort during his long and frequent fits of dejection ; for his religion partook of his own character. The light from heaven shone on him indeed, but not in a direct line, or with its own pure splendour. The rays had to struggle through a disturbing medium : they reached him refracted, dulled and discoloured by the thick gloom which had settled on his soul ; and, though they might be sufficiently clear to guide him, were too dim to cheer him.

With such infirmities of body and of mind, this celebrated man was left, at two-and-twenty, to fight his way through the world. He remained during about five years in the midland counties. At Lichfield, his birth-place and his early home, he had inherited some friends and acquired others. He was kindly noticed by Henry Hervey, a gay officer of noble family, who happened to be quartered there. Gilbert Walmesley, registrar of the ecclesiastical court of the diocese, a man of distinguished parts, learning, and knowledge of the world, did himself honour by patronizing the young adventurer, whose repulsive person, unpolished manners, and squalid garb, moved many of the petty aristocracy of the neighbourhood to laughter or to disgust.   At Lich-field, however, Johnson could find no way of earning a livelihood.   He became usher of a grammar school in Leicestershire; he resided as a humble companion in the house of a country gentleman; but a life of dependence was insupportable to his haughty spirit. He repaired to Birmingham, and there earned a few guineas by literary drudgery.   In that town he printed a translation, little noticed at the time, and long forgotten, of a Latin book about Abyssinia. He then put forth proposals for publishing by sub-scription the poems of Politian, with notes containing a history of modern Latin verse; but subscriptions did not come in; and the volume never appeared.

While leading this vagrant and miserable life, Johnson fell in love.   The object of his passion was Mrs. Elizabeth Porter, a widow who had children as old as himself.   To ordinary spectators, the lady appeared to be a short, fat, coarse woman, painted half an inch thick, dressed in gaudy colours, and fond of exhibiting provincial airs and graces which were not exactly those of the Queensberrys and Lepels.   To Johnson, however, whose passions were strong, whose eyesight was too weak to distinguish ceruse from natural bloom, and who had seldom or never been in the same room with a woman of real fashion, his Titty, as he called her, was the most beautiful, graceful, and accomplished of her sex.

That his admiration was unfeigned cannot be doubted; for she was as poor as himself. She accepted, with a readiness which did her little honour, the addresses of a suitor who might have been her son. The marriage, however, in spite of occasional wranglings, proved happier than might have been expected. The lover continued to be under the illusions of the wedding-day till the lady died in her sixty-fourth year. On her monument he placed an inscription extolling the charms of her person and of her manners; and when, long after her decease, he had occasion to mention her, he exclaimed, with a tenderness half ludicrous, half pathetic, "Pretty creature!"

His marriage made it necessary for him to exert himself more strenuously than he had hitherto done, He took a house in the neighbourhood of his native town, and advertised for pupils. But eighteen months passed away; and only three pupils came to his academy. Indeed, his appearance was so strange, and his temper so violent, that his schoolroom must have resembled an ogre's den. Nor was the tawdry painted grandmother whom he called his Titty well qualified to make provision for the comfort of young gentlemen. David Garrick, who was one of the pupils, used many years later, to throw the best company of London into convulsions of laughter by mimicking the endearments of this extraordinary pair.

At length Johnson, in the twenty-eighth year of his age, determined to seek his fortune in the capital as a literary adventurer. He set out with a few guineas, three acts of the tragedy of Irene in manuscript, and two or three letters of introduction from his friend Walmesley.

Never since literature became a calling in England had it been a less gainful calling than at the time when Johnson took up his residence in London. In the preceding generation a writer of eminent merit was sure to be munificently rewarded by the government. The least that he could expect was a pension or a sinecure place ; and, if he showed any aptitude for politics, he might hope to be a member of parliament, a lord of the treasury, an ambassador, a secretary of state. It would be easy, on the other hand, to name several writers of the nineteenth century of whom the least successful has received forty thousand pounds from the booksellers. But Johnson entered on his vocation in the most dreary part of the dreary interval which separated two ages of prosperity. Literature had ceased to flourish under the patronage of the great, and had not begun to flourish under the patronage of the public. One man of letters, indeed, Pope, had acquired by his pen what was then considered as a handsome fortune, and lived on a footing of equality with nobles and ministers of state. But this was a solitary exception. Even an author whose reputation was established, and whose works were popular, such an author as Thomson, whose Seasons were in every library, such an author as Fielding, whose Pasquin had had a greater run than any drama since the Beggar's Opera, was sometimes glad to obtain, by pawning his best coat, the means of dining on tripe at a cookshop underground, where he could wipe his hands, after his greasy meal, on the back of a Newfoundland dog. It is easy, therefore, to imagine what humiliations and privations must have awaited the novice who had still to earn a name. One of the publishers to whom Johnson applied for employment measured with a scornful eye that athletic though uncouth frame, and exclaimed, " You had better get a porter's knot, and carry trunks." Nor was the advice bad, for a porter was likely to be as plentifully fed, and as comfortably lodged, as a poet.

Some time appears to have elapsed before Johnson was able to form any literary connection from which he could expect more than bread for the day which was passing over him. He never forgot the generosity with which Hervey, who was now residing in London, relieved his wants during this time of trial. " Harry Hervey," said the old philosopher many years later, " was a vicious man ; but he was very kind to me. If you call a dog Hervey, I shall love him." At Hervey's table Johnson sometimes enjoyed feasts which were made more agreable by contrast. But in general he dined, and thought that he dined well, on sixpenny worth of meat and a pennyworth of bread at an alehouse near Drury Lane.

The effect of the privations and sufferings which he endured at this time was discernible to the last in his temper and his deportment. His manners had never been courtly. They now became almost savage. Being frequently under the necessity of wearing shabby coats and dirty shirts, he became a confirmed sloven. Being often very hungry when he sate down to his meals, he contracted a habit of eating with ravenous greediness. Even to the end of his life, and even at the tables of the great, the sight of food affected him as it affects wild beasts and birds of prey. His taste in cookery, formed in subterranean ordinaries and *Alamode* beef-shops, was far from delicate. Whenever he was so fortunate as to have near him a hare that had been kept too long, or a meat pie made with rancid butter, he gorged himself with such violence that his veins swelled, and the moisture broke out on his forehead. The affronts which his poverty emboldened stupid and low-minded men to offer to him would have broken a mean spirit into sycophancy, but made him rude even to ferocity. Unhappily the insolence which, while it was defensive, was pardonable, and in some sense respectable, accompanied him into societies where he was treated with courtesy and kindness. He was repeatedly provoked into striking those who had taken liberties with him. All the sufferers, however, were wise enough to abstain from talking about their beatings, except Osborne, the most rapacious and brutal of booksellers, who proclaimed everywhere that he had been knocked down by the huge fellow whom he had hired to puff the Harleian Library.

About a year after Johnson had begun to reside in London, he was fortunate enough to obtain regular employment from Cave, an enterprising and intelligent bookseller, who was proprietor and editor of the Gentleman's Magazine. That journal, just entering on the ninth year of its long existence, was the only periodical work in the kingdom which then had what would now be called a large circulation. It was indeed, the chief source of parliamentary intelligence. It was not then safe, even during a recess, to publish an account of the proceedings of either House without some disguise. Cave, however, ventured to entertain his readers with what he called Reports of the Debates of the Senate of Lilliput. France was Blefuscu: London was Mildendo : pounds were sprugs : the Duke of Newcastle was the Nardac secretary of state : Lord Hardwicke was the Hugo Hickrad ; and William Pulteney was Wingul Pulnub. To write the speeches was, during several years, the business of Johnson. He was generally furnished with notes, meagre indeed, and inaccurate, of what had been said ; but sometimes he had to find arguments and eloquence both for

K

the ministry and for the opposition. He was himself a Tory, not from rational conviction—for his
serious opinion was that one form of government
was just as good or as bad as another—but from
mere passion, such as inflamed the Capulets against
the Montagues, or the Blues of the Roman circus
against the Greens. In his infancy he had heard so
much talk about the villanies of the Whigs, and
the dangers of the Church, that he had become a
furious partisan when he could scarcely speak.
Before he was three he had insisted on being taken
to hear Sacheverell preach at Lichfield Cathedral,
and had listened to the sermon with as much respect, and probably with as much intelligence, as any
Staffordshire squire in the congregation. The work
which had been begun in the nursery had been
completed by the university. Oxford, when Johnson resided there, was the most Jacobitical place in
England; and Pembroke was one of the most
Jacobitical colleges in Oxford. The prejudices
which he brought up to London were scarcely less
absurd than those of his own Tom Tempest.
Charles II. and James II. were two of the best
kings that ever reigned. Laud, a poor creature who
never did, said, or wrote any thing indicating more
than the ordinary capacity of an old woman, was a
prodigy of parts and learning over whose tomb Art
and Genius still continued to weep. Hampden
deserved no more honourable name than that of

"the zealot of rebellion." Even the ship money, condemned not less decidedly by Falkland and Clarendon than by the bitterest Roundheads, Johnson would not pronounce to have been an unconstitutional impost. Under a government the mildest that had ever been known in the world, under a government which allowed to the people an unprecedented liberty of speech and action, he fancied that he was a slave ; he assailed the ministry with obloquy which refuted itself, and regretted the lost freedom and happiness of those golden days in which a writer who had taken but one-tenth part of the license allowed to him would have been pilloried, mangled with the shears, whipped at the cart's tail, and flung into a noisome dungeon to die. He hated dissenters and stock-jobbers, the excise and the army, septennial parliaments, and continental connections. He long had an aversion to the Scotch, an aversion of which he could not remember the commencement, but which, he owned, had probably originated in his abhorrence of the conduct of the nation during the Great Rebellion. It is easy to guess in what manner debates on great party questions were likely to be reported by a man whose judgment was so much disordered by party spirit. A show of fairness was indeed necessary to the prosperity of the Magazine. But Johnson long afterwards owned that, though he had saved appearances, he had taken care that the Whig dogs should

not have the best of it; and, in fact, every passage
which has lived, every passage which bears the
marks of his higher faculties, is put into the mouth
of some member of the opposition.

A few weeks after Johnson had entered on these
obscure labours, he published a work which at once
placed him high among the writers of his age. It
is probable that what he had suffered during his
first year in London had often reminded him of
some parts of that noble poem in which Juvenal
had described the misery and degradation of a needy
man of letters, lodged among the pigeons' nests in
the tottering garrets which overhung the streets of
Rcme. Pope's admirable imitations of Horace's
Satires and Epistles had recently appeared, were in
every hand, and were by many readers thought
superior to the originals. What Pope had done
for Horace, Johnson aspired to do for Juvenal.
The enterprise was bold, and yet judicious. For
between Johnson and Juvenal there was much in
common, much more certainly than between Pope
and Horace.

Johnson's London appeared without his name
in May 1738. He received only ten guineas for
this stately and vigorous poem : but the sale was
rapid, and the success complete. A second edition was required within a week. Those small
critics who are always desirous to lower established
reputations ran about proclaiming that the anony-

mous satirist was superior to Pope in Pope's own peculiar department of literature. It ought to be remembered, to the honour of Pope, that he joined heartily in the applause with which the appearance of a rival genius was welcomed. He made inquiries about the author of London. Such a man, he said, could not long be concealed. The name was soon discovered; and Pope, with great kindness, exerted himself to obtain an academical degree and the mastership of a grammar school for the poor young poet. The attempt failed, and Johnson remained a bookseller's hack.

It does not appear that these two men, the most eminent writer of the generation which was going out, and the most eminent writer of the generation which was coming in, ever saw each other. They lived in very different circles, one surrounded by dukes and earls, the other by starving pamphleteers and index-makers. Among Johnson's associates at this time may be mentioned Boyse, who, when his shirts were pledged, scrawled Latin verses sitting up in bed with his arms through two holes in his blankets who composed very respectable sacred poetry when he was sober, and who was at last run over by a hackney coach when he was drunk; Hoole, surnamed the metaphysical tailor, who, instead of attending to his measures, used to trace geometrical diagrams on the board where he sate cross-legged; and the penitent imposter, George

Psalmanazar, who, after poring all day, in a humble lodging, on the folios of Jewish rabbis and Christian fathers, indulged himself at night with literary and theological conversation at an alehouse in the city. But the most remarkable of the persons with whom at this time Johnson consorted, was Richard Savage, an earl's son, a shoemaker's apprentice, who had seen life in all its forms, who had feasted among blue ribands in Saint James's Square, and had lain with fifty pounds weight of irons on his legs, in the condemned ward of Newgate. This man had, after many vicissitudes of fortune, sunk at last into abject and hopeless poverty. His pen had failed him. His patrons had been taken away by death, or estranged by the riotous profusion with which he squandered their bounty, and the ungrateful insolence with which he rejected their advice. He now lived by begging. He dined on venison and Champagne whenever he had been so fortunate as to borrow a guinea. If his questing had been unsuccessful, he appeased the rage of hunger with some scraps of broken meat, and lay down to rest under the Piazza of Covent Garden in warm weather, and, in cold weather, as near as he could get to the furnace of a glass house. Yet, in his misery, he was still an agreeable companion. He had an inexhaustible store of anecdotes about that gay and brilliant world from which he was now an outcast. He had observed the great men of both parties in hours of careless relaxation, had seen the leaders of opposition without the mask of patriotism, and had heard the prime minister roar with laughter and tell stories not over decent. During some months Savage lived in the closest familiarity with Johnson ; and then the friends parted, not without tears. Johnson remained in London to drudge for Cave. Savage went to the West of England, lived there as he had lived everywhere, and, in 1743, died, penniless and heart-broken, in Bristol gaol.

Soon after his death, while the public curiosity was strongly excited about his extraordinary character, and his not less extraordinary adventures, a life of him appeared widely different from the catch-penny lives of eminent men which were then a staple article of manufacture in Grub Street. The style was indeed deficient in ease and variety ; and the writer was evidently too partial to the Latin element of our language. But the little work, with all its faults, was a masterpiece. No finer specimen of literary biography existed in any language, living or dead ; and a discerning critic might have confidently predicted that the author was destined to be the founder of a new school of English eloquence.

The Life of Savage was anonymous ; but it was well known in literary circles that Johnson was the writer. During the three years which followed, he produced no important work ; but he was not, and indeed could not be, idle. The fame of his abilities

and learning continued to grow.   Warburton pronounced him a man of parts and genius ; and the
praise of Warburton was then no light thing.
Such was Johnson's reputation that, in 1747, several
eminent booksellers combined to employ him in the
arduous work of preparing a Dictionary of the English Language, in two folio volumes.   The sum
which they agreed to pay him was only fifteen
hundred guineas ; and out of this sum he had to
pay several poor men of letters who assisted him in
the humbler parts of his task.

The Prospectus of the Dictionary he addressed to
the Earl of Chesterfield.   Chesterfield had long
been celebrated for the politeness of his manners,
the brilliancy of his wit, and the delicacy of his taste.
He was acknowledged to be the finest speaker in the
House of Lords.   He had recently governed Ireland,
at a momentous conjuncture, with eminent firmness,
wisdom, and humanity ; and he had since become
Secretary of State.   He received Johnson's homage
with the most winning affability, and requited it
with a few guineas, bestowed doubtless in a very
graceful manner, but was by no means desirous to
see all his carpets blackened with the London mud,
and his soups and wines thrown to right and left
over the gowns of fine ladies and the waistcoats of
fine gentlemen, by an absent, awkward scholar, who
gave strange starts and uttered strange growls, who
dressed like a scarecrow, and ate like a cormorant.

During some time Johnson continued to call on his patron, but, after being repeatedly told by the porter that his lordship was not at home, took the hint, and ceased to present himself at the inhospitable door.

Johnson had flattered himself that he should have completed his Dictionary by the end of 1750 ; but it was not till 1755 that he at length gave his huge volumes to the world. During the seven years which he passed in the drudgery of penning definitions and marking quotations for transcription, he sought for relaxation in literary labour of a more agreeable kind. In 1749 he published the Vanity of Human Wishes, an excellent imitation of the Tenth Satire of Juvenal. It is in truth not easy to say whether the palm belongs to the ancient or to the modern poet. The couplets in which the fall of Wolsey is described, though lofty and sonorous, are feeble when compared with the wonderful lines which bring before us all Rome in tumult on the day of the fall of Sejanus, the laurels on the doorposts, the white bull stalking towards the Capitol, the statues rolling down from their pedestals, the flatterers of the disgraced minister running to see him dragged with a hook through the streets, and to have a kick at his carcass before it is hurled into the Tiber. It must be owned too that in the concluding passage the Christian moralist has not made the most of his advantages, and has fallen decidedly short of the sublimity of his Pagan model. On the other hand, Juvenal's Hannibal must yield to Johnson's Charles; and Johnson's vigorous and pathetic enumeration of the miseries of a literary life must be allowed to be superior to Juvenal's lamentation over the fate of Demosthenes and Cicero.

For the copyright of the Vanity of Human Wishes Johnson received only fifteen guineas.

A few days after the publication of this poem, his tragedy, begun many years before, was brought on the stage. His pupil, David Garrick, had, in 1741, made his appearance on a humble stage in Goodman's Fields, had at once risen to the first place among actors, and was now, after several years of almost uninterrupted success, manager of Drury Lane Theatre. The relation between him and his old preceptor was of a very singular kind. They repelled each other strongly, and yet attracted each other strongly. Nature had made them of very different clay; and circumstances had fully brought out the natural peculiarities of both. Sudden prosperity had turned Garrick's head. Continued adversity had soured Johnson's temper. Johnson saw with more envy than became so great a man the villa, the plate, the china, the Brussels carpet, which the little mimic had got by repeating, with grimaces and gesticulations, what wiser men had written; and the exquisitely sensitive vanity of Garrick was galled by the thought that, while all the rest of the world was applauding him, he could obtain from one morose cynic, whose opinion it was impossible to despise, scarcely any compliment not acidulated with scorn. Yet the two Lichfield men had so many early recollections in common, and sympathized with each other on so many points on which they sympathized with nobody else in the vast population of the capital, that, though the master was often provoked by the monkey-like impertinence of the pupil, and the pupil by the bearish rudeness of the master, they remained friends till they were parted by death. Garrick now brought Irene out, with alterations sufficient to displease the author, yet not sufficient to make the piece pleasing to the audience. The public, however, listened, with little emotion, but with much civility, to five acts of monotonous declamation. After nine representations the play was withdrawn. It is, indeed, altogether unsuited to the stage, and, even when perused in the closet, will be found hardly worthy of the author. He had not the slightest notion of what blank verse should be. A change in the last syllable of every other line would make the versification of the Vanity of Human Wishes closely resemble the versification of Irene. The poet, however, cleared, by his benefit nights, and by the sale of the copyright of his tragedy, about three hundred pounds, then a great sum in his estimation.

About a year after the representation of Irene, he

began to publish a series of short essays on morals, manners, and literature. This species of composition had been brought into fashion by the success of the Tatler, and by the still more brilliant success of the Spectator. A crowd of small writers had vainly attempted to rival Addison. The Lay Monastery, the Censor, the Freethinker, the Plain Dealer, the Champion, and other works of the same kind, had had their short day. None of them had obtained a permanent place in our literature; and they are now to be found only in the libraries of the curious. At length Johnson undertook the adventure in which so many aspirants had failed. In the thirty-sixth year after the appearance of the last number of the Spectator appeared the first number of the Rambler. From March 1750 to March 1752, this paper continued to come out every Tuesday and Saturday.

From the first the Rambler was enthusiastically admired by a few eminent men. Richardson, when only five numbers had appeared, pronounced it equal, if not superior to the Spectator. Young and Hartley expressed their approbation not less warmly. Bubb Dodington, among whose many faults indifference to the claims of genius and learning cannot be reckoned, solicited the acquaintance of the writer. In consequence probably of the good offices of Dodington, who was then the confidential adviser of Prince Frederick, two of his Royal Highness's gentlemen carried a gracious message to the printing-office, and ordered seven copies for Leicester House. But these overtures seem to have been very coldly received. Johnson had had enough of the patronage of the great to last him all his life, and was not disposed to haunt any other door as he had haunted the door of Chesterfield.

By the public the Rambler was at first very coldly received. Though the price of a number was only twopence, the sale did not amount to five hundred. The profits were therefore very small. But as soon as the flying leaves were collected and reprinted they became popular. The author lived to see thirteen thousand copies spread over England alone. Separate editions were published for the Scotch and Irish markets. A large party pronounced the style perfect, so absolutely perfect that in some essays it would be impossible for the writer himself to alter a single word for the better. Another party, not less numerous, vehemently accused him of having corrupted the purity of the English tongue. The best critics admitted that his diction was too monotonous, too obviously artificial, and now and then turgid even to absurdity. But they did justice to the acuteness of his observations on morals and manners, to the constant precision and frequent brilliancy of his language, to the weighty and magnificent eloquence of many serious passages, and to the solemn yet pleasing humour of some of the lighter papers. On the question of precedence between Addison and

Johnson, a question which, seventy years ago, was much disputed, posterity has pronounced a decision from which there is no appeal. Sir Roger, his chaplain and his butler, Will Wimble and Will Honeycomb, the Vision of Mirza, the Journal of the Retired Citizen, the Everlasting Club, the Dunmow Flitch, the Loves of Hilpah and Shalum, the Visit to the Exchange, and the Visit to the Abbey, are known to everybody. But many men and women, even of highly cultivated minds, are unacquainted with Squire Bluster and Mrs. Busy, Quisquilius and Venustulus, the Allegory of Wit and Learning, the Chronicle of the Revolutions of a Garret, and the sad fate of Aningait and Ajut.

The last Rambler was written in a sad and gloomy hour. Mrs. Johnson had been given over by the physicians. Three days later she died. She left her husband almost broken-hearted. Many people had been surprised to see a man of his genius and learning stooping to every drudgery, and denying himself almost every comfort, for the purpose of supplying a silly, affected old woman with superfluities, which she accepted with but little gratitude. But all his affection had been concentrated on her. He had neither brother nor sister, neither son nor daughter. To him she was beautiful as the Gunnings, and witty as Lady Mary. Her opinion of his writings was more important to him than the voice of the pit of Drury Lane Theatre, or the judgment of the

Monthly Review. The chief support which had sustained him through the most arduous labour of his life was the hope that she would enjoy the fame and the profit which he anticipated from his Dictionary. She was gone; and, in that vast labyrinth of streets, peopled by eight hundred thousand human beings, he was alone. Yet it was necessary for him to set himself, as he expressed it, doggedly to work. After three more laborious years, the Dictionary was at length complete.

It had been generally supposed that this great work would be dedicated to the eloquent and accomplished nobleman to whom the Prospectus had been addressed. He well knew the value of such a compliment; and therefore, when the day of publication drew near, he exerted himself to soothe, by a show of zealous and at the same time of delicate and judicious kindness, the pride which he had so cruelly wounded. Since the Ramblers had ceased to appear, the town had been entertained by a journal called The World, to which many men of high rank and fashion contributed. In two successive numbers of the World, the Dictionary was, to use the modern phrase, puffed with wonderful skill. The writings of Johnson were warmly praised. It was proposed that he should be invested with the authority of a Dictator, nay, of a Pope, over our language, and that his decisions about the meaning and the spelling of words should be received as final. His two folios,

it was said, would of course be bought by everybody
who could afford to buy them.   It was soon known
that these papers were written by Chesterfield.
But the just resentment of Johnson was not to be
so appeased.   In a letter written with singular
energy and dignity of thought and language, he
repelled the tardy advances of his patron.   The
Dictionary came forth without a dedication.   In the
preface the author truly declared that he owed
nothing to the great, and described the difficulties
with which he had been left to struggle so forcibly
and pathetically that the ablest and most malevolent
of all the enemies of his fame, Horne Tooke, never
could read that passage without tears.

The public, on this occasion, did Johnson full
justice, and something more than justice.   The best
lexicographer may well be content if his productions
are received by the world with cold esteem.   But
Johnson's Dictionary was hailed with an enthusiasm
such as no similar work has ever excited.   It was
indeed the first dictionary which could be read with
pleasure.   The definitions show so much acuteness
of thought and command of language, and the passages quoted from poets, divines, and philosophers,
are so skilfully selected, that a leisure hour may
always be very agreeably spent in turning over the
pages.   The faults of the book resolve themselves,
for the most part, into one great fault.   Johnson
was a wretched etymologist.   He knew little or

nothing of any Teutonic language except English, which indeed, as he wrote it, was scarcely a Teutonic language; and thus he was absolutely at the mercy of Junius and Skinner.

The Dictionary, though it raised Johnson's fame, added nothing to his pecuniary means. The fifteen hundred guineas which the booksellers had agreed to pay him had been advanced and spent before the last sheets issued from the press. It is painful to relate that, twice in the course of the year which followed the publication of this great work, he was arrested and carried to spunging-houses, and that he was twice indebted for his liberty to his excellent friend Richardson. It was still necessary for the man who had been formally saluted by the highest authority as Dictator of the English language to supply his wants by constant toil. He abridged his Dictionary. He proposed to bring out an edition of Shakspeare by subscription; and many subscribers sent in their names, and laid down their money; but he soon found the task so little to his taste that he turned to more attractive employments. He contributed many papers to a new monthly journal, which was called the Literary Magazine. Few of these papers have much interest; but among them was the very best thing that he ever wrote, a masterpiece both of reasoning and of satirical pleasantry, the review of Jenyns's Inquiry into the Nature and Origin of Evil.

In the spring of 1758 Johnson put forth the first of a series of essays, entitled The Idler. During two years these essays continued to appear weekly. They were eagerly read, widely circulated, and, indeed, impudently pirated while they were still in the original form, and had a large sale when collected into volumes. The Idler may be described as a second part of the Rambler, somewhat livelier and somewhat weaker than the first part.

While Johnson was busied with his Idlers, his mother, who had accomplished her ninetieth year, died at Lichfield. It was long since he had seen her; but he had not failed to contribute largely, out of his small means, to her comfort. In order to defray the charges of her funeral, and to pay some debts which she had left, he wrote a little book in a single week, and sent off the sheets to the press without reading them over. A hundred pounds were paid him for the copyright; and the purchasers had great cause to be pleased with their bargain; for the book was Rasselas.

The success of Rasselas was great, though such ladies as Miss Lydia Languish must have been grievously disappointed when they found that the new volume from the circulating library was little more than a dissertation on the author's favourite theme, the Vanity of Human Wishes; that the Prince of Abyssinia was without a mistress, and the Princess without a lover; and that the story set the hero and the heroine down exactly where it had taken them up. The style was the subject of much eager controversy. The Monthly Review and the Critical Review took different sides. Many readers pronounced the writer a pompous pedant, who would never use a word of two syllables where it was possible to use a word of six, and who could not make a waiting woman relate her adventures without balancing every noun with another noun, and every epithet with another epithet. Another party, not less zealous, cited with delight numerous passages in which weighty meaning was expressed with accuracy and illustrated with splendour. And both the censure and the praise were merited.

About the plan of Rasselas little was said by the critics; and yet the faults of the plan might seem to invite severe criticism. Johnson has frequently blamed Shakspeare for neglecting the proprieties of time and place, and for ascribing to one age or nation the manners and opinions of another. Yet Shakspeare has not sinned in this way more grievously than Johnson. Rasselas and Imlac, Nekayah and Pekuah, are evidently meant to be Abyssinians of the eighteenth century: for the Europe which Imlac describes is the Europe of the eighteenth century; and the inmates of the Happy Valley talk familiarly of that law of gravitation which Newton discovered, and which was not fully received even at Cambridge till the eighteenth century. What a real company

of Abyssinians would have been may be learned from
Bruce's Travels.   But Johnson, not content with
turning filthy savages, ignorant of their letters, and
gorged with raw steaks cut from living cows, into
philosophers as eloquent and enlightened as himself
or his friend Burke, and into ladies as highly accomplished as Mrs. Lennox or Mrs. Sheridan, transferred
the whole domestic system of England to Egypt.
Into a land of harems, a land of polygamy, a land
where women are married without ever being seen,
he introduced the flirtations and jealousies of our
ball-rooms.   In a land where there is boundless
liberty of divorce, wedlock is described as the indissoluble compact.   "A youth and maiden meeting
by chance, or brought together by artifice, exchange
glances, reciprocate civilities, go home, and dream of
each other.   Such," says Rasselas, "is the common
process of marriage."   Such it may have been, and
may still be, in London, but assuredly not at Cairo.
A writer who was guilty of such improprieties had
little right to blame the poet who made Hector quote
Aristotle, and represented Julio Romano as flourishing
in the days of the oracle of Delphi.

By such exertions as have been described, Johnson
·supported himself till the year 1762.   In that year
a great change in his circumstances took place.   He
had from a child been an enemy of the reigning
dynasty. His Jacobite prejudices had been exhibited
with little disguise both in his works and in his

conversation. Even in his massy and elaborate Dictionary, he had, with a strange want of taste and judgment, inserted bitter and contumelious reflections on the Whig party. The excise, which was a favourite resource of Whig financiers, he had designated as a hateful tax. He had railed against the commissioners of excise in language so coarse that they had seriously thought of prosecuting him. He had with difficulty been prevented from holding up the Lord Privy Seal by name as an example of the meaning of the word "renegade." A pension he had defined as pay given to a state hireling to betray his country; a pensioner as a slave of state hired by a stipend to obey a master. It seemed unlikely that the author of these definitions would himself be pensioned. But that was a time of wonders. George the Third had ascended the throne; and had, in the course of a few months, disgusted many of the old friends, and conciliated many of the old enemies of his house. The city was becoming mutinous. Oxford was becoming loyal. Cavendishes and Bentincks were murmuring. Somersets and Wyndhams were hastening to kiss hands. The head of the treasury was now Lord Bute, who was a Tory, and could have no objection to Johnson's Toryism. Bute wished to be thought a patron of men of letters; and Johnson was one of the most eminent and one of the most needy men of letters in Europe. A pension of three hundred a year was graciously offered, and with very little hesitation accepted.

This event produced a change in Johnson's whole way of life. For the first time since his boyhood he no longer felt the daily goad urging him to the daily toil. He was at liberty, after thirty years of anxiety and drudgery, to indulge his constitutional indolence, to lie in bed till two in the afternoon, and to sit up talking till four in the morning, without fearing either the printer's devil or the sheriff's officer.

One laborious task indeed he had bound himself to perform. He had received large subscriptions for his promised edition of Shakspeare; he had lived on those subscriptions during some years; and he could not without disgrace omit to perform his part of the contract. His friends repeatedly exhorted him to make an effort; and he repeatedly resolved to do so. But, notwithstanding their exhortations and his resolutions, month followed month, year followed year, and nothing was done. He prayed fervently against his idleness; he determined, as often as he received the sacrament, that he would no longer doze away and trifle away his time; but the spell under which he lay resisted prayer and sacrament. His private notes at this time are made up of self-reproaches. "My indolence," he wrote on Easter eve in 1764, "has sunk into grosser sluggishness. A kind of strange oblivion has overspread me, so that I know not what has become of the last year." Easter 1765 came, and found him still in the same state. "My time," he wrote, "has been unprofitably spent, and seems as a dream that has left nothing behind. My memory grows confused, and I know not how the days pass over me." Happily for his honour, the charm which held him captive was at length broken by no gentle or friendly hand. He had been weak enough to pay serious attention to a story about a ghost which haunted a house in Cock Lane, and had actually gone himself, with some of his friends, at one in the morning, to St. John's Church, Clerkenwell, in the hope of receiving a communication from the perturbed spirit. But the spirit, though adjured with all solemnity, remained obstinately silent; and it soon appeared that a naughty girl of eleven had been amusing herself by making fools of so many philosophers. Churchill, who, confident in his powers, drunk with popularity, and burning with party spirit, was looking for some man of established fame and Tory politics to insult, celebrated the Cock Lane Ghost in three cantos, nicknamed Johnson Pomposo, asked where the book was which had been so long promised and so liberally paid for, and directly accused the great moralist of cheating. This terrible word proved effectual; and in October 1765 appeared, after a delay of nine years, the new edition of Shakspeare.

This publication saved Johnson's character for

honesty, but added nothing to the fame of his
abilities and learning. The preface, though it
contains some good passages, is not in his best
manner. The most valuable notes are those in
which he had an opportunity of showing how atten-
tively he had during many years observed human
life and human nature. The best specimen is the
note on the character of Polonius. Nothing so
good is to be found even in Wilhelm Meister's
admirable examination of Hamlet. But here praise
must end. It would be difficult to name a more
slovenly, a more worthless edition of any great
classic. The reader may turn over play after play
without finding one happy conjectural emendation,
or one ingenious and satisfactory explanation of a
passage which had baffled preceding commentators.
Johnson had, in his Prospectus, told the world that
he was peculiarly fitted for the task which he had
undertaken, because he had, as a lexicographer, been
under the necessity of taking a wider view of the
English language than any of his predecessors.
That his knowledge of our literature, was extensive
is indisputable. But, unfortunately, he had altogether neglected that very part of our literature with
which it is especially desirable that an editor of
Shakespeare should be conversant. It is dangerous
to assert a negative. Yet little will be risked by
the assertion, that in the two folio volumes of the
English Dictionary there is not a single passage

quoted from any dramatist of the Elizabethan age, except Shakspeare and Ben. Even from Ben the quotations are few. Johnson might easily, in a few months, have made himself well acquainted with every old play that was extant. But it never seems to have occurred to him that this was a necessary preparation for the work which he had undertaken. He would doubtless have admitted that it would be the height of absurdity in a man who was not familiar with the works of Æschylus and Euripides to publish an edition of Sophocles. Yet he ventured to publish an edition of Shakspeare, without having ever in his life, as far as can be discovered, read a single scene of Massinger, Ford, Decker, Webster, Marlow, Beaumont, or Fletcher. His detractors were noisy and scurrilous. Those who most loved and honoured him had little to say in praise of the manner in which he had discharged the duty of a commentator. He had, however, acquitted himself of a debt which had long lain heavy on his conscience, and he sank back into the repose from which the sting of satire had roused him. He long continued to live upon the fame which he had already won. He was honoured by the University of Oxford with a Doctor's degree, by the Royal Academy with a professorship, and by the King with an interview, in which his Majesty most graciously expressed a hope that so excellent a writer would not cease to write. In the interval,

however, between 1765 and 1775, Johnson published
only two or three political tracts, the longest of
which he could have produced in forty-eight hours,
if he had worked as he worked on the Life of Savage
and on Rasselas.

But though his pen was now idle, his tongue was
active. The influence exercised by his conversation,
directly upon those with whom he lived, and indirectly on the whole literary world, was altogether
without a parallel. His colloquial talents were
indeed of the highest order. He had strong sense,
quick discernment, wit, humour, immense knowledge
of literature and of life, and an infinite store of curious anecdotes. As respected style, he spoke far
better than he wrote. Every sentence which dropped from his lips was as correct in structure as the
most nicely balanced period of the Rambler. But
in his talk there were no pompous triads, and little
more than a fair proportion of words in *osity* and
ation. All was simplicity, ease, and vigour. He
uttered his short, weighty, and pointed sentences
with a power of voice, and a justness and energy of
emphasis, of which the effect was rather increased
than diminished by the rollings of his huge form,
and by the asthmatic gaspings and puffings in which
the peals of his eloquence generally ended. Nor did
the laziness which made him unwilling to sit down
to his desk prevent him from giving instruction or
entertainment orally. To discuss questions of taste,

of learning, of casuistry, in language so exact and so forcible that it might have been printed without the alteration of a word, was to him no exertion, but a pleasure. He loved, as he said, to fold his legs and have his talk out. He was ready to bestow the overflowings of his full mind on anybody who would start a subject, on a fellow-passenger in a stage coach, or on the person who sate at the same table with him in an eating-house. But his conversation was nowhere so brilliant and striking as when he was surrounded by a few friends, whose abilities and knowledge enabled them, as he once expressed it, to send him back every ball that he threw. Some of these, in 1764, formed themselves into a club, which gradually became a formidable power in the commonwealth of letters. The verdicts pronounced by this conclave on new books were speedily known over all London, and were sufficient to sell off a whole edition in a day, or to condemn the sheets to the service of the trunk-maker and the pastrycook. Nor shall we think this strange when we consider what great and various talents and acquirements met in the little fraternity. Goldsmith was the representative of poetry and light literature, Reynolds of the arts, Burke of political eloquence and political philosophy. There, too, were Gibbon, the greatest historian, and Jones the greatest linguist, of the age. Garrick brought to the meetings his inexhaustible pleasantry, his incomparable mimicry, and his consummate knowledge of stage effect. Among the most constant attendants were two high-born and high-bred gentlemen, closely bound together by friendship, but of widely different characters and habits; Bennet Langton, distinguished by his skill in Greek literature, by the orthodoxy of his opinions, and by the sanctity of his life; and Topham Beauclerk, renowned for his amours, his knowledge of the gay world, his fastidious taste, and his sarcastic wit. To predominate over such a society was not easy. Yet even over such a society Johnson predominated. Burke might indeed have disputed the supremacy to which others were under the necessity of submitting. But Burke, though not generally a very patient listener, was content to take the second part when Johnson was present; and the club itself, consisting of so many eminent men, is to this day popularly designated as Johnson's club.

Among the members of this celebrated body was one to whom it has owed the greater part of its celebrity, yet who was regarded with little respect by his brethren, and had not without difficulty obtained a seat among them. This was James Boswell, a young Scotch lawyer, heir to an honourable name and a fair estate. That he was a coxcomb and a bore, weak, vain, pushing, curious, garrulous, was obvious to all who were acquainted with him. That he could not reason, that he had no wit, no humour, no eloquence, is apparent from his writings. And yet his writings are read beyond the Mississippi, and under the Southern Cross, and are likely to be read as long as the English exists, either as a living or as a dead language. Nature had made him a slave and an idolater. His mind resembled those creepers which the botanists call parasites, and which can subsist only by clinging round the stems and imbibing the juices of stronger plants. He must have fastened himself on somebody. He might have fastened himself on Wilkes, and have become the fiercest patriot in the Bill of Rights Society. He might have fastened himself on Whitfield, and have became the loudest field preacher among the Calvinistic Methodists. In a happy hour he fastened himself on Johnson. The pair might seem ill matched. For Johnson had early been prejudiced against Boswell's country. To a man of Johnson's strong understanding and irritable temper, the silly egotism and adulation of Boswell must have been as teasing as the constant buzz of a fly. Johnson hated to be questioned; and Boswell was eternally catechizing him on all kinds of subjects, and sometimes propounded such questions as, "What would you do, sir, if you were locked up in a tower with a baby?" Johnson was a water drinker and Boswell was a winebibber, and indeed little better than a habitual sot. It was impossible that there should be perfect harmony between two such companions. Indeed, the great man was sometimes provoked into fits of passion, in which he said things which the small man, during a few hours, seriously resented. Every quarrel, however, was soon made up. During twenty years the disciple continued to worship the master: the master continued to scold the disciple, to sneer at him, and to love him. The two friends ordinarily resided at a great distance from each other. Boswell practised in the Parliament House of Edinburgh, and could pay only occasional visits to London. During those visits his chief business was to watch Johnson, to discover all Johnson's habits, to turn the conversation to subjects about which Johnson was likely to say something remarkable, and to fill quarto note-books with minutes of what Johnson had said. In this way were gathered the materials, out of which was afterwards constructed the most interesting biographical work in the world.

Soon after the club began to exist, Johnson formed a connection less important indeed to his fame, but much more important to his happiness, than his connection with Boswell. Henry Thrale, one of the most opulent brewers in the kingdom, a man of sound and cultivated understanding, rigid principles, and liberal spirit, was married to one of those clever, kind-hearted, engaging, vain, pert, young women, who are perpetually doing or saying what is not exactly right, but who, do or say what they may, are always agreeable. In 1765 the

Thrales became acquainted with Johnson, and the acquaintance ripened fast into friendship. They were astonished and delighted by the brilliancy of his conversation. They were flattered by finding that a man so widely celebrated preferred their house to any other in London. Even the peculiarities which seemed to unfit him for civilised society, his gesticulations, his rollings, his puffings, his mutterings, the strange way in which he put on his clothes, the ravenous eagerness with which he devoured his dinner, his fits of melancholy, his fits of anger, his frequent rudeness, his occasional ferocity, increased the interest which his new associates took in him. For these things were the cruel marks left behind by a life which had been one long conflict with disease and with adversity. In a vulgar hack writer, such oddities would have excited only disgust. But in a man of genius, learning, and virtue, their effect was to add pity to admiration and esteem. Johnson soon had an apartment at the brewery in Southwark, and a still more pleasant apartment at the villa of his friends on Streatham Common. A large part of every year he passed in those abodes—abodes which must have seemed magnificent and luxurious indeed, when compared with the dens in which he had generally been lodged. But his chief pleasures were derived from what the astronomer of his Abyssinian tale called " the endearing elegance of female friendship." Mrs. Thrale rallied him, soothed him,

coaxed him, and, if she sometimes provoked him by
her flippancy, made ample amends by listening to
his reproofs with angelic sweetness of temper.
When he was diseased in body and in mind, she
was the most tender of nurses. No comfort that
wealth could purchase, no contrivance that womanly
ingenuity, set to work by womanly compassion,
could devise was wanting to his sick room. He
requited her kindness by an affection pure as the
affection of a father, yet delicately tinged with a
gallantry, which, though awkward, must have been
more flattering than the attentions of a crowd of the
fools who gloried in the names, now obsolete, of
Buck and Maccaroni. It should seem that a full
half of Johnson's life, during about sixteen years,
was passed under the roof of the Thrales. He accompanied the family sometimes to Bath, and sometimes
to Brighton, once to Wales and once to Paris. But
he had at the same time a house in one of the
narrow and gloomy courts on the north of Fleet
Street. In the garrets was his library, a large and
miscellaneous collection of books, falling to pieces
and begrimed with dust. On a lower floor he
sometimes, but very rarely, regaled a friend with a
plain dinner, a veal pie, or a leg of lamb and spinage,
and a rice pudding. Nor was the dwelling unin-
habited during his long absences. It was the
home of the most extraordinary assemblage of inmates that ever was brought together. At the head

of the establishment Johnson had placed an old lady named Williams, whose chief recommendations were her blindness and her poverty. But, in spite of her murmurs and reproaches, he gave an asylum to another lady who was as poor as herself, Mrs. Desmoulins, whose family he had known many years before in Staffordshire. Room was found for the daughter of Mrs. Desmoulins, and for another destitute damsel, who was generally addressed as Miss Carmichael, but whom her generous host called Polly. An old quack doctor named Levett, who bled and dosed coal-heavers and hackney coachmen, and received for fees crusts of bread, bits of bacon, glasses of gin, and sometimes a little copper, completed this strange menagerie. All these poor creatures were at constant war with each other, and with Johnson's negro servant Frank. Sometimes, indeed, they transferred their hostilities from the servant to the master, complained that a better table was not kept for them, and railed or maundered till their benefactor was glad to make his escape to Streatham, or to the Mitre Tavern. And yet he, who was generally the haughtiest and most irritable of mankind, who was but too prompt to resent anything which looked like a slight on the part of a purse-proud bookseller, or of a noble and powerful patron, bore patiently from mendicants, who, but for his bounty, must have gone to the workhouse, insults more provoking than those for which he had

knocked down Osborne and bidden defiance to
Chesterfield.   Year after year Mrs. Williams and
Mrs. Desmoulins, Polly and Levett, continued to
torment him and to live upon him.

The course of life which has been described was
interrupted in Johnson's sixty-fourth year by an
important event.   He had early read an account of
the Hebrides, and had been much interested by
learning that there was so near him a land peopled
by a race which was still as rude and simple as in
the middle ages.   A wish to become intimately
acquainted with a state of society so utterly unlike
all that he had ever seen frequently crossed his
mind.   But it is not probable that his curiosity
would have overcome his habitual sluggishness, and
his love of the smoke, the mud, and the cries of
London, had not Boswell importuned him to attempt
the adventure, and offered to be his squire.   At
length, in August 1773, Johnson crossed the High-
land line, and plunged courageously into what was
then considered, by most Englishmen, as a dreary
and perilous wilderness.   After wandering about
two months through the Celtic region, sometimes in
rude boats which did not protect him from the rain,
and sometimes on small shaggy ponies which could
hardly bear his weight, he returned to his old haunts
with a mind full of new images and new theories.
During the following year he employed himself in
recording his adventures.   About the beginning of

1775, his Journey to the Hebrides was published,
and was, during some weeks, the chief subject of
conversation in all circles in which any attention
was paid to literature. The book is still read with
pleasure. The narrative is entertaining; the specula-
tions, whether sound or unsound, are always ingenious; and the style, though too stiff and pompous,
is somewhat easier and more graceful than that of
his early writings. His prejudice against the Scotch
had at length become little more than matter of jest;
and whatever remained of the old feeling had been
effectually removed by the kind and respectful
hospitality with which he had been received in every
part of Scotland. It was, of course, not to be expected
that an Oxonian Tory should praise the Presbyterian
polity and ritual, or that an eye accustomed to the
hedgerows and parks of England should not be struck
by the bareness of Berwickshire and East Lothian.
But even in censure Johnson's tone is not unfriendly.
The most enlightened Scotchmen, with Lord Mans-
field at their head, were well pleased. But some
foolish and ignorant Scotchmen were moved to anger
by a little unpalatable truth which was mingled with
much eulogy, and assailed him whom they chose to
consider as the enemy of their country with libels
much more dishonourable to their country than
anything that he had ever said or written. They
published paragraphs in the newspapers, articles in
the magazines, sixpenny pamphlets, five shilling

books.   One scribbler abused Johnson for being
blear-eyed; another for being a pensioner; a third
informed the world that one of the Doctor's uncles
had been convicted of felony in Scotland, and had
found that there was in that country one tree
capable of supporting the weight of an Englishman.
Macpherson, whose Fingal had been proved in the
Journey to be an impudent forgery, threatened to
take vengeance with a cane.   The only effect of this
threat was that Johnson reiterated the charge of
forgery in the most contemptuous terms, and walked
about, during some time, with a cudgel, which, if
the impostor had not been too wise to encounter it,
would assuredly have descended upon him, to borrow
the sublime language of his own epic poem, "like a
hammer on the red son of the furnace."

Of other assailants Johnson took no notice whatever.   He had early resolved never to be drawn into
controversy; and he adhered to his resolution with
a steadfastness which is the more extraordinary,
because he was, both intellectually and morally, of
the stuff of which controversialists are made.   In
conversation, he was a singularly eager, acute, and
pertinacious disputant.   When at a loss for good
reasons, he had recourse to sophistry; and when
heated by altercation, he made unsparing use of
sarcasm and invective.   But when he took his pen
in his hand, his whole character seemed to be changed.
A hundred bad writers misrepresented him and

reviled him; but not one of the hundred could boast of having been thought by him worthy of a refutation, or even of a retort. The Kenricks, Campbells, MacNicols, and Hendersons, did their best to annoy him, in the hope that he would give them importance by answering them. But the reader will in vain search his works for any allusion to Kenrick or Campbell, to MacNicol or Henderson. One Scotchman, bent on vindicating the fame of Scotch learning, defied him to the combat in a detestable Latin hexameter.

"Maxime, si tu vis, cupio contendere tecum."

But Johnson took no notice of the challenge. He had learned, both from his own observation and from literary history, in which he was deeply read, that the place of books in the public estimation is fixed, not by what is written about them, but by what is written in them ; and that an author whose works are likely to live is very unwise if he stoops to wrangle with detractors whose works are certain to die. He always maintained that fame was a shuttlecock which could be kept up only by being beaten back, as well as beaten forward, and which would soon fall if there were only one battledore. No saying was oftener in his mouth than that fine apophthegm of Bentley, that no man was ever written down but by himself.

Unhappily, a few months after the appearance

of the Journey to the Hebrides, Johnson did what
none of his envious assailants could have done, and
to a certain extent succeeded in writing himself down.
The disputes between England and her American
colonies had reached a point at which no amicable
adjustment was possible. Civil war was evidently
impending; and the ministers seem to have thought
that the eloquence of Johnson might with advantage
be employed to inflame the nation against the opposition here, and against the rebels beyond the
Atlantic. He had already written two or three
tracts in defence of the foreign and domestic policy
of the government; and those tracts, though hardly
worthy of him, were much superior to the crowd of
pamphlets which lay on the counters of Almon and
Stockdale. But his Taxation No Tyranny was a
pitiable failure. The very title was a silly phrase,
which can have been recommended to his choice by
nothing but a jingling alliteration which he ought
to have despised. The arguments were such as boys
use in debating societies. The pleasantry was as
awkward as the gambols of a hippopotamus. Even
Boswell was forced to own that, in this unfortunate
piece, he could detect no trace of his master's powers.
The general opinion was that the strong faculties
which had produced the Dictionary and the Rambler
were beginning to feel the effect of time and of disease, and that the old man would best consult his
credit by writing no more.

But this was a great mistake. Johnson had failed, not because his mind was less vigorous than when he wrote Rasselas in the evenings of a week, but because he had foolishly chosen, or suffered others to choose for him, a subject such as he would at no time have been competent to treat. He was in no sense a statesman. He never willingly read or thought or talked about affairs of state. He loved biography, literary history, the history of manners; but political history was positively distasteful to him. The question at issue between the colonies and the mother country was a question about which he had really nothing to say. He failed, therefore, as the greatest men must fail when they attempt to do that for which they are unfit; as Burke would have failed if Burke had tried to write comedies like those of Sheridan; as Reynolds would have failed if Reynolds had tried to paint landscapes like those of Wilson. Happily, Johnson soon had an opportunity of proving most signally that his failure was not to be ascribed to intellectual decay.

On Easter eve 1777, some persons, deputed by a meeting which consisted of forty of the first booksellers in London, called upon him. Though he had some scruples about doing business at that season, he received his visitors with much civility. They came to inform him that a new edition of the English poets, from Cowley downwards, was in contemplation, and to ask him to furnish short bio-

graphical prefaces. He readily undertook the task,
a task for which he was pre-eminently qualified.
His knowledge of the literary history of England
since the Restoration was unrivalled. That knowledge he had derived partly from books, and partly
from sources which had long been closed; from old
Grub Street traditions; from the talk of forgotten
poetasters and pamphleteers who had long been
lying in parish vaults; from the recollections of such
men as Gilbert Walmesley, who had conversed with
the wits of Button; Cibber, who had mutilated the
plays of two generations of dramatists; Orrery, who
had been admitted to the society of Swift; and
Savage, who had rendered services of no very
honourable kind to Pope. The biographer therefore
sate down to his task with a mind full of matter.
He had at first intended to give only a paragraph to
every minor poet, and only four or five pages to the
greatest name. But the flood of anecdote and criticism overflowed the narrow channel. The work,
which was originally meant to consist only of a few
sheets, swelled into ten volumes, small volumes, it is
true, and not closely printed. The first four appeared in 1779, the remaining six in 1781.

The Lives of the Poets are, on the whole, the best
of Johnson's works. The narratives are as entertaining as any novel. The remarks on life and on human
nature are eminently shrewd and profound. The
criticisms are often excellent, and, even when grossly

and provokingly unjust, well deserve to be studied. For, however erroneous they may be, they are never silly. They are the judgments of a mind trammelled by prejudice and deficient in sensibility, but vigorous and acute. They, therefore, generally contain a portion of valuable truth which deserves to be separated from the alloy; and, at the very worst, they mean something, a praise to which much of what is called criticism in our time has no pretensions.

Savage's Life Johnson reprinted nearly as it had appeared in 1744. Whoever, after reading that life, will turn to the other lives will be struck by the difference of style. Since Johnson had been at ease in his circumstances he had written little and had talked much. When, therefore, he, after the lapse of years, resumed his pen, the mannerism which he had contracted while he was in the constant habit of elaborate composition was less perceptible than formerly; and his diction frequently had a colloquial ease which it had formerly wanted. The improvement may be discerned by a skilful critic in the Journey to the Hebrides, and in the Lives of the Poets is so obvious that it cannot escape the notice of the most careless reader.

Among the Lives the best are perhaps those of Cowley, Dryden, and Pope. The very worst is, beyond all doubt, that of Gray.

This great work at once became popular. There was, indeed, much just and much unjust censure;

but even those who were loudest in blame were attracted by the book in spite of themselves. Malone computed the gains of the publishers at five or six thousand pounds. But the writer was very poorly remunerated. Intending at first to write very short prefaces, he had stipulated for only two hundred guineas. The booksellers, when they saw how far his performance had surpassed his promise, added only another hundred. Indeed, Johnson, though he did not despise, or affect to despise money, and though his strong sense and long experience ought to have qualified him to protect his own interests, seems to have been singularly unskilful and unlucky in his literary bargains. He was generally reputed the first English writer of his time. Yet several writers of his time sold their copyrights for sums such as he never ventured to ask. To give a single instance, Robertson received four thousand five hundred pounds for the history of Charles V.; and it is no disrespect to the memory of Robertson to say that the History of Charles V. is both a less valuable and a less amusing book than the Lives of the Poets.

Johnson was now in his seventy-second year. The infirmities of age were coming fast upon him. That inevitable event of which he never thought without horror was brought near to him; and his whole life was darkened by the shadow of death. He had often to pay the cruel price of longevity.

Every year he lost what could never be replaced. The strange dependants to whom he had given shelter, and to whom, in spite of their faults, he was strongly attached by habit, dropped off one by one; and, in the silence of his home, he regretted even the noise of their scolding matches. The kind and generous Thrale was no more; and it would have been well if his wife had been laid beside him. But she survived to be the laughing-stock of those who had envied her, and to draw from the eyes of the old man who had loved her beyond anything in the world, tears far more bitter than he would have shed over her grave. With some estimable, and many agreeable qualities, she was not made to be independent. The control of a mind more steadfast than her own was necessary to her respectability. While she was restrained by her husband, a man of sense and firmness, indulgent to her taste in trifles, but always the undisputed master of his house, her worst offences had been impertinent jokes, white lies, and short fits of pettishness ending in sunny good humour. But he was gone; and she was left an opulent widow of forty, with strong sensibility, volatile fancy, and slender judgment. She soon fell in love with a music-master from Brescia, in whom nobody but herself could discover anything to admire. Her pride, and perhaps some better feelings, struggled hard against this degrading passion. But the struggle irritated her nerves, soured her temper,

and at length endangered her health. Conscious
that her choice was one which Johnson could not
approve, she became desirous to escape from his
inspection. Her manner towards him changed.
She was sometimes cold and sometimes petulant.
She did not conceal her joy when he left Streatham;
she never pressed him to return; and, if he came
unbidden, she received him in a manner which convinced him that he was no longer a welcome guest.
He took the very intelligible hints which she gave.
He read, for the last time, a chapter of the Greek
Testament in the library which had been formed by
himself. In a solemn and tender prayer he com-
mended the house and its inmates to the Divine
protection, and, with emotions which choked his
voice and convulsed his powerful frame, left for ever
that beloved home for the gloomy and desolate
house behind Fleet Street, where the few and evil
days which still remained to him were to run out.
Here, in June 1783, he had a paralytic stroke, from
which, however, he recovered, and which does not
appear to have at all impaired his intellectual
faculties. But other maladies came thick upon
him. His asthma tormented him day and night.
Dropsical symptoms made their appearance. While
sinking under a complication of diseases, he heard
that the woman whose friendship had been the chief
happiness of sixteen years of his life, had married an
Italian fiddler; that all London was crying shame

upon her ; and that the newspapers and magazines were filled with allusions to the Ephesian matron and the two pictures in Hamlet. He vehemently said that he would try to forget her existence. He never uttered her name. Every memorial of her which met his eye he flung into the fire. She meanwhile fled from the laughter and hisses of her countrymen and countrywomen to a land where she was unknown, hastened across Mount Cenis, and learned, while passing a merry Christmas of concerts and lemonade parties at Milan, that the great man with whose name hers is inseparably associated, had ceased to exist.

He had, in spite of much mental and much bodily affliction, clung vehemently to life. The feeling described in that fine but gloomy paper which closes the series of his Idlers seemed to grow stronger in him as his last hour drew near. He fancied that he should be able to draw his breath more easily in a southern climate, and would probably have set out for Rome and Naples but for his fear of the expense of the journey. That expense, indeed, he had the means of defraying; for he had laid up about two thousand pounds, the fruit of labours which had made the fortune of several publishers. But he was unwilling to break in upon this hoard, and he seems to have wished even to keep its existence a secret. Some of his friends hoped that the government might be induced to

increase his pension to six hundred pounds a year,
but this hope was disappointed, and he resolved to
stand one English winter more. That winter was
his last. His legs grew weaker ; his breath grew
shorter; the fatal water gathered fast, in spite of in-
cisions which he, courageous against pain, but timid
against death, urged his surgeons to make deeper
and deeper. Though the tender care which had
mitigated his sufferings during months of sickness
at Streatham was withdrawn, he was not left desolate. The ablest physicians and surgeons attended
him, and refused to accept fees from him. Burke
parted from him with deep emotion. Windham
sate much in the sick room, arranged the pillows,
and sent his own servant to watch at night by the
bed. Frances Burney, whom the old man had
cherished with fatherly kindness, stood weeping at
the door ; while Langton, whose piety eminently
qualified him to be an adviser and comforter at such
a time, received the last pressure of his friend's hand
within. When at length the moment, dreaded
through so many years, came close, the dark cloud
passed away from Johnson's mind. His temper became unusually patient and gentle ; he ceased to
think with terror of death, and of that which lies
beyond death; and he spoke much of the mercy of
God, and of the propitiation of Christ. In this
serene frame of mind he died on the 13th of December
1784. He was laid, a week later, in Westminster

Abbey, among the eminent men of whom he had been the historian,—Cowley and Denham, Dryden and Congreve, Gay, Prior, and Addison.

Since his death the popularity of his works—the Lives of the Poets, and, perhaps, the Vanity of Human Wishes, excepted—has greatly diminished. His Dictionary has been altered by editors till it can scarcely be called his. An allusion to his Rambler or his Idler is not readily apprehended in literary circles. The fame even of Rasselas has grown somewhat dim. But though the celebrity of the writings may have declined, the celebrity of the writer, strange to say, is as great as ever. Boswell's book has done for him more than the best of his own books could do. The memory of other authors is kept alive by their works. But the memory of Johnson keeps many of his works alive. The old philosopher is still among us in the brown coat with the metal buttons and the shirt which ought to be at wash, blinking, puffing, rolling his head, drumming with his fingers, tearing his meat like a tiger, and swallowing his tea in oceans. No human being who has been more than seventy years in the grave is so well known to us. And it is but just to say that our intimate acquaintance with what he would himself have called the anfractuosities of his intellect and of his temper, serves only to strengthen our conviction that he was both a great and a good man.

WILLIAM PITT.

WILLIAM PITT, the second son of William Pitt, Earl
of Chatham, and of Lady Hester Grenville, daughter
of Hester, Countess Temple, was born on the 28th
of May 1759. The child inherited a name which,
at the time of his birth, was the most illustrious in
the civilized world, and was pronounced by every
Englishman with pride, and by every enemy of
England with mingled admiration and terror. During
the first year of his life, every month had its illumi-
nations and bonfires, and every wind brought some
messenger charged with joyful tidings and hostile
standards. In Westphalia the English infantry won
a great battle which arrested the armies of Louis
the Fifteenth in the midst of a career of conquest:
Boscawen defeated one French fleet on the coast of
Portugal: Hawke put to flight another in the Bay
of Biscay: Johnson took Niagara: Amherst took
Ticonderoga: Wolfe died by the most enviable of
deaths under the walls of Quebec: Clive destroyed
a Dutch armament in the Hoogley, and established

the English supremacy in Bengal: Coote routed
Lally at Wandewash, and established the English
supremacy in the Carnatic.   The nation, while loudly
applauding the successful warriors, considered them
all, on sea and on land, in Europe, in America, and
in Asia, merely as instruments which received their
direction from one superior mind.   It was the great
William Pitt, the great commoner, who had vanquished French marshals in Germany, and French
admirals on the Atlantic; who had conquered for
his country one great empire on the frozen shores of
Ontario, and another under the tropical sun near
the mouths of the Ganges.   It was not in the nature
of things that popularity such as he at this time
enjoyed should be permanent.   That popularity had
lost its gloss before his children were old enough to
understand that their father was a great man.   He
was at length placed in situations in which neither
his talents for administration nor his talents for
debate appeared to the best advantage.   The energy
and decision which had eminently fitted him for the
direction of war were not needed in time of peace.
The lofty and spirit-stirring eloquence, which had
made him supreme in the House of Commons, often
fell dead on the House of Lords.   A cruel malady
racked his joints, and left his joints only to fall on
his nerves and on his brain.   During the closing
years of his life, he was odious to the court, and yet
was not on cordial terms with the great body of the

opposition. Chatham was only the ruin of Pitt, but an awful and majestic ruin, not to be contemplated by any man of sense and feeling without emotions resembling those which are excited by the remains of the Parthenon and of the Coliseum. In one respect the old statesman was eminently happy. Whatever might be the vicissitudes of his public life, he never failed to find peace and love by his own hearth. He loved all his children, and was loved by them ; and, of all his children, the one of whom he was fondest and proudest was his second son.

The child's genius and ambition displayed themselves with a rare and almost unnatural precocity. At seven, the interest which he took in grave subjects, the ardour with which he pursued his studies, and the sense and vivacity of his remarks on books and on events, amazed his parents and instructors. One of his sayings of this date was reported to his mother by his tutor. In August 1766, when the world was agitated by the news that Mr. Pitt had become Earl of Chatham, little William exclaimed, "I am glad that I am not the eldest son. I want to speak in the House of Commons like papa." A letter is extant in which Lady Chatham, a woman of considerable abilities, remarked to her lord, that their younger son at twelve had left far behind him his elder brother, who was fifteen. "The fineness," she wrote, "of William's mind makes him enjoy with the greatest pleasure what would be above the reach of any other creature of his small age." At fourteen the lad was in intellect a man. Hayley, who met him at Lyme in the summer of 1773, was astonished, delighted, and somewhat overawed, by hearing wit and wisdom from so young a mouth. The poet, indeed, was afterwards sorry that his shyness had prevented him from submitting the plan of an extensive literary work, which he was then meditating, to the judgment of this extraordinary boy. The boy, indeed, had already written a tragedy, bad of course, but not worse than the tragedies of his friend. This piece is still preserved at Chevening, and is in some respects highly curious. There is no love. The whole plot is political; and it is remarkable that the interest, such as it is, turns on a contest about a regency. On one side is a faithful servant of the Crown, on the other an ambitious and unprincipled conspirator. At length the king, who had been missing, re-appears, resumes his power, and rewards the faithful defender of his rights. A reader who should judge only by internal evidence would have no hesitation in pronouncing that the play was written by some Pittite poetaster at the time of the rejoicings for the recovery of George the Third in 1789.

The pleasure with which William's parents observed the rapid development of his intellectual powers was alloyed by apprehensions about his health.

He shot up alarmingly fast; he was often ill, and always weak; and it was feared that it would be impossible to rear a stripling so tall, so slender, and so feeble. Port wine was prescribed by his medical advisers; and it is said that he was, at fourteen, accustomed to take this agreeable physic in quantities which would, in our abstemious age, be thought much more than sufficient for any full-grown man. This regimen, though it would probably have killed ninety-nine boys out of a hundred, seems to have been well suited to the peculiarities of William's constitution; for at fifteen he ceased to be molested by disease, and, though never a strong man, continued, during many years of labour and anxiety, of nights passed in debate and of summers passed in London, to be a tolerably healthy one. It was probably on account of the delicacy of his frame that he was not educated like other boys of the same rank. Almost all the eminent English statesmen and orators to whom he was afterwards opposed or allied, North, Fox, Shelburne, Windham, Grey, Wellesley, Grenville, Sheridan, Canning, went through the training of great public schools. Lord Chatham had himself been a distinguished Etonian; and it is seldom that a distinguished Etonian forgets his obligations to Eton. But William's infirmities required a vigilance and tenderness such as could be found only at home. He was therefore bred under the paternal roof. His studies were superintended by a clergyman named

Wilson; and those studies, though often interrupted by illness, were prosecuted with extraordinary success. Before the lad had completed his fifteenth year, his knowledge both of the ancient languages and of mathematics was such as very few men of eighteen then carried up to college. He was therefore sent, towards the close of the year 1773, to Pembroke Hall, in the university of Cambridge. So young a student required much more than the ordinary care which a college tutor bestows on undergraduates. The governor, to whom the direction of William's academical life was confided, was a bachelor of arts named Pretyman, who had been senior wrangler in the preceding year, and who, though not a man of prepossessing appearance or brilliant parts, was eminently acute and laborious, a sound scholar, and an excellent geometrician. At Cambridge, Pretyman was, during more than two years, the inseparable companion, and indeed almost the only companion, of his pupil. A close and lasting friendship sprang up between the pair. The disciple was able, before he completed his twenty-eighth year, to make his preceptor bishop of Lincoln and dean of St. Paul's; and the preceptor showed his gratitude by writing a Life of the disciple, which enjoys the distinction of being the worst biographical work of its size in the world.

Pitt, till he graduated, had scarcely one acquaintance, attended chapel regularly morning and evening, dined every day in hall, and never went to a single evening party. At seventeen, he was admitted, after the bad fashion of those times, by right of birth, without any examination, to the degree of Master of Arts. But he continued during some years to reside at college, and to apply himself vigorously, under Pretyman's direction, to the studies of the place, while mixing freely in the best academic society.

The stock of learning which Pitt laid in during this part of his life was certainly very extraordinary. In fact, it was all that he ever possessed; for he very early became too busy to have any spare time for books. The work in which he took the greatest delight was Newton's Principia. His liking for mathematics, indeed, amounted to a passion, which, in the opinion of his instructors, themselves distinguished mathematicians, required to be checked rather than encouraged. The acuteness and readiness with which he solved problems was pronounced by one of the ablest of the moderators, who in those days presided over the disputations in the schools, and conducted the examinations of the Senate-House, to be unrivalled in the university. Nor was the youth's proficiency in classical learning less remarkable. In one respect, indeed, he appeared to disadvantage when compared with even second-rate and third-rate men from public schools. He had never, while under Wilson's care, been in the habit of composing in the ancient languages; and he therefore never acquired that knack of versification which is sometimes possessed by clever boys whose knowledge of the language and literature of Greece and Rome is very superficial. It would have been utterly out of his power to produce such charming elegiac lines as those in which Wellesley bade farewell to Eton, or such Virgilian hexameters as those in which Canning described the pilgrimage to Mecca. But it may be doubted whether any scholar has ever, at twenty, had a more solid and profound knowledge of the two great tongues of the old civilized world. The facility with which he penetrated the meaning of the most intricate sentences in the Attic writers astonished veteran critics. He had set his heart on being intimately acquainted with all the extant poetry of Greece, and was not satisfied till he had mastered Lycophron's Cassandra, the most obscure work in the whole range of ancient literature. This strange rhapsody, the difficulties of which have perplexed and repelled many excellent scholars, "he read," says his preceptor, "with an ease at first sight, which, if I had not witnessed it, I should have thought beyond the compass of human intellect."

To modern literature Pitt paid comparatively little attention. He knew no living language except French; and French he knew very imperfectly. With a few of the best English writers he was intimate, particularly with Shakspeare and Milton. The debate in Pandemonium was, as it well deserved to be, one of his favourite passages ; and his early friends used to talk, long after his death, of the just emphasis and the melodious cadence with which they had heard him recite the incomparable speech of Belial. He had indeed been carefully trained from infancy in the art of managing his voice, a voice naturally clear and deep-toned. His father, whose oratory owed no small part of its effect to that art, had been a most skilful and judicious instructor. At a later period, the wits of Brookes's, irritated by observing, night after night, how powerfully Pitt's sonorous elocution fascinated the rows of country gentlemen, reproached him with having been " taught by his dad on a stool."

His education, indeed, was well adapted to form a great parliamentary speaker. One argument often urged against those classical studies which occupy so large a part of the early life of every gentleman bred in the south of our island is, that they prevent him from acquiring a command of his mother tongue, and that it is not unusual to meet with a youth of excellent parts, who writes Ciceronian Latin prose and Horatian Latin Alcaics, but who would find it impossible to express his thoughts in pure, perspicuous, and forcible English. There may perhaps be some truth in this observation. But the classical studies of Pitt were carried on in a peculiar manner,

and had the effect of enriching his English vocabu-
lary, and of making him wonderfully expert in the
art of constructing correct English sentences. His
practice was to look over a page or two of a Greek
or Latin author, to make himself master of the
meaning, and then to read the passage straight forward into his own language. This practice, begun
under his first teacher Wilson, was continued under
Pretyman. It is not strange that a young man of
great abilities, who had been exercised daily in this
way during ten years, should have acquired an
almost unrivalled power of putting his thoughts,
without premeditation, into words well selected and
. well arranged. .

Of all the remains of antiquity, the orations were
those on which he bestowed the most minute
examination. His favourite employment was to
compare harangues on opposite sides of the same
question, to analyse them, and to observe which of
the arguments of the first speaker were refuted by
the second, which were evaded, and which were left
untouched. Nor was it only in books that he at
this time studied the art of parliamentary fencing.
When he was at home, he had frequent opportunities of hearing important debates at Westminster ;
and he heard them, not only with interest and
enjoyment, but with a close scientific attention
resembling that with which a diligent pupil at
Guy's Hospital watches every turn of the hand of a

great surgeon through a difficult operation. On one of these occasions, Pitt, a youth whose abilities were as yet known only to his own family and to a small knot of college friends, was introduced on the steps of the throne in the House of Lords to Fox, who was his senior by eleven years, and who was already the greatest debater, and one of the greatest orators, that had appeared in England. Fox used afterwards to relate that, as the discussion proceeded, Pitt repeatedly turned to him, and said, "But surely, Mr. Fox, that might be met thus;" or, "Yes; but he lays himself open to this retort." What the particular criticisms were Fox had forgotten; but he said that he was much struck at the time by the precocity of a lad who, through the whole sitting, seemed to be thinking only how all the speeches on both sides could be answered.

One of the young man's visits to the House of Lords was a sad and memorable era in his life. He had not quite completed his nineteenth year, when, on the 7th of April 1778, he attended his father to Westminster. A great debate was expected. It was known that France had recognized the independence of the United States. The Duke of Richmond was about to declare his opinion that all thought of subjugating those states ought to be relinquished. Chatham had always maintained that the resistance of the colonies to the mother country was justifiable. But he conceived, very erroneously, that on the day on which their independence should be acknowledged the greatness of England would be at an end. Though sinking under the weight of years and infirmities, he determined, in spite of the entreaties of his family, to be in his place. His son supported him to a seat. The excitement and exertion were too much for the old man. In the very act of addressing the peers, he fell back in convulsions. A few weeks later his corpse was borne, with gloomy pomp, from the Painted Chamber to the Abbey. The favourite child and namesake of the deceased statesman followed the coffin as chief mourner, and saw it deposited in the transept where his own was destined to lie.

His elder brother, now Earl of Chatham, had means sufficient, and barely sufficient, to support the dignity of the peerage. The other members of the family were poorly provided for. William had little more than three hundred a year. It was necessary for him to follow a profession. He had already begun to eat his terms. In the spring of 1780 he came of age. He then quitted Cambridge, was called to the bar, took chambers in Lincoln's Inn, and joined the western circuit. In the autumn of that year a general election took place; and he offered himself as a candidate for the university; but he was at the bottom of the poll. It is said that the grave doctors who then sate, robed in scarlet, on the benches of Golgotha, thought it great presumption in so young a man to solicit so high a distinction. He was, however, at the request of a hereditary friend, the Duke of Rutland, brought into Parliament by Sir James Lowther for the borough of Appleby.

The dangers of the country were at that time such as might well have disturbed even a constant mind. Army after army had been sent in vain against the rebellious colonists of North America. On pitched fields of battle the advantage had been with the disciplined troops of the mother country. But it was not on pitched fields of battle that the event of such a contest could be decided. An armed nation, with hunger and the Atlantic for auxiliaries, was not to be subjugated. Meanwhile the House of Bourbon, humbled to the dust a few years before by the genius and vigour of Chatham, had seized the opportunity of revenge. France and Spain were united against us, and had recently been joined by Holland. The command of the Mediterranean had been for a time lost. The British flag had been scarcely able to maintain itself in the British Channel. The northern powers professed neutrality; but their neutrality had a menacing aspect. In the East, Hyder had descended on the Carnatic, had destroyed the little army of Baillie, and had spread terror even to the ramparts of Fort Saint George. The discontents of Ireland threatened nothing less than civil war. In England the authority of the government had sunk to the lowest point. The King and the House of Commons were alike unpopular. The cry for parliamentary reform was scarcely less loud and vehement than in the autumn of 1830. Formidable associations, headed, not by ordinary demagogues, but by men of high rank, stainless character, and distinguished ability, demanded a revision of the representative system. The populace, emboldened by the impotence and irresolution of the government, had recently broken loose from all restraint, besieged the chambers of the legislature, hustled peers, hunted bishops, attacked the residences of ambassadors, opened prisons, burned and pulled down houses. London had presented during some days the aspect of a city taken by storm; and it had been necessary to form a camp among the trees of Saint James's Park.

In spite of dangers and difficulties abroad and at home, George the Third, with a firmness which had little affinity with virtue or with wisdom, persisted in his determination to put down the American rebels by force of arms; and his ministers submitted their judgment to his. Some of them were probably actuated merely by selfish cupidity; but their chief, Lord North, a man of high honour, amiable temper, winning manners, lively wit, and excellent talents both for business and for debate, must be acquitted of all sordid motives. He remained at a post from which he had long wished and had repeatedly tried

to escape, only because he had not sufficient fortitude to resist the entreaties and reproaches of the
King, who silenced all arguments by passionately
asking whether any gentleman, any man of spirit,
could have the heart to desert a kind master in the
hour of extremity.

The opposition consisted of two parties which
had once been hostile to each other, and which had
been very slowly, and, as it soon appeared, very
imperfectly reconciled, but which at this conjuncture
seemed to act together with cordiality. The larger
of these parties consisted of the great body of the
Whig aristocracy. Its head was Charles, Marquess
of Rockingham, a man of sense and virtue, and in
wealth and parliamentary interest equalled by very
few of the English nobles, but afflicted with a
nervous timidity which prevented him from taking
a prominent part in debate. In the House of
Commons, the adherents of Rockingham were led
by Fox, whose dissipated habits and ruined fortunes
were the talk of the whole town, but whose commanding genius, and whose sweet, generous, and
affectionate disposition, extorted the admiration and
love of those who most lamented the errors of
his private life. Burke, superior to Fox in largeness
of comprehension, in extent of knowledge, and in
splendour of imagination, but less skilled in that
kind of logic and in that kind of rhetoric which
convince and persuade great assemblies, was willing

to be the lieutenant of a young chief who might have been his son.

A smaller section of the opposition was composed of the old followers of Chatham. At their head was William, Earl of Shelburne, distinguished both as a statesman and as a lover of science and letters. With him were leagued Lord Camden, who had formerly held the Great Seal, and whose integrity, ability, and constitutional knowledge commanded the public respect; Barré, an eloquent and acrimonious declaimer; and Dunning, who had long held the first place at the English bar. It was to this party that Pitt was naturally attracted.

On the 26th of February 1781 he made his first speech in favour of Burke's plan of economical reform. Fox stood up at the same moment, but instantly gave way. The lofty yet animated deportment of the young member, his perfect self-possession, the readiness with which he replied to the orators who had preceded him, the silver tones of his voice, the perfect structure of his unpremeditated sentences, astonished and delighted his hearers. Burke, moved even to tears, exclaimed, "It is not a chip of the old block; it is the old block itself." "Pitt will be one of the first men in Parliment," said a member of the opposition to Fox. "He is so already," answered Fox, in whose nature envy had no place. It is a curious fact, well remembered by some who were very recently living, that soon after this debate Pitt's name was put up by Fox at Brookes's.

On two subsequent occasions during that session Pitt addressed the House, and on both fully sustained the reputation which he had acquired on his first appearance. In the summer, after the prorogation, he again went the western circuit, held several briefs, and acquitted himself in such a manner that he was highly complimented by Buller from the bench, and by Dunning at the bar.

On the 27th of November the Parliament reassembled. Only forty-eight hours before had arrived tidings of the surrender of Cornwallis and his army; and it had consequently been necessary to re-write the royal speech. Every man in the kingdom, except the King, was now convinced that it was mere madness to think of conquering the United States. In the debate on the report of the address, Pitt spoke with even more energy and brilliancy than on any former occasion. He was warmly applauded by his allies; but it was remarked that no person on his own side of the house was so loud in eulogy as Henry Dundas, the Lord Advocate of Scotland, who spoke from the ministerial ranks. That able and versatile politician distinctly foresaw the approaching downfall of the government with which he was connected, and was preparing to make his own escape from the ruin. From that night dates his connection with Pitt, a connection which soon became a close intimacy, and which lasted till it was dissolved by death.

About a fortnight later, Pitt spoke in the committee of supply on the army estimates. Symptoms of dissension had begun to appear on the Treasury bench. Lord George Germaine, the Secretary of State who was especially charged with the direction of the war in America, had held language not easily to be reconciled with declarations made by the First Lord of the Treasury. Pitt noticed the discrepancy with much force and keenness. Lord George and Lord North began to whisper together; and Welbore Ellis, an ancient placeman who had been drawing salary almost every quarter since the days of Henry Pelham, bent down between them to put in a word. Such interruptions sometimes discompose veteran speakers. Pitt stopped, and looking at the group, said, with admirable readiness, " I shall wait till Nestor has composed the dispute between Agamemnon and Achilles."

After several defeats, or victories hardly to be distinguished from defeats, the ministry resigned. The King, reluctantly and ungraciously, consented to accept Rockingham as first minister. Fox and Shelburne became Secretaries of State. Lord John Cavendish, one of the most upright and honourable of men, was made Chancellor of the Exchequer. Thurlow, whose abilities and force of character had made him the dictator of the House of Lords, continued to hold the great seal.

To Pitt was offered, through Shelburne, the Vice-Treasurership of Ireland, one of the easiest and most highly paid places in the gift of the Crown; but the offer was, without hesitation, declined. The young statesman had resolved to accept no post which did not entitle him to a seat in the cabinet; and a few days later, he announced that resolution in the House of Commons. It must be remembered that the cabinet was then a much smaller and more select body than at present. We have seen cabinets of sixteen. In the time of our grandfathers a cabinet of ten or eleven was thought inconveniently large. Seven was a usual number. Even Burke, who had taken the lucrative office of Paymaster, was not in the cabinet. Many therefore thought Pitt's declaration indecent. He himself was sorry that he had made it. The words, he said in private, had escaped him in the heat of speaking; and he had no sooner uttered them than he would have given the world to recall them. They, however, did him no harm with the public. The second William Pitt, it was said, had shown that he had inherited the spirit, as well as the genius, of the first. In the son, as in the father, there might perhaps be too much pride; but there was nothing low or sordid. It might be called arrogance in a young barrister, living in chambers on three hundred a year, to refuse a salary of five thousand a year, merely because he did not choose to bind himself to speak or vote for plans which he had no share in framing; but surely such arrogance was not very far removed from virtue.

Pitt gave a general support to the administration of Rockingham, but omitted, in the meantime, no opportunity of courting that Ultra-Whig party which the persecution of Wilkes and the Middlesex election had called into existence, and which the disastrous events of the war, and the triumph of republican principles in America, had made formidable both in numbers and in temper. He supported a motion for shortening the duration of Parliaments. He made a motion for a committee to examine into the state of the representation, and, in the speech by which that motion was introduced, avowed himself the enemy of the close boroughs, the strongholds of that corruption to which he attributed all the calamities of the nation, and which, as he phrased it in one of those exact and sonorous sentences of which he had a boundless command, had grown with the growth of England and strengthened with her strength, but had not diminished with her diminution or decayed with her decay. On this occasion he was supported by Fox. The motion was lost by only twenty votes in a house of more than three hundred members. The reformers never again had so good a division till the year 1831.

The new administration was strong in abilities, and was more popular than any administration which had held office since the first year of George the Third, but was hated by the King, hesitatingly supported by the Parliament, and torn by internal dissensions. The Chancellor was disliked and distrusted by almost all his colleagues. The two Secretaries of State regarded each ,other with no friendly feeling. The line between their departments had not been traced with precision; and there were consequently jealousies, encroachments, and complaints. It was all that Rockingham could do to keep the peace in his cabinet; and, before the cabinet had existed three months, Rockingham died.

In an instant all was confusion. The adherents of the deceased statesman looked on the Duke of Portland as their chief. The King placed Shelburne at the head of the Treasury. Fox, Lord John Cavendish, and Burke, immediately resigned their offices; and the new prime minister was left to constitute a government out of very defective materials. His own parliamentary talents were great; but he could not be in the place where parliamentary talents were most needed. It was necessary to find some member of the House of Commons who could confront the great orators of the opposition; and Pitt alone had the eloquence and the courage which were required. He was

offered the great place of Chancellor of the Exchequer, and he accepted it. He had scarcely completed
his twenty-third year.

The Parliament was speedily prorogued. During
the recess, a negotiation for peace which had been
commenced under Rockingham was brought to a
successful termination. England acknowledged the
independence of her revolted colonies; and she ceded
to her European enemies some places in the Mediterranean and in the Gulf of Mexico. But the terms
which she obtained were quite as advantageous and
honourable as the events of the war entitled her to
expect, or as she was likely to obtain by persevering
in a contest against immense odds. All her vital
parts, all the real sources of her power, remained
uninjured. She preserved even her dignity; for
she ceded to the House of Bourbon only part of
what she had won from that House in previous
wars. She retained her Indian empire undimin-
ished; and, in spite of the mightiest efforts of two
great monarchies, her flag still waved on the rock of
Gibraltar. There is not the slightest reason to believe
that Fox, if he had remained in office, would have
hesitated one moment about concluding a treaty on
such conditions. Unhappily that great and most
amiable man was, at this crisis, hurried by his passions into an error which made his genius and his
virtues, during a long course of years, almost useless
to his country.

He saw that the great body of the House of Commons was divided into three parties, his own, that of North, and that of Shelburne; that none of those three parties was large enough to stand alone; that, therefore, unless two of them united, there must be a miserably feeble administration, or, more probably, a rapid succession of miserably feeble administrations, and this at a time when a strong government was essential to the prosperity and respectability of the nation. It was then necessary and right that there should be a coalition. To every possible coalition there were objections. But, of all possible coalitions, that to which there were the fewest objections was undoubtedly a coalition between Shelburne and Fox. It would have been generally applauded by the followers of both. It might have been made without any sacrifice of public principle on the part of either. Unhappily, recent bickerings had left in the mind of Fox a profound dislike and distrust of Shelburne. Pitt attempted to mediate, and was authorized to invite Fox to return to the service of the Crown. "Is Lord Shelburne," said Fox, "to remain prime minister?" Pitt answered in the affirmative. "It is impossible that I can act under him," said Fox. "Then negotiation is at an end," said Pitt; "for I cannot betray him." Thus the two statesmen parted. They were never again in a private room together.

As Fox and his friends would not treat with

Shelburne, nothing remained to them but to treat with North. That fatal coalition which is emphatically called "The Coalition," was formed. Not three quarters of a year had elapsed since Fox and Burke had threatened North with impeachment, and had described him, night after night, as the most arbitrary, the most corrupt, the most incapable of ministers. They now allied themselves with him for the purpose of driving from office a statesman with whom they cannot be said to have differed as to any important question. Nor had they even the prudence and the patience to wait for some occasion on which they might, without inconsistency, have combined with their old enemies in opposition to the government. That nothing might be wanting to the scandal, the great orators who had, during seven years, thundered against the war, determined to join with the authors of that war in passing a vote of censure on the peace.

The Parliament met before Christmas 1782. But it was not till January 1783 that the preliminary treaties were signed. On the 17th of February they were taken into consideration by the House of Commons. There had been, during some days, floating rumours that Fox and North had coalesced; and the debate indicated but too clearly that those rumours were not unfounded. Pitt was suffering from indisposition: he did not rise till his own strength and that of his hearers were exhausted;

and he was consequently less successful than on any former occasion. His admirers owned that his speech was feeble and petulant. He so far forgot himself as to advise Sheridan to confine himself to amusing theatrical audiences. This ignoble sarcasm gave Sheridan an opportunity of retorting with great felicity. "After what I have seen and heard to-night," he said, "I really feel strongly tempted to venture on a competition with so great an artist as Ben Jonson, and to bring on the stage a second Angry Boy." On a division, the address proposed by the supporters of the government was rejected by a majority of sixteen.

But Pitt was not a man to be disheartened by a single failure, or to be put down by the most lively repartee. When, a few days later, the opposition proposed a resolution directly censuring the treaties, he spoke with an eloquence, energy, and dignity, which raised his fame and popularity higher than ever. To the coalition of Fox and North he alluded in language which drew forth tumultuous applause from his followers. "If," he said, "this ill-omened and unnatural marriage be not yet consummated, I know of a just and lawful impediment; and, in the name of the public weal, I forbid the banns."

The ministers were again left in a minority, and Shelburne consequently tendered his resignation. It was accepted: but the King struggled long and hard before he submitted to the terms dictated by

Fox, whose faults he detested, and whose high spirit and powerful intellect he detested still more. The first place at the board of Treasury was repeatedly offered to Pitt : but the offer, though tempting, was steadfastly declined. The young man, whose judgment was as precocious as his eloquence, saw that his time was coming, but was not come, and was deaf to royal importunities and reproaches. His Majesty, bitterly complaining of Pitt's faintheartedness, tried to break the coalition. Every art of seduction was practised on North, but in vain. During several weeks the country remained without a government. It was not till all devices had failed, and till the aspect of the House of Commons became threatening, that the King gave way. The Duke of Portland was declared First Lord of the Treasury. Thurlow was dismissed. Fox and North became Secretaries of State, with power ostensibly equal. But Fox was the real prime minister.

The year was far advanced before the new arrangements were completed ; and nothing very important was done during the remainder of the session. Pitt, now seated on the opposition bench, brought the question of parliamentary reform a second time under the consideration of the Commons. He proposed to add to the House at once a hundred county members and several members for metropolitan districts, and to enact that every borough of which an election committee should report that the majority of voters appeared to be corrupt should lose the franchise. The motion was rejected by 293 votes to 149.

After the prorogation, Pitt visited the Continent for the first and last time. His travelling companion was one of his most intimate friends, a young man of his own age, who had already distinguished himself in Parliament by an engaging natural eloquence, set off by the sweetest and most exquisitely modulated of human voices, and whose affectionate heart, caressing manners, and brilliant wit, made him the most delightful of companions, William Wilberforce. That was the time of Anglomania in France; and at Paris the son of the great Chatham was absolutely hunted by men of letters and women of fashion, and forced, much against his will, into political disputation. One remarkable saying which dropped from him during this tour has been preserved. A French gentleman expressed some surprise at the immense influence which Fox, a man of pleasure, ruined by the dice-box and the turf, exercised over the English nation. "You have not," said Pitt, "been under the wand of the magician."

In November 1783 the Parliament met again. The government had irresistible strength in the House of Commons, and seemed to be scarcely less strong in the House of Lords, but was, in truth, surrounded on every side by dangers. The King was impatiently waiting for the moment at which he

could emancipate himself from a yoke which galled
him so severely that he had more than once seriously
thought of retiring to Hanover; and the King was
scarcely more eager for a change than the nation.
Fox and North had committed a fatal error.   They
ought to have known that coalitions between parties
which have long been hostile can succeed only when
the wish for coalition pervades the lower ranks of
both.   If the leaders unite before there is any disposition to union among the followers, the probability is that there will be a mutiny in both camps,
and that the two revolted armies will make a truce
with each other, in order to be revenged on those
by whom they think that they have been betrayed.
Thus it was in 1783. At the beginning of that
eventful year, North had been the recognized head
of the old Tory party, which, though for a moment
prostrated by the disastrous issue of the American
war, was still a great power in the state.   To him
the clergy, the universities, and that large body of
country gentlemen whose rallying cry was "Church
and King," had long looked up with respect and
confidence.   Fox had, on the other hand, been the
idol of the Whigs, and of the whole body of Protestant dissenters.   The coalition at once alienated
the most zealous Tories from North, and the most
zealous Whigs from Fox.   The University of Oxford,
which had marked its approbation of North's orthodoxy by electing him chancellor, the city of London,

which had been during two and twenty years at war with the Court, were equally disgusted. Squires and, rectors, who had inherited the principles of the cavaliers of the preceding century, could not forgive their old leader for combining with disloyal subjects in order to put a force on the sovereign. The members of the Bill of Rights Society and of the Reform Associations were enraged by learning that their favourite orator now called the great champion of tyranny and corruption his noble friend. Two great multitudes were at once left without any head, and both at once turned their eyes on Pitt. One party saw in him the only man who could rescue the King; the other saw in him the only man who could purify the Parliament. He was supported on one side by Archbishop Markham, the preacher of divine right, and by Jenkinson, the captain of the Prætorian band of the King's friends; on the other side by Jebb and Priestley, Sawbridge and Cartwright, Jack Wilkes and Horne Tooke. On the benches of the House of Commons, however, the ranks of the ministerial majority were unbroken; and that any statesman would venture to brave such a majority was thought impossible. No prince of the Hanoverian line had ever, under any provocation, ventured to appeal from the representative body to the constituent body. The ministers, therefore, notwithstanding the sullen looks and muttered words of displeasure with which their suggestions were received in the closet, notwithstanding the roar of obloquy which was rising louder and louder every day from every corner of the island, thought themselves secure.

Such was their confidence in their strength that, as soon as the Parliament had met, they brought forward a singularly bold and original plan for the government of the British territories in India. What was proposed was that the whole authority, which till that time had been exercised over those territories by the East India Company, should be transferred to seven commissioners who were to be named by Parliament, and were not to be removable at the pleasure of the Crown. Earl Fitzwilliam, the most intimate personal friend of Fox, was to be chairman of this board, and the eldest son of North was to be one of the members.

As soon as the outlines of the scheme were known, all the hatred which the coalition had excited burst forth with an astounding explosion. The question which ought undoubtedly to have been considered as paramount to every other was, whether the proposed change was likely to be beneficial or injurious to the thirty millions of people who were subject to the Company. But that question cannot be said to have been even seriously discussed. Burke, who, whether right or wrong in the conclusions to which he came, had at least the merit of looking at the subject in the right point of view, vainly reminded

his hearers of that mighty population whose daily
rice might depend on a vote of the British Parliament. He spoke with even more than his wonted
power of thought and language, about the desolation
of Rohilcund, about the spoliation of Benares, about
the evil policy which had suffered the tanks of the
Carnatic to go to ruin ; but he could scarcely obtain
a hearing. The contending parties, to their shame
it must be said, would listen to none but English
topics. Out of doors the cry against the ministry
was almost universal. Town and country were
united. Corporations exclaimed against the violation
of the charter of the greatest corporation in the
realm. Tories and democrats joined in pronouncing
the proposed board an unconstitutional body. It
was to consist of Fox's nominees. The effect of his
bill was to give, not to the Crown, but to him
personally, whether in office or in opposition, an
enormous power,. a patronage sufficient to counter-
balance the patronage of the Treasury and of the
Admiralty, and to decide the elections for fifty
boroughs. He knew, it was said, that he was hateful alike to King and people ; and he had devised a
plan which would make him independent of both.
Some nicknamed him Cromwell, and some Carlo
Khan. Wilberforce, with his usual felicity of expression, and with very unusual bitterness of feeling,
described the scheme as the genuine offspring of the
coalition, as marked with the features of both its

parents, the corruption of one and the violence o
the other. In spite of all opposition, however, th
bill was supported in every stage by great majorities
was rapidly passed, and was sent up to the Lords
To the general astonishment, when the second read
ing was moved in the Upper House, the opposition
proposed an adjournment, and carried it by eighty
seven votes to seventy-nine. The cause of thi
strange turn of fortune was soon known. Pitt'
cousin, Earl Temple, had been in the royal closet
and had there been authorized to let it be know1
that His Majesty would consider all who voted fo
the bill as his enemies. The ignominous commissio1
was performed, and instantly a troop of Lords o
the Bedchamber, of Bishops who wished to b
translated, and of Scotch peers who wished to b
re-elected, made haste to change sides. On a late1
day, the Lords rejected the bill. Fox and Nortl
were immediately directed to send their seals to the
palace by their Under Secretaries; and Pitt wa
appointed First Lord of the Treasury and Chancello1
of the Exchequer.

The general opinion was, that there would be a1
immediate dissolution. But Pitt wisely determined
to give the public feeling time to gather strength
On this point he differed from his kinsman Temple.
The consequence was, that Temple, who had been
appointed one of the Secretaries of State, resigned
his office forty-eight hours after he had accepted it,

and thus relieved the new government from a great
load of unpopularity : for all men of sense and
honour, however strong might be their dislike of
the India Bill, disapproved of the manner in which
that bill had been thrown out. Temple carried
away with him the scandal which the best friends
of the new government could not but lament. The
fame of the young prime minister preserved its
whiteness. He could declare with perfect truth that,
if unconstitutional machinations had been employed,
he had been no party to them.

He was, however, surrounded by difficulties and
dangers. In the House of Lords, indeed, he had a
majority ; nor could any orator of the opposition in
that assembly be considered as a match for Thurlow,
who was now again Chancellor, or for Camden, who
cordially supported the son of his old friend Chatham.
But in the other House there was not a single
eminent speaker among the official men who sate
round Pitt. His most useful assistant was Dundas,
who, though he had not eloquence, had sense, knowledge, readiness, and boldness. On the opposite
benches was a powerful majority, led by Fox, who
was supported by Burke, North, and Sheridan. The
heart of the young minister, stout as it was, almost
died within him. He could not once close his eyes
on the night which followed Temple's resignation.
But, whatever his internal emotions might be, his
language and deportment indicated nothing but

P

unconquerable firmness and haughty confidence in
his own powers. His contest against the House
of Commons lasted from the 17th of December 1783
to the 8th of March 1784. In sixteen divisions the
opposition triumphed. Again and again the King
was requested to dismiss his ministers. But he
was determined to go to Germany rather than yield
Pitt's resolution never wavered. The cry of the nation
in his favour became vehement and almost furious
Addresses assuring him of public support came up
daily from every part of the kingdom. The freedom
of the city of London was presented to him in a
gold box. He went in state to receive this mark of
distinction. He was sumptuously feasted in Grocers
Hall; and the shopkeepers of the Strand and Fleet
Street illuminated their houses in his honour. These
things could not but produce an effect within the
walls of Parliament. The ranks of the majority
began to waver; a few passed over to the enemy
some skulked away; many were for capitulating
while it was still possible to capitulate with the
honours of war. Negotiations were opened with the
view of forming an administration on a wide basis
but they had scarcely been opened when they were
closed. The opposition demanded, as a preliminary
article of the treaty, that Pitt should resign the
Treasury; and with this demand Pitt steadfastly
refused to comply. While the contest was raging
the Clerkship of the Pells, a sinecure place for life

worth three thousand a year, and tenable with a seat in the House of Commons, became vacant. The appointment was with the Chancellor of the Exchequer: nobody doubted that he would appoint himself; and nobody could have blamed him if he had done so: for such sinecure offices had always been defended on the ground that they enabled a few men of eminent abilities and small incomes to live without any profession, and to devote themselves to the service of the state. Pitt, in spite of the remonstrances of his friends, gave the Pells to his father's old adherent, Colonel Barré, a man distinguished by talent and eloquence, but poor and afflicted with blindness. By this arrangement a pension which the Rockingham administration had granted to Barré was saved to the public. Never was there a happier stroke of policy. About treaties, wars, expeditions, tariffs, budgets, there will always be room for dispute. The policy which is applauded by half the nation may be condemned by the other half. But pecuniary disinterestedness everybody comprehends. It is a great thing for a man who has only three hundred a year to be able to show that he considers three thousand a year as mere dirt beneath his feet, when compared with the public interest and the public esteem. Pitt had his reward. No minister was ever more rancorously libelled; but even when he was known to be overwhelmed with debt, when millions were passing through his hands, when

the wealthiest magnates of the realm were solicitin
him for marquisates and garters, his bitterest enemie
did not dare to accuse him of touching unlawful gair

At length the hard fought fight ended. A fina
remonstrance, drawn up by Burke with admirabl
skill, was carried on the 8th of March by a singl
vote in a full House. Had the experiment beer
repeated, the supporters of the coalition would pro
bably have been in a minority. But the supplie
had been voted; the Mutiny Bill had been passed
and the Parliament was dissolved.

The popular constituent bodies all over th
country were in general enthusiastic on the side o
the new government. A hundred and sixty of th
supporters of the coalition lost their seats. The Firs
Lord of the Treasury himself came in at the head o
the poll for the University of Cambridge. His youn
friend, Wilberforce, was elected Knight of the grea
shire of York, in opposition to the whole influenc
of the Fitzwilliams, Cavendishes, Dundases, an
Saviles. In the midst of such triumphs Pitt com
pleted his twenty-fifth year. He was now th
greatest subject that England had seen during man
generations. He domineered absolutely over th
cabinet, and was the favourite at once of the Sove
reign, of the Parliament, and of the nation. Hi
father had never been so powerful, nor Walpole, no
Marlborough.

This narrative has now reached a point, beyon

which a full history of the life of Pitt would be a
history of England, or rather of the whole civilized
world; and for such a history this is not the proper
place. Here a very slight sketch must suffice; and
in that sketch prominence will be given to such
points as may enable a reader who is already acquainted with the general course of events to form a
just notion of the character of the man on whom so
much depended.

If we wish to arrive at a correct judgment of
Pitt's merits and defects, we must never forget that
he belonged to a peculiar class of statesmen, and
that he must be tried by a peculiar standard. It is
not easy to compare him fairly with such men as
Ximenes and Sully, Richelieu and Oxenstiern, John
De Witt and Warren Hastings. The means by
which those politicians governed great communities
were of quite a different kind from those which
Pitt was under the necessity of employing. Some
talents, which they never had any opportunity of
showing that they possessed, were developed in him
to an extraordinary degree. In some qualities, on
the other hand, to which they owe a large part of
their fame, he was decidedly their inferior. They
transacted business in their closets, or at boards
where a few confidential councillors sate. It was
his lot to be born in an age and in a country, in
which parliamentary government was completely
established; his whole training from infancy was

such as fitted him to bear a part in parliamentary
government; and, from the prime of his manhood
to his death, all the powers of his vigorous mind
were almost constantly exerted in the work of parliamentary government. He accordingly became
the greatest master of the whole art of parliamentary
government that has ever existed, a greater than
Montague or Walpole, a greater than his father
Chatham or his rival Fox, a greater than either of
his illustrious successors Canning and Peel.

Parliamentary government, like every other contrivance of man, has its advantages and its disadvan-
tages. On the advantages there is no need to dilate.
The history of England during the hundred and
seventy years which have elapsed since the House
of Commons became the most powerful body in the
state, her immense and still growing prosperity, her
freedom, her tranquillity, her greatness in arts, in
sciences, and in arms, her maritime ascendancy, the
marvels of her public credit, her American, her
African, her Australian, her Asiatic empires, sufficiently prove the excellence of her institutions. But
those institutions, though excellent, are assuredly
not perfect. Parliamentary government is government by speaking. In such a government, the
power of speaking is the most highly prized of all
the qualities which a politician can possess; and
that power may exist, in the highest degree, without
judgment, without fortitude, without skill in reading

the characters of men or the signs of the times, without any knowledge of the principles of legislation or of political economy, and without any skill in diplomacy or in the administration of war. Nay, it may well happen that those very intellectual qualities which give a peculiar charm to the speeches of a public man may be incompatible with the qualities which would fit him to meet a pressing emergency with promptitude and firmness. It was thus with Charles Townshend. It was thus with Windham. It was a privilege to listen to those accomplished and ingenious orators. But in a perilous crisis they would have been found far inferior in all the qualities of rulers to such a man as Oliver Cromwell, who talked nonsense, or as William the Silent, who did not talk at all. When parliamentary government is established, a Charles Townshend or a Windham will almost always exercise much greater influence than such men as the great Protector of England, or as the founder of the Batavian commonwealth. In such a government, parliamentary talent, though quite distinct from the talents of a good executive or judicial officer, will be a chief qualification for executive and judicial office. From the Book of Dignities a curious list might be made out of Chancellors ignorant of the principles of equity, and First Lord of the Admiralty ignorant of the principles of navigation, of Colonial ministers who could not repeat the names of the Colonies, of Lords of the Treasury who did not know the difference between funded and unfunded debt, and of Secretaries of the India Board who did not know whether the Mahrattas were Mahometans or Hindoos. On these grounds, some persons, incapable of seeing more than one side of a question, have pronounced parliamentary government a positive evil, and have maintained that the administration would be greatly improved if the power, now exercised by a large assembly, were transferred to a single person. Men of sense will probably think the remedy very much worse than the disease, and will be of opinion that there would be small gain in exchanging Charles Townshend and Windham for the Prince of the Peace, or the poor slave and dog Steenie.

Pitt was emphatically the man of parliamentary government, the type of his class, the minion, the child, the spoiled child, of the House of Commons. For the House of Commons he had a hereditary, an infantine love. Through his whole boyhood, the House of Commons was never out of his thoughts, or out of the thoughts of his instructors. Reciting at his father's knee, reading Thucydides and Cicero into English, analyzing the great Attic speeches on the Embassy and on the Crown, he was constantly in training for the conflicts of the House of Commons. He was a distinguished member of the House of Commons at twenty-one. The ability which he had displayed in the House of Commons made him the most powerful subject in Europe before he was twenty-five. It would have been happy for himself and for his country if his elevation had been deferred. Eight or ten years, during which he would have had leisure and opportunity for reading and reflection, for foreign travel, for social intercourse and free exchange of thought on equal terms with a great variety of companions, would have supplied what, without any fault on his part, was wanting to his powerful intellect. He had all the knowledge that he could be expected to have; that is to say, all the knowledge that a man can acquire while he is a student at Cambridge, and all the knowledge that a man can acquire when he is First Lord of the Treasury and Chancellor of the Exchequer. But the stock of general information which he brought from college, extraordinary for a boy, was far inferior to what Fox possessed, and beggarly when compared with the massy, the splendid, the various treasures laid up in the large mind of Burke. After Pitt became minister, he had no leisure to learn more than was necessary for the purposes of the day which was passing over him. What was necessary for those purposes such a man could learn with little difficulty. He was surrounded by experienced and able public servants. He could at any moment command their best assistance. From the stores which they produced his vigorous mind rapidly collected the materials for a good parliamentary case: and that was enough. Legislation and administration were with him secondary matters. To the work of framing statutes, of negotiating treaties, of organizing fleets and armies, of sending forth expeditions, he gave only the leavings of his time and the dregs of his fine ·intellect. The strength and sap of his mind were all drawn in a different direction. It was when the House of Commons was to be convinced and persuaded that he put forth all his powers.

Of those powers we must form our estimate chiefly from tradition; for of all the eminent speakers of the last age, Pitt has suffered most from the reporters. Even while he was still living, critics remarked that his eloquence could not be preserved, that he must be heard to be appreciated. They more than once applied to him the sentence in which Tacitus describes the fate of a senator whose rhetoric was admired in the Augustan age: "Haterii canorum illud et profluens cum ipso simul exstinctum est." There is, however, abundant evidence that nature had bestowed on Pitt the talents of a great orator; and those talents had been developed in a very peculiar manner, first by his education, and secondly by the high official position to which he rose early, and in which he passed the greater part of his public life.

At his first appearance in Parliament he showed himself superior to all his contemporaries in command of language. He could pour forth a long succession of round and stately periods, without premeditation, without ever pausing for a word, without ever repeating a word, in a voice of silver clearness, and with a pronunciation so articulate that not a letter was slurred over. He had less amplitude of mind and less richness of imagination than Burke, less ingenuity than Windham, less wit than Sheridan, less perfect mastery of dialectical fence, and less of that highest sort of eloquence which consists of reason and passion fused together, than Fox. Yet the almost unanimous judgment of those who were in the habit of listening to that remarkable race of men placed Pitt, as a speaker, above Burke, above Windham, above Sheridan, and not below Fox. His declamation was copious, polished, and splendid. In power of sarcasm he was probably not surpassed by any speaker, ancient or modern; and of this formidable weapon he made merciless use. In two parts of the oratorical art which are of the highest value to a minister of state he was singularly expert. No man knew better how to be luminous or how to be obscure. When he wished to be understood, he never failed to make himself understood. He could with ease present to his audience, not perhaps an exact or profound, but a clear, popular, and plausible view of the most extensive and complicated subject. Nothing was out of place; nothing was forgotten; minute details, dates, sums of money, were all faithfully preserved in his memory. Even intricate questions of finance, when explained by him, seemed clear to the plainest man among his hearers. On the other hand, when he did not wish to be explicit,—and no man who is at the head of affairs always wishes to be explicit,—he had a marvellous power of saying nothing in language which left on his audience the impression that he had said a great deal. He was at once the only man who could open a budget without notes, and the only man who, as Windham said, could speak that most elaborately evasive and unmeaning of human compositions, a King's speech, without premeditation.

The effect of oratory will always to a great extent depend on the character of the orator. There perhaps never were two speakers whose eloquence had more of what may be called the race, more of the flavour imparted by moral qualities, than Fox and Pitt. The speeches of Fox owe a great part of their charm to that warmth and softness of heart, that sympathy with human suffering, that admiration for everything great and beautiful, and that hatred of cruelty and injustice, which interest and delight us even in the most defective reports. No person, on the other hand, could hear Pitt without perceiving him to be a man of high, intrepid, and commanding spirit, proudly conscious of his own rectitude and of his own intellectual superiority, incapable of the low vices of fear and envy, but too prone to feel and to show disdain. Pride, indeed, pervaded the whole man, was written in the harsh, rigid lines of his face, was marked by the way in which he walked, in which he sate, in which he stood, and, above all, in which he bowed. Such pride, of course, inflicted many wounds. It may confidently be affirmed that there cannot be found, in all the ten thousand invectives written against Fox, a word indicating that his demeanour had ever made a single personal enemy. On the other hand, several men of note who had been partial to Pitt, and who to the last continued to approve his public conduct and to support his administration, Cumberland for example, Boswell, and Matthias, were so much irritated by the contempt with which he treated them, that they complained in print of their wrongs. But his pride, though it made him bitterly disliked by individuals, inspired the great body of his followers in Parliament and throughout the country with respect and confidence. They took him at his own valuation. They saw that his self-esteem was not that of an upstart who was drunk with good luck and with applause, and who, if fortune turned, would sink from arrogance into abject humility. It was that of the magnanimous man so finely described by Aristotle in the Ethics, of the man who thinks himself worthy of great things, being in truth worthy. It sprang from a consciousness of great powers and great virtues, and was never so conspicuously displayed as in the midst of difficulties and dangers which would have unnerved and bowed down any ordinary mind. It was closely connected, too, with an ambition which had no mixture of low cupidity. There was something noble in the cynical disdain with which the mighty ministers scattered riches and titles to right and left among those who valued them, while he spurned them out of his own way. 'Poor himself, he was surrounded by friends on whom he had bestowed three thousand, six thousand, ten thousand a year. Plain Mister himself, he had made more lords than any three ministers that had preceded him. The garter, for which the first dukes in the kingdom were contending, was repeatedly offered to him, and offered in vain.

The correctness of his private life added much to the dignity of his public character. In the relations of son, brother, uncle, master, friend, his conduct was exemplary. In the small circle of his intimate associates, he was amiable, affectionate, even playful. They loved him sincerely; they regretted him long; and they would hardly admit that he who was so kind and gentle with them could be stern and haughty with others. He indulged, indeed, somewhat too freely in wine, which he had early been directed to take as a medicine, and which use had made a necessary of life to him. But it was very seldom that any indication of undue excess could be detected in his tones or gestures; and, in truth, two bottles of port were little more to him than two dishes of tea. He had, when he was first introduced into the clubs of Saint James's Street, shown a strong taste for play; but he had the prudence and the resolution to stop before this taste had acquired the strength of habit. From the passion which generally exercises the most tyrannical dominion over the young he possessed an immunity, which is probably to be ascribed partly to his temperament and partly to his situation. His constitution was feeble: he was very shy; and he was very busy. The strictness of his morals furnished such buffoons as Peter Pindar and Captain Morris with an inexhaustible theme for merriment of no very delicate kind. But the great body of the middle class of Englishmen could not see the joke. They warmly praised the young statesman for commanding his passions, and for covering his frailties, if he had frailties, with decorous obscurity, and would have been very far indeed from thinking better of him if he had vindicated himself from the taunts of his enemies by taking under his protection a Nancy Parsons or a Marianne Clark.

No part of the immense popularity which Pitt long enjoyed is to be attributed to the eulogies of wits and poets. It might have been naturally expected that a man of genius, of learning, of taste, an orator whose diction was often compared to that of Tully, the representative, too, of a great university, would have taken a peculiar pleasure in befriending

eminent writers, to whatever political party they
might have belonged. The love of literature had
induced Augustus to heap benefits on Pompeians,
Somers to be the protector of nonjurors, Harley to
make the fortunes of Whigs. But it could not
move Pitt to show any favour even to Pittites. He
was doubtless right in thinking that, in general,
poetry, history, and philosophy, ought to be suffered,
like calico and cutlery, to find their proper price in
the market, and that to teach men of letters to look
habitually to the state for their recompense is bad
for the state and bad for letters. Assuredly nothing
can be more absurd or mischievous than to waste
the public money in bounties for the purpose of
inducing people who ought to be weighing out
grocery or measuring out drapery to write bad or
middling books. But, though the sound rule is
that authors should be left to be remunerated by
their readers, there will, in every generation, be a
few exceptions to this rule. To distinguish these
special cases from the mass is an employment well
worthy of the faculties of a great and accomplished
ruler; and Pitt would assuredly have had little
difficulty in finding such cases. While he was in
power, the greatest philologist of the age, his own
contemporary at Cambridge, was reduced to earn a
livelihood by the lowest literary drudgery, and to
spend in writing squibs for the Morning Chronicle
years to which we might have owed an all but

perfect text of the whole tragic and comic drama of Athens. The greatest historian of the age, forced by poverty to leave his country, completed his immortal work on the shores of Lake Leman. The political heterodoxy of Porson, and the religious heterodoxy of Gibbon, may perhaps be pleaded in defence of the minister by whom those eminent men were neglected. But there were other cases in which no such excuse could be set up. Scarcely had Pitt obtained possession of unbounded power when an aged writer of the highest eminence, who had made very little by his writings, and who was sinking into the grave under a load of infirmities and sorrows, wanted five or six hundred pounds to enable him, during the winter or two which might still remain to him, to draw his breath more easily in the soft climate of Italy. Not a farthing was to be obtained; and before Christmas the author of the English Dictionary and of the Lives of the Poets had gasped his last in the river fog and coal smoke of Fleet Street. A few months after the death of Johnson appeared the Task, incomparably the best poem that any Englishman then living had produced—a poem, too, which could hardly fail to excite in a well constituted mind a feeling of esteem and compassion for the poet, a man of genius and virtue, whose means were scanty, and whom the most cruel of all the calamities incident to humanity had made incapable of supporting himself by vigorous and sustained exertion. Nowhere had Chatham been praised with more enthusiasm, or in verse more worthy of the subject, than in the Task. The son of Chatham, however, contented himself with reading and admiring the book, and left the author to starve. The pension which, long after, enabled poor Cowper to close his melancholy life, unmolested by duns and bailiffs, was obtained for him by the strenuous kindness of Lord Spencer. What a contrast between the way in which Pitt acted towards Johnson and the way in which Lord Grey acted towards his political enemy Scott, when Scott, worn out by misfortune and disease, was advised to try the effect of the Italian air! What a contrast between the way in which Pitt acted towards Cowper and the way in which Burke, a poor man and out of place, acted towards Crabbe! Even Dundas, who made no pretensions to literary taste, and was content to be considered as a hard-headed and somewhat coarse man of business, was, when compared with his eloquent and classically educated friend, a Mæcenas or a Leo. Dundas made Burns an exciseman, with seventy pounds a year; and this was more than Pitt, during his long tenure of power, did for the encouragement of letters. Even those who may think that it is, in general, no part of the duty of a government to reward literary merit, will hardly deny that a government, which has much lucrative church preferment in its gift, is bound, in distributing that preferment, not to overlook divines whose writings have rendered great service to the cause of religion. But it seems never to have occurred to Pitt that he lay under any such obligation. All the theological works of all the numerous bishops whom he made and translated are not, when put together, worth fifty pages of the Horæ Paulinæ, of the Natural Theology, or of the View of the Evidences of Christianity. But on Paley the all-powerful minister never bestowed the smallest benefice. Artists Pitt treated as contemptuously as writers. For painting he did simply nothing. Sculptors, who had been selected to execute monuments voted by Parliament, had to haunt the ante-chambers of the Treasury during many years before they could obtain a farthing from him. One of them, after vainly soliciting the minister for payment during fourteen years, had the courage to present a memorial to the King, and thus obtained tardy and ungracious justice. Architects it was absolutely necessary to employ; and the worst that could be found seem to have been employed. Not a single fine public building of any kind or in any style was erected during his long administration. It may be confidently affirmed that no ruler whose abilities and attainments would bear any comparison with his has ever shown such cold disdain for what is excellent in arts and letters.

His first administration lasted seventeen years. That long period is divided by a strongly marked line into two almost exactly equal parts. The first part ended and the second began in the autumn of 1792. Throughout both parts Pitt displayed in the highest degree the talents of a parliamentary leader. During the first part he was a fortunate, and, in many respects, a skilful administrator. With the difficulties which he had to encounter during the second part he was altogether incapable of contending: but his eloquence and his perfect mastery of the tactics of the House of Commons concealed his incapacity from the multitude.

The eight years which followed the general election of 1784 were as tranquil and prosperous as any eight years in the whole history of England. Neighbouring nations which had lately been in arms against her, and which had flattered themselves that, in losing her American colonies, she had lost a chief source of her wealth and of her power, saw, with wonder and vexation, that she was more wealthy and more powerful than ever. Her trade increased. Her manufactures flourished. Her exchequer was full to overflowing. Very idle apprehensions were generally entertained, that the public debt, though much less than a third of the debt which we now bear with ease, would be found too heavy for the strength of the nation. Those apprehensions might not perhaps have been easily quieted by reason. But Pitt quieted them by a juggle. He succeeded in persuading first himself, and then the whole nation, his opponents included, that a new sinking fund, which, so far as it differed from former sinking funds, differed for the worse, would, by virtue of some mysterious power of propagation belonging to money, put into the pocket of the public creditor great sums not taken out of the pocket of the tax-payer. The country, terrified by a danger which was no danger, hailed with delight and boundless confidence a remedy which was no remedy. The minister was almost universally extolled as the greatest of financiers. Meanwhile both the branches of the House of Bourbon found that England was as formidable an antagonist as she had ever been. France had formed a plan for reducing Holland to vassalage. But England interposed, and France receded. Spain interrupted by violence the trade of our merchants with the regions near the Oregon. But England armed, and Spain receded. Within the island there was profound tranquillity. The King was, for the first time, popular. During the twenty-three years which had followed his accession he had not been loved by his subjects. His domestic virtues were acknowledged. But it was generally thought that the good qualities by which he was distinguished in private life were wanting to his political character. As a Sovereign, he was resentful, unforgiving, stubborn, cunning. Under his rule the country had sustained cruel disgraces and disasters; and every one of those disgraces and disasters was imputed to his strong antipathies,

and to his perverse obstinacy in the wrong. One
statesman after another complained that he had been
induced by royal caresses, entreaties, and promises,
to undertake the direction of affairs at a difficult
.conjuncture, and that, as soon as he had, not without
sullying his fame and alienating his best friends,
served the turn for which he was wanted, his ungrateful master began to intrigue against him, and
to canvass against him. Grenville, Rockingham,
Chatham, men of widely different characters, but all
three upright and high-spirited, agreed in thinking
that the Prince under whom they had successively
held the highest place in the government was one of
the most insincere of mankind. His confidence was
reposed, they said, not in those known and respon-
sible counsellors to whom he had delivered the seals
of office, but in secret advisers who stole up the back
stairs into his closet. In Parliament, his ministers,
while defending themselves against the attacks of the
opposition in front, were perpetually, at his instiga-
tion, assailed on the flank or in the rear by a vile
band of mercenaries who called themselves his
friends. These men constantly, while in possession
of lucrative places in his service, spoke and voted
against bills which he had authorized the First Lord
of the Treasury or the Secretary of State to bring in.
But from the day on which Pitt was placed at the
head of affairs there was an end of secret influence.
His haughty and aspiring spirit was not to be satis-

fied with the mere show of power. Any attempt to undermine him at Court, any mutinous movement among his followers in the House of Commons, was certain to be at once put down. He had only to tender his resignation; and he could dictate his own terms. For he, and he alone, stood between the King and the Coalition. He was therefore little less than Mayor of the Palace. The nation loudly applauded the King for having the wisdom to repose entire confidence in so excellent a minister. His Majesty's private virtues now began to produce their full effect. He was generally regarded as the model of a respectable country gentleman, honest, good-natured, sober, religious. He rose early: he dined temperately: he was strictly faithful to his wife: he never missed church; and at church he never missed a response. His people heartily prayed that he might long reign over them; and they prayed the more heartily because his virtues were set off to the best advantage by the vices and follies of the Prince of Wales, who lived in close intimacy with the chiefs of the opposition.

How strong this feeling was in the public mind appeared signally on one great occasion. In the autumn of 1788 the King became insane. The opposition, eager for office, committed the great indiscretion of asserting that the heir apparent had, by the fundamental laws of England, a right to be Regent with the full powers of royalty. Pitt, on the other hand, maintained it to be the constitutional doctrine that, when a Sovereign is, by reason of infancy, disease, or absence, incapable of exercising the regal functions, it belongs to the estates of the realm to determine who shall be the vicegerent, and with what portion of the executive authority such vicegerent shall be entrusted. A long and violent contest followed, in which Pitt was supported by the great body of the people with as much enthusiasm as during the first months of his administration. Tories with one voice applauded him for defending the sick-bed of a virtuous and unhappy Sovereign against a disloyal faction and an undutiful son. Not a few Whigs applauded him for asserting the authority of Parliaments and the principles of the Revolution, in opposition to a doctrine which seemed to have too much affinity with the servile theory of indefeasible hereditary right. The middle class, always zealous on the side of decency and the domestic virtues, looked forward with dismay to a reign resembling that of Charles II. The palace, which had now been, during thirty years, the pattern of an English home, would be a public nuisance, a school of profligacy. To the good King's repast of mutton and lemonade, despatched at three o'clock, would succeed midnight banquets, from which the guests would be carried home speechless. To the backgammon board at which the good King played for a little silver with his equerries, would succeed faro tables from which young patricians who had sate down rich would rise up beggars. The drawing-room, from which the frown of the Queen had repelled a whole generation of frail beauties, would now be again what it had been in the days of Barbara Palmer and Louisa de Querouaille. Nay, severely as the public reprobated the Prince's many illicit attachments, his one virtuous attachment was reprobated more severely still. Even in grave and pious circles his Protestant mistresses gave less scandal than his Popish wife. That he must be Regent nobody ventured to deny. But he and his friends were so unpopular that Pitt could, with general approbation, propose to limit the powers of the Regent by restrictions to which it would have been impossible to subject a Prince beloved and trusted by the country. Some interested men, fully expecting a change of administration, went over to the opposition. But the majority, purified by these desertions, closed its ranks, and presented a more firm array than ever to the enemy. In every division Pitt was victorious. When at length, after a stormy interregnum of three months, it was announced, on the very eve of the inauguration of the Regent, that the King was himself again, the nation was wild with delight. On the evening of the day on which His Majesty resumed his functions, a spontaneous illumination, the most general that had ever been seen in England, brightened the whole vast space from Highgate to Tooting, and from Hammersmith to Greenwich. On the day on which he returned thanks in the cathedral of his capital, all the horses and carriages within a hundred miles of London were too few for the multitudes which flocked to see him pass through the streets. A second illumination followed, which was even superior to the first in magnificence. Pitt with difficulty escaped from the tumultuous kindness of an innumerable multitude which insisted on drawing his coach from Saint Paul's Churchyard to Downing Street. This was the moment at which his fame and fortune may be said to have reached the zenith. His influence in the closet was as great as that of Carr or Villiers had been. His dominion over the Parliament was more absolute than that of Walpole or Pelham had been. He was at the same time as high in the favour of the populace as ever Wilkes or Sacheverell had been. Nothing did more to raise his character than his noble poverty. It was well known that, if he had been dismissed from office after more than five years of boundless power, he would hardly have carried out with him a sum sufficient to furnish the set of chambers in which, as he cheerfully declared, he meant to resume the practice of the law. His admirers, however, were by no means disposed to suffer him to depend on daily toil for his daily bread. The voluntary contributions which were awaiting his acceptance in the city of

London alone would have sufficed to make him a rich man. But it may be doubted whether his haughty spirit would have stooped to accept a provision so honourably earned and so honourably bestowed.

To such a height of power and glory had this extraordinary man risen at twenty-nine years of age. And now the tide was on the turn. Only ten days after the triumphant procession to Saint Paul's, the States-General of France, after an interval of a hundred and seventy-four years, met at Versailles.

The nature of the great Revolution which followed was long very imperfectly understood in this country. Burke saw much further than any of his contemporaries; but whatever his sagacity descried was refracted and discoloured by his passions and his imagination. More than three years elapsed before the principles of the English administration underwent any material change. Nothing could as yet be milder or more strictly constitutional than the minister's domestic policy. Not a single act indicating an arbitrary temper or a jealousy of the people could be imputed to him. He had never applied to Parliament for any extraordinary powers. He had never used with harshness the ordinary powers entrusted by the constitution to the executive government. Not a single state prosecution which would even now be called 'oppressive had been instituted by him. Indeed, the only oppressive state prosecution instituted during the first eight years of his administration was that of Stockdale, which is to be attributed, not to the government, but to the chiefs of the opposition. In office, Pitt had redeemed the pledges which he had, at his entrance into public life, given to the supporters of parliamentary reform. He had, in 1785, brought forward a judicious plan for the improvement of the representative system, and had prevailed on the King, not only to refrain from talking against that plan, but to recommend it to the Houses in a speech from the throne.* This attempt failed : but there can be little doubt that, if the French Revolution had not produced a violent reaction of public feeling, Pitt would have performed, with little difficulty and no danger, that great work which, at a later period, Lord Grey could accomplish only by means which for a time loosened the very foundations of the commonwealth. When the atrocities of the slave trade were first brought under the consideration of Parliament, no abolitionist was more zealous than Pitt. When sickness prevented Wilberforce from appearing in public, his place was most efficiently supplied by his friend the minister. A humane bill, which mitigated the horrors of the middle passage, was, in 1788, carried by the eloquence

---

* The speech with which the King opened the session of 1785 concluded with an assurance that His Majesty would heartily concur in every measure which could tend to secure the true principles of the constitution. These words were at the time understood to refer to Pitt's Reform Bill.

and determined spirit of Pitt, in spite of the opposition of some of his own colleagues; and it ought always to be remembered to his honour that, in order to carry that bill, he kept the Houses sitting, in spite of many murmurs, long after the business of the government had been done, and the Appropriation Act passed. In 1791 he cordially concurred with Fox in maintaining the sound constitutional doctrine, that an impeachment is not terminated by a dissolution. In the course of the same year the two great rivals contended side by side in a far more important cause. They are fairly entitled to divide the high honour of having added to our statute-book the inestimable law which places the liberty of the press under the protection of juries. On one occasion, and one alone, Pitt, during the first half of his long administration, acted in a manner unworthy of an enlightened Whig. In the debate on the Test Act, he stooped to gratify the master whom he served, the university which he represented, and the great body of clergymen and country gentlemen on whose support he rested, by talking, with little heartiness, indeed, and with no asperity, the language of a Tory. With this single exception, his conduct from the end of 1783 to the middle of 1792 was that of an honest friend of civil and religious liberty.

Nor did anything, during that period, indicate that he loved war, or harboured any malevolent feeling against any neighbouring nation. Those

French writers who have represented him as a Hannibal sworn in childhood by his father to bear eternal hatred to France, as having, by mysterious intrigues and lavish bribes, instigated the leading Jacobins to commit those excesses which dishonoured the Revolution, as having been the real author of the first coalition, know nothing of his character or of his history. So far was he from being a deadly enemy to France, that his laudable attempts to bring about a closer connection with that country by means of a wise and liberal treaty of commerce brought on him the severe censure of the opposition. He was told in the House of Commons that he was a degenerate son, and that his partiality for the hereditary foes of our island was enough to make his great father's bones stir under the pavement of the Abbey.

And this man, whose name, if he had been so fortunate as to die in 1792, would now have been associated with peace, with freedom, with philanthropy, with temperate reform, with mild and constitutional administration, lived to associate his name with arbitrary government, with harsh laws harshly executed, with alien bills, with gagging bills, with suspensions of the Habeas Corpus Act, with cruel punishments inflicted on some political agitators, with unjustifiable prosecutions instituted against others, and with the most costly and most sanguinary wars of modern times. He lived to be held up to obloquy as the stern oppressor of England, and the indefatigable disturber of Europe. Poets, contrasting his earlier with his later years, likened him sometimes to the apostle who kissed in order to betray, and sometimes to the evil angels who kept not their first estate. A satirist of great genius introduced the fiends of Famine, Slaughter, and Fire, proclaiming that they had received their commission from One whose name was formed of four letters, and promising to give their employer ample proofs of gratitude. Famine would gnaw the multitude till they should rise up against him in madness. The demon of Slaughter would impel them to tear him from limb to limb. But Fire boasted that she alone could reward him as he deserved, and that she would cling round him to all eternity. By the French press and the French tribune every crime that disgraced and every calamity that afflicted France was ascribed to the monster Pitt and his guineas. While the Jacobins were dominant, it was he who had corrupted the Gironde, who had raised Lyons and Bordeaux against the Convention, who had suborned Paris to assassinate Lepelletier, and Cecilia Regnault to assassinate Robespierre. When the Thermidorian reaction came, all the atrocities of the Reign of Terror were imputed to him. Collot D'Herbois and Fouquier Thinville had been his pensioners. It was he who had hired the murderers of September, who had dictated the pamphlets of

Marat and the Carmagnoles of Barrere, who had paid Lebon to deluge Arras with blood, and Carrier to choke the Loire with corpses.

The truth is, that he liked neither war nor arbitrary government. He was a lover of peace and freedom, driven, by a stress against which it was hardly possible for any will or any intellect to struggle, out of the course to which his inclinations pointed, and for which his abilities and acquirements fitted him, and forced into a policy repugnant to his feelings and unsuited to his talents.

The charge of apostasy is grossly unjust. A man ought no more to be called an apostate because his opinions alter with the opinions of the great body of his contemporaries than he ought to be called an oriental traveller because he is always going round from west to east with the globe and everything that is upon it. Between the spring of 1789 and the close of 1792, the public mind of England underwent a great change. If the change of Pitt's sentiments attracted peculiar notice, it was not because he changed more than his neighbours; for in fact he changed less than most of them; but because his position was far more conspicuous than theirs, because he was, till Bonaparte appeared, the individual who filled the greatest space in the eyes of the inhabitants of the civilized word. During a short time the nation, and Pitt, as one of the nation, looked with interest and approbation on the French

Revolution. But soon vast confiscations, the violent sweeping away of ancient institutions, the domination of clubs, the barbarities of mobs maddened by famine and hatred, produced a reaction here. The court, the nobility, the gentry, the clergy, the manufacturers, the merchants, in short, nineteen twentieths of those who had good roofs over their heads and good coats on their backs, became eager and intolerant Antijacobins. This feeling was at least as strong among the minister's adversaries as among his supporters. Fox in vain attempted to restrain his followers. All his genius, all his vast personal influence, could not prevent them from rising up against him in general mutiny. Burke set the example of revolt; and Burke was in no long time joined by Portland, Spencer, Fitzwilliam, Loughborough, Carlisle, Malmesbury, Windham, Elliot. In the House of Commons, the followers of the great Whig statesman and orator diminished from about a hundred and sixty to fifty. In the House of Lords he had but ten or twelve adherents left. There can be no doubt that there would have been a similar mutiny on the ministerial benches, if Pitt had obstinately resisted the general wish. Pressed at once by his master and by his colleagues, by old friends and by old opponents, he abandoned, slowly and reluctantly, the policy which was dear to his heart. He laboured hard to avert the European war. When the European war broke out, he still

R

flattered himself that it would not be necessary for this country to take either side. In the spring of 1792 he congratulated the Parliament on the prospect of long and profound peace, and proved his sincerity by proposing large remissions of taxation. Down to the end of that year he continued to cherish the hope that England might be able to preserve neutrality. But the passions which raged on both sides of the Channel were not to be restrained. The republicans who ruled France were inflamed by a fanaticism resembling that of the Mussulmans, who, with the Koran in one hand and the sword in the other, went forth, conquering and converting, eastward to the Bay of Bengal, and westward to the Pillars of Hercules. The higher and middle classes of England were animated by zeal not less fiery than that of the Crusaders who raised the cry of *Deus vult* at Clermont. The impulse which drove the two nations to a collision was not to be arrested by the abilities or by the authority of any single man. As Pitt was in front of his fellows, and towered high above them, he seemed to lead them. But in fact he was violently pushed on by them, and, had he held back but a little more than he did, would have been thrust out of their way or trampled under their feet.

He yielded to the current: and from that day his misfortunes began. The truth is that there were only two consistent courses before him. Since he

did not choose to oppose himself, side by side with
Fox, to the public feeling, he should have taken the
advice of Burke, and should have availed himself of
that feeling to the full extent. If it was impossible
to preserve peace, he should have adopted the only
policy which could lead to victory. He should have
proclaimed a Holy War for religion, morality, property, order, public law, and should have thus
opposed to the Jacobins an energy equal to their own.
Unhappily he tried to find a middle path; and he
found one which united all that was worst in both
extremes. He went to war: but he would not
understand the peculiar character of that war. He
was obstinately blind to the plain fact, that he was
contending against a state which was also a sect,
and that the new quarrel between England and
France was of quite a different kind from the old
quarrels about colonies in America and fortresses in
the Netherlands. He had to combat frantic enthusiasm, boundless ambition, restless activity, the
wildest and most audacious spirit of innovation;
and he acted as if he had had to deal with the
harlots and fops of the old Court of Versailles, with
Madame De Pompadour and the Abbé de Bernis.
It was pitiable to hear him, year after year, proving
to an admiring audience that the wicked Republic
was exhausted, that she could not hold out, that
her credit was gone, that her assignats were not
worth more than the paper of which they were

made; as if credit was necessary to a government of which the principle was rapine, as if Alboin could not turn Italy into a desert till he had negotiated a loan at five per cent, as if the exchequer bills of Attila had been at par. It was impossible that a man who so completely mistook the nature of a contest could carry on that contest successfully. Great as Pitt's abilities were, his military administration was that of a driveller. He was at the head of a nation engaged in a struggle for life and death, of a nation eminently distinguished by all the physical and all the moral qualities which make excellent soldiers. The resources at his command were unlimited. The Parliament was even more ready to grant him men and money than he was to ask for them. In such an emergency, and with such means, such a statesman as Richelieu, as Louvois, as Chatham, as Wellesley, would have created in a few months one of the finest armies in the world, and would soon have discovered and brought forward generals worthy to command such an army. Germany might have been saved by another Blenheim; Flanders recovered by another Ramilies; another Poitiers might have delivered the Royalist and Catholic provinces of France from a yoke which they abhorred, and might have spread terror even to the barriers of Paris. But the fact is, that, after eight years of war, after a vast destruction of life, after an expenditure of wealth far exceeding the expenditure of the American war, of the Seven Years' War, of the war of the Austrian Succession, and of the war of the Spanish Succession united, the English army, under Pitt, was the laughing-stock of all Europe. It could not boast of one single brilliant exploit. It had never shown itself on the Continent but to be beaten, chased, forced to re-embark, or forced to capitulate. To take some sugar island in the West Indies, to scatter some mob of half naked Irish peasants, such were the most splendid victories won by the British troops under Pitt's auspices.

The English navy no mismanagement could ruin. But during a long period whatever mismanagement could do was done. The Earl of Chatham, without a single qualification for high public trust, was made, by a fraternal partiality, First Lord of the Admiralty, and was kept in that great post during two years of a war in which the very existence of the state depended on the efficiency of the fleet. He continued to doze away and trifle away the time which ought to have been devoted to the public service, till the whole mercantile body, though generally disposed to support the government, complained bitterly that our flag gave no protection to our trade. Fortunately he was succeeded by George Earl Spencer, one of those chiefs of the Whig party who, in the great schism caused by the French Revolution, had followed Burke. Lord Spencer, though inferior to many of his colleagues as an orator, was decidedly the best administrator among them. To him it was owing that a long and gloomy succession of days of fasting, and, most emphatically, of humiliation, was interrupted, twice in the short space of eleven months, by days of thanksgiving for great victories.

It may seem paradoxical to say that the incapacity which Pitt showed in all that related to the conduct of the war is, in some sense, the most decisive proof that he was a man of very extraordinary abilities. Yet this is the simple truth. For assuredly one-tenth part of his errors and disasters would have been fatal to the power and influence of any minister who had not possessed, in the highest degree, the talents of a parliamentary leader. While his schemes were confounded, while his predictions were falsified, while the coalitions which he had laboured to form were falling to pieces, while the expeditions which he had sent forth at enormous cost were ending in rout and disgrace, while the enemy against whom he was feebly contending was subjugating Flanders and Brabant, the Electorate of Mentz and the Electorate of Treves, Holland, Piedmont, Liguria, Lombardy, his authority over the House of Commons was constantly becoming more and more absolute. There was his empire. There were his victories, his Lodi and his Arcola, his Rivoli and his Marengo. If some great misfortune, a pitched battle lost by the allies, the annexation of a new department to the French

Republic, a sanguinary insurrection in Ireland, a mutiny in the fleet, a panic in the city, a run on the bank, had spread dismay through the ranks of his majority, that dismay lasted only till he rose from the Treasury bench, drew up his haughty head, stretched his arm with commanding gesture, and poured forth, in deep and sonorous tones, the lofty language of inextinguishable hope and inflexible resolution. Thus, through a long and calamitous period, every disaster that happened without the walls of Parliament was regularly followed by a triumph within them. At length he had no longer an opposition to encounter. Of the great party which had contended against him during the first eight years of his administration more than one half now marched under his standard, with his old competitor the Duke of Portland at their head; and the rest had, after many vain struggles, quitted the field in despair. Fox had retired to the shades of St. Anne's Hill, and had there found, in the society of friends whom no vicissitude could estrange from him, of a woman whom he tenderly loved, and of the illustrious dead of Athens, of Rome, and of Florence, ample compensation for all the misfortunes of his public life. Session followed session with scarcely a single division. In the eventful year 1799, the largest minority that could be mustered against the government was twenty-five.

In Pitt's domestic policy there was at this time

assuredly no want of vigour. While he offered to French Jacobinism a resistance so feeble that it only encouraged the evil which he wished to suppress, he put down English Jacobinism with a strong hand. The Habeas Corpus Act was repeatedly suspended. Public meetings were placed under severe restraints. The government obtained from Parliament power to send out of the country aliens who were suspected of evil designs ; and that power was not suffered to be idle. Writers who propounded doctrines adverse to monarchy and aristocracy were proscribed and punished without mercy. It was hardly safe for a republican to avow his political creed over his beef-steak and his bottle of port at a chop-house. The old laws of Scotland against sedition, laws which were considered by Englishmen as barbarous, and which a succession of governments had suffered to rust, were now furbished up and sharpened anew. Men of cultivated minds and polished manners were, for offences which at Westminster would have been treated as mere misdemeanours, sent to herd with felons at Botany Bay. Some reformers, whose opinions were extravagant, and whose language was intemperate, but who had never dreamed of subverting the government by physical force, were indicted for high treason, and were saved from the gallows only by the righteous verdicts of juries. This severity was at the time loudly applauded by alarmists whom fear had made cruel, but will be seen in a

very different light by posterity. The truth is, that
the Englishmen who wished for a revolution were,
even in number, not formidable, and, in everything
but number, a faction utterly contemptible, without
arms, or funds, or plans, or organisation, or leader.
There can be no doubt that Pitt, strong as he was in
the support of the great body of the nation, might
easily have repressed the turbulence of the discon-
tented minority by firmly yet temperately enforcing
the ordinary law. Whatever vigour he showed
during this unfortunate part of his life was vigour
out of place and season. He was all feebleness and
languor in his conflict with the foreign enemy who
was really to be dreaded, and reserved all his energy
and resolution for the domestic enemy who might
safely have been despised.

One part only of Pitt's conduct during the last
eight years of the eighteenth century deserves high
praise. He was the first English minister who formed
great designs for the benefit of Ireland. The manner
in which the Roman Catholic population of that
unfortunate country had been kept down during
many generations seemed to him unjust and cruel ;
and it was scarcely possible for a man of his abilities
not to perceive that, in a contest against the Jacobins, the Roman Catholics were his natural allies.
Had he been able to do all that he wished, it is
probable that a wise and liberal policy would have
averted the rebellion of 1798. But the difficulties

which he encountered were great, perhaps insurmountable; and the Roman Catholics were, rather by his misfortune than by his fault, thrown into the hands of the Jacobins. There was a third great rising of the Irishry against the Englishry, a rising not less formidable than the risings of 1641 and 1689. The Englishry remained victorious; and it was necessary for Pitt, as it had been necessary for Oliver Cromwell and William of Orange before him, to consider how the victory should be used. It is only just to his memory to say that he formed a scheme of policy, so grand and so simple, so righteous and so humane, that it would alone entitle him to a high place among statesmen. He determined to make Ireland one kingdom with England, and, at the same time, to relieve the Roman Catholic laity from civil disabilities, and to grant a public maintenance to the Roman Catholic clergy. Had he been able to carry these noble designs into effect, the Union would have been a Union indeed. It would have been inseparably associated in the minds of the great majority of Irishmen with civil and religious freedom; and the old Parliament in College Green would have been regretted only by a small knot of discarded jobbers and oppressors, and would have been remembered by the body of the nation with the loathing and contempt due to the most tyrannical and the most corrupt assembly that had ever sate in Europe. But Pitt could execute only one half of what he had projected. He succeeded in obtaining the consent of the Parliaments of both kingdoms to the Union : but that reconciliation of races and sects, without which the Union could exist only in name, was not accomplished. He was well aware that he was likely to find difficulties in the closet. But he flattered himself that, by cautious and dexterous management, those difficulties might be overcome. Unhappily, there were traitors and sycophants in high place who did not suffer him to take his own time and his own way, but prematurely disclosed his scheme to the king, and disclosed it in the manner most likely to irritate and alarm a weak and diseased mind. His Majesty absurdly imagined that his coronation oath bound him to refuse his assent to any bill for relieving Roman Catholics from civil disabilities. To argue with him was impossible. Dundas tried to explain the matter, but was told to keep his Scotch metaphysics to himself. Pitt, and Pitt's ablest colleagues, resigned their offices. It was necessary that the King should make a new arrangement. But by this time his anger and distress had brought back the malady which had, many years before, incapacitated him for the discharge of his functions. He actually assembled his family, read the Coronation oath to them, and told them that, if he broke it, the Crown would immediately pass to the House of Savoy. It was not until after an interregnum of several weeks that he regained the full use of his small faculties, and that a ministry after his own heart was at length formed.

The materials out of which he had to construct a government were neither solid nor splendid. To that party, weak in numbers, but strong in every kind of talent, which was hostile to the domestic and foreign policy of his late advisers, he could not have recourse. For that party, while it differed from his late advisers on every point on which they had been honoured with his approbation, cordially agreed with them as to the single matter which had brought on them his displeasure. All that was left to him was to call up the rear ranks of the old ministry to form the front rank of a new ministry. In an age pre-eminently fruitful of parliamentary talents, a cabinet was formed containing hardly a single man who, in parliamentary talents, could be considered as even of the second rate. The most important offices in the state were bestowed on decorous and laborious mediocrity. Henry Addington was at the head of the Treasury. He had been an early, indeed a hereditary, friend of Pitt, and had by Pitt's influence been placed, while still a young man, in the chair of the House of Commons. He was universally admitted to have been the best speaker that had sate in that chair since the retirement of Onslow. But nature had not bestowed on him very vigorous faculties; and the highly respectable situation which he had long occupied with honour had rather unfitted than fitted him for the discharge of his new duties. His business had been to bear himself evenly between contending factions. He had taken no part in the war of words; and he had always been addressed with marked deference by the great orators who thundered against each other from his right and from his left. It was not strange that when, for the first time, he had to encounter keen and vigorous antagonists, who dealt hard blows without the smallest ceremony, he should have been awkward and unready, or that the air of dignity and authority which he had acquired in his former post, and of which he had not divested himself, should have made his helplessness laughable and pitiable. Nevertheless, during many months, his power seemed to stand firm. He was a favourite with the King, whom he resembled in narrowness of mind, and to whom he was more obsequious than Pitt had ever been. The nation was put into high good humour by a peace with France. The enthusiasm with which the upper and middle classes had rushed into the war had spent itself. Jacobinism was no longer formidable. Everywhere there was a strong reaction against what was called the atheistical and anarchical philosophy of the eighteenth century. Bonaparte, now First Consul, was busied in constructing out of the ruins of old institutions a new ecclesiastical establishment and a new order of knighthood. That nothing less than the dominion of the whole civilized world would satisfy his selfish ambition was not yet suspected; nor did even wise men see any reason to doubt that he might be as safe a neighbour as any prince of the House of Bourbon had been. The treaty of Amiens was therefore hailed by the great body of the English people with extravagant joy. The popularity of the minister was for the moment immense. His want of parliamentary ability was, as yet, of little consequence: for he had scarcely any adversary to encounter. The old opposition, delighted by the peace, regarded him with favour. A new opposition, had indeed been formed by some of the late ministers, and was led by Grenville in the House of Lords, and by Windham in the House of Commons. But the new opposition could scarcely muster ten votes, and was regarded with no favour by the country. On Pitt the ministers relied ·as on their firmest support. He had not, like some of his colleagues, retired in anger. He had expressed the greatest respect for the conscientious scruple which had taken possession of the royal mind; and he had promised his successors all the help in his power. In private his advice was at their service. In Parliament he took his seat on the bench behind them; and, in more than one debate, defended them with powers far superior to their own. The King perfectly understood the value of such assistance. On one occasion, at the palace, he took the old minister and the new minister aside.

"If we three," he said, "keep together, all will go well."

But it was hardly possible, human nature being what it is, and, more especially, Pitt and Addington being what they were, that this union should be durable. Pitt, conscious of superior powers, imagined that the place which he had quitted was now occupied by a mere puppet which he had set up, which he was to govern while he suffered it to remain, and which he was to fling aside as soon as he wished to resume his old position. Nor was it long before he began to pine for the power which he had relinquished. He had been so early raised to supreme authority in the state, and had enjoyed that authority so long, that it had become necessary to him. In retirement his days passed heavily. He could not, like Fox, forget the pleasures and cares of ambition in the company of Euripides or Herodotus. Pride restrained him from intimating, even to his dearest friends, that he wished to be again minister. But he thought it strange, almost ungrateful, that his wish had not been divined, that it had not been anticipated, by one whom he regarded as his deputy.

Addington, on the other hand, was by no means inclined to descend from his high position. He was, indeed, under a delusion much resembling that of Abon Hassan in the Arabian tale. His brain was turned by his short and unreal Caliphate. He took his elevation quite seriously, attributed it to his own merit, and considered himself as one of the great triumvirate of English statesmen, as worthy to make a third with Pitt and Fox.

Such being the feelings of the late minister and of the present minister, a rupture was inevitable ; and there was no want of persons bent on making that rupture speedy and violent. Some of these persons wounded Addington's pride by representing him as a lacquey, sent to keep a place on the Treasury bench till his master should find it convenient to come. Others took every opportunity of praising him at Pitt's expense. Pitt had waged a long, a bloody, a costly, an unsuccessful war. Addington had made peace. Pitt had suspended the constitutional liberties of Englishmen. Under Addington those liberties were again enjoyed. Pitt had wasted the public resources. Addington was carefully nursing them. It was sometimes but too evident that these compliments were not unpleasing to Addington. Pitt became cold and reserved. During many months he remained at a distance from London. Meanwhile his most intimate friends, in spite of his declarations that he made no complaint, and that he had no wish for office, exerted themselves to effect a change of ministry. His favourite disciple, George Canning, young, ardent, ambitious, with great powers and great virtues, but with a temper too restless and a wit too satirical for his own happiness, was indefatigable. He spoke; he wrote; he intrigued; he tried to induce a large number of the supporters of the government to sign a round robin desiring a change; he made game of Addington and of Addington's relations in a succession of lively pasquinades. The minister's partisans retorted with equal acrimony, if not with equal vivacity. Pitt could keep out of the affray only by keeping out of politics altogether; and this it soon became impossible for him to do. Had Napoleon, content with the first place among the sovereigns of the Continent, and with a military reputation surpassing that of Marlborough or of Turenne, devoted himself to the noble task of making France happy by mild administration and wise legislation, our country might have long continued to tolerate a government of fair intentions and feeble abilities. Unhappily, the treaty of Amiens had scarcely been signed, when the restless ambition and the insupportable insolence of the First Consul convinced the great body of the English people that the peace, so eagerly welcomed, was only a precarious armistice. As it became clearer and clearer that a war for the dignity, the independence, the very existence of the nation was at hand, men looked with increasing uneasiness on the weak and languid cabinet which would have to contend against an enemy who united more than the power of Lewis the Great to more than the genius of Frederick the

s

Great. It is true that Addington might easily have been a better war minister than Pitt, and could not possibly have been a worse. But Pitt had cast a spell on the public mind. The eloquence, the judgment, the calm and disdainful firmness which he had, during many years, displayed in Parliament, deluded the world into the belief that he must be eminently qualified to superintend every department of politics; and they imagined, even after the miserable failures of Dunkirk, of Quiberon, and of the Helder, that he was the only statesman who could cope with Bonaparte. This feeling was nowhere stronger than among Addington's own colleagues. The pressure put on him was so strong, that he could not help yielding to it; yet, even in yielding, he showed how far he was from knowing his own place. His first proposition was, that some insignificant nobleman should be First Lord of the Treasury and nominal head of the administration, and that the real power should be divided between Pitt and himself, who were to be secretaries of state. Pitt, as might have been expected, refused even to discuss such a scheme, and talked of it with bitter mirth. "Which secretaryship was offered to you?" his friend Wilberforce asked. "Really," said Pitt, "I had not the curiosity to inquire." Addington was frightened into bidding higher. He offered to resign the Treasury to Pitt, on condition that there should be no extensive change in the government.

But Pitt would listen to no such terms. Then came a dispute such as often arises after negotiations orally conducted, even when the negotiators are men of strict honour. Pitt gave one account of what had passed; Addington gave another; and though the discrepancies were not such as necessarily implied any intentional violation of truth on either side, both were greatly exasperated.

Meanwhile the quarrel with the First Consul had come to a crisis. On the 16th of May 1803, the King sent a message calling on the House of Commons to support him in withstanding the ambitious and encroaching policy of France; and on the 22d, the House took the message into consideration.

Pitt had now been living many months in retirement. There had been a general election since he had spoken in Parliament, and there were two hundred members who had never heard him. It was known that on this occasion he would be in his place, and curiosity was wound up to the highest point. Unfortunately, the short-hand writers were, in consequence of some mistake, shut out on that day from the gallery, so that the newspapers contained only a very meagre report of the proceedings. But several accounts of what passed are extant; and of those accounts the most interesting is contained in an unpublished letter written by a very young member, John William Ward, afterwards Earl of

Dudley. When Pitt rose, he was received with loud
cheering. At every pause in his speech there was a
burst of applause. The peroration is said to have
been one of the most animated and magnificent ever
heard in Parliament. " Pitt's speech," Fox wrote a
few days later, " was admired very much, and very
justly. I think it was the best he ever made in
that style. The debate was adjourned; and on the
second night Fox replied in an oration which, as
the most zealous Pittites were forced to acknowledge, left the palm of eloquence doubtful. Addington made a pitiable appearance between the two
great rivals; and it was observed that Pitt, while
exhorting the Commons to stand resolutely by the
executive government against France, said not a
word indicating esteem or friendship for the prime
minister.

.War was speedily declared. The First Consul
threatened to invade England at the head of the
conquerors of Belgium and Italy, and formed a great
camp near the Straits of Dover. On the other side
of those Straits the whole population of our island
was ready to rise up as one man in defence of the
soil. At this conjuncture, as at some other great
conjunctures in our history, the conjuncture of 1660,
for example, and the conjuncture of 1688, there was
a general disposition among honest and patriotic men
to forget old quarrels, and to regard as a friend every
person who was ready, in the existing emergency, to

do his part towards the saving of the state. A coalition of all the first men in the country would, at that moment, have been as popular as the coalition of 1783 had been unpopular. Alone in the kingdom the King looked with perfect complacency on a cabinet in which no man superior to himself in genius was to be found, and was so far from being willing to admit all his ablest subjects to office that he was bent on excluding them all.

A few months passed before the different parties which agreed in regarding the government with dislike and contempt came to an understanding with each other. But in the spring of 1804 it became evident that the weakest of ministries would have to defend itself against the strongest of oppositions, an opposition made up of three oppositions, each of which would, separately, have been formidable from ability, and which, when united, were also formidable from number. The party which had opposed the peace, headed by Grenville and Windham, and the party which had opposed the renewal of the war, headed by Fox, concurred in thinking that the men now in power were incapable of either making a good peace or waging a vigorous war. Pitt had, in 1802, spoken for peace against the party of Grenville, and had, in 1803, spoken for war against the party of Fox. But of the capacity of the cabinet, and especially of its chief, for the conduct of great affairs, he thought as meanly as either Fox or Grenville.

Questions were easily found on which all the enemies of the government could act cordially together. The unfortunate First Lord of the Treasury, who had, during the earlier months of his administration, been supported by Pitt on one side, and by Fox on the other, now had to answer Pitt, and to be answered by Fox. Two sharp debates, followed by close divisions, made him weary of his post. It was known, too, that the Upper House was ever more hostile to him than the Lower, that the Scotch representative peers wavered, that there were signs of mutiny among the Bishops. In the cabinet itself there was discord, and, worse than discord, treachery. It was necessary to give way: the ministry was dissolved; and the task of forming a government was entrusted to Pitt.

Pitt was of opinion that there was now an opportunity, such as had never before offered itself, and such as might never offer itself again, of uniting in the public service, on honourable terms, all the eminent talents of the kingdom. The passions to which the French Revolution had given birth were extinct. The madness of the innovator and the madness of the alarmist had alike had their day. Jacobinism and Anti-jacobinism had gone out of fashion together. The most liberal statesman did not think that season propitious for schemes of parliamentary reform; and the most conservative statesman could not pretend that there was any occasion for gagging bills and suspensions of the Habeas Corpus Act. The great struggle for independence and national honour occupied all minds; and those who were agreed as to the duty of maintaining that struggle with vigour might well postpone to a more convenient time all disputes about matters comparatively unimportant. Strongly impressed by these considerations, Pitt wished to form a ministry including all the first men in the country. The Treasury he reserved for himself; and to Fox he proposed to assign a share of power little inferior to his own.

The plan was excellent: but the King would not hear of it. Dull, obstinate, unforgiving, and, at that time, half mad, he positively refused to admit Fox into his service. Anybody else, even men who had gone as far as Fox, or further than Fox, in what His Majesty considered as Jacobinism, Sheridan, Grey, Erskine, should be graciously received; but Fox never. During several hours Pitt laboured in vain to reason down this senseless antipathy. That he was perfectly sincere there can be no doubt; but it was not enough to be sincere; he should have been resolute. Had he declared himself determined not to take office without Fox, the royal obstinacy would have given way, as it gave way a few months later, when opposed to the immutable resolution of Lord Grenville. In an evil hour Pitt yielded. He flattered himself with the hope that, though he consented to forego the aid of his illustrious rival, there would still remain ample materials for the formation of an efficient ministry. That hope was cruelly disappointed. Fox entreated his friends to leave personal considerations out of the question, and declared that he would support with the utmost cordiality, an efficient and patriotic ministry from which he should be himself excluded. Not only his friends, however, but Grenville and Grenville's adherents, answered with one voice, that the question was not personal, that a great constitutional principle was at stake, and that they would not take office while a man eminently qualified to render service to the commonwealth was placed under a ban merely because he was disliked at Court. All that was left to Pitt was to construct a government out of the wreck of Addington's feeble administration. The small circle of his personal retainers furnished him with a very few useful assistants, particularly Dundas, who had been created Viscount Melville, Lord Harrowby, and Canning.

Such was the inauspicious manner in which Pitt entered on his second administration. The whole history of that administration was of a piece with the commencement. Almost every month brought some new disaster or disgrace. To the war with France was soon added a war with Spain. The opponents of the minister were numerous, able, and active. His most useful coadjutors he soon lost.

Sickness deprived him of the help of Lord Harrowby. It was discovered that Lord Melville had been guilty of highly culpable laxity in transactions relating to public money. He was censured by the House of Commons, driven from office, ejected from the Privy Council, and impeached of high crimes and misdemeanours. The blow fell heavy on Pitt. It gave him, he said in Parliament, a deep pang; and, as he uttered the word pang, his lip quivered; his voice shook; he paused; and his hearers thought that he was about to burst into tears. Such tears shed by Eldon would have moved nothing but laughter. Shed by the warm-hearted and open-hearted Fox, they would have moved sympathy, but would have caused no surprise. But a tear from Pitt would have been something portentous. He suppressed his emotion, however, and proceeded with his usual majestic self-possession.

His difficulties compelled him to resort to various expedients. At one time Addington was persuaded to accept office with a peerage; but he brought no additional strength to the government. Though he went through the form of reconciliation it was impossible for him to forget the past. While he remained in place he was jealous and punctilious; and he soon retired again. At another time Pitt renewed his efforts to overcome his master's aversion to Fox; and it was rumoured that the King's obstinacy was gradually giving way. But, meanwhile, it was impossible for the minister to conceal from the public eye the decay of his health and the constant anxiety which gnawed at his heart. His sleep was broken. His food ceased to nourish him. All who passed him in the Park, all who had interviews with him in Downing Street, saw misery written in his face. The peculiar look which he wore during the last months of his life was often pathetically described by Wilberforce, who used to call it the Austerlitz look.

Still the vigour of Pitt's intellectual faculties, and the intrepid haughtiness of his spirit, remained unaltered. He had staked everything on a great venture. He had succeeded in forming another mighty coalition against the French ascendancy. The united forces of Austria, Russia, and England might, he hoped, oppose an insurmountable barrier to the ambition of the common enemy. But the genius and energy of Napoleon prevailed. While the English troops were preparing to embark for Germany, while the Russian troops were slowly coming up from Poland, he, with rapidity unprecedented in modern war, moved a hundred thousand men from the shores of the Ocean to the Black Forest, and compelled a great Austrian army to surrender at Ulm. To the first faint rumours of this calamity Pitt would give no credit. He was irritated by the alarms of those around him. "Do not believe a word of it," he said: "it is all a fiction." The next day he received a Dutch newspaper containing the capitulation. He knew no Dutch. It was Sunday; and the public offices were shut. He carried the paper to Lord Malmesbury, who had been minister in Holland; and Lord Malmesbury translated it. Pitt tried to bear up; but the shock was too great; and he went away with death in his face.

The news of the battle of Trafalgar arrived four days later, and seemed for a moment to revive him. Forty-eight hours after that most glorious and most mournful of victories had been announced to the country came the Lord Mayor's day; and Pitt dined at Guildhall. His popularity had declined. But on this occasion, the multitude, greatly excited by the recent tidings, welcomed him enthusiastically, took off his horses in Cheapside, and drew his carriage up King Street. When his health was drunk, he returned thanks in two or three of those stately sentences of which he had a boundless command. Several of those who heard him laid up his words in their hearts; for they were the last words that he ever uttered in public: "Let us hope that England, having saved herself by her energy, may save Europe by her example."

This was but a momentary rally. Austerlitz soon completed what Ulm had begun. Early in December Pitt had retired to Bath, in the hope that he might there gather strength for the approaching session. While he was languishing there on his sofa arrived the news that a decisive battle had been fought and lost in Moravia, that the coalition was dissolved, that the Continent was at the feet of France. He sank down under the blow. Ten days later, he was so emaciated that his most intimate friends hardly knew him. He came up from Bath by slow journeys, and, on the 11th of January 1806, reached his villa at Putney. Parliament was to meet on the 21st. On the 20th was to be the parliamentary dinner at the house of the First Lord of the Treasury in Downing Street; and the cards were already issued. But the days of the great minister were numbered. The only chance for his life, and that a very slight chance, was, that he should resign his office, and pass some months in profound repose. His colleagues paid him very short visits, and carefully avoided political conversation. But his spirit, long accustomed to dominion, could not, even in that extremity, relinquish hopes which everybody but himself perceived to be vain. On the day on which he was carried into his bedroom at Putney, the Marquess Wellesley, whom he had long loved, whom he had sent to govern India, and whose administration had been eminently able, energetic, and successful, arrived in London after an absence of eight years. The friends saw each other once more. There was an affectionate meeting, and a last parting. That it was a last parting Pitt did not seem to be aware.

He fancied himself to be recovering, talked on various subjects cheerfully, and with an unclouded mind, and pronounced a warm and discerning eulogium on the Marquess's brother Arthur. "I never," he said, "met with any military man with whom it was so satisfactory to converse." The excitement and exertion of this interview were too much for the sick man. He fainted away; and Lord Wellesley left the house, convinced that the close was fast approaching.

And now members of Parliament were fast coming up to London. The chiefs of the opposition met for the purpose of considering the course to be taken on the first day of the session. It was easy to guess what would be the language of the King's speech, and of the address which would be moved in answer to that speech. An amendment condemning the policy of the government had been prepared, and was to have been proposed in the House of Commons by Lord Henry Petty, a young nobleman who had already won for himself that place in the esteem of his country which, after the lapse of more than half a century, he still retains. He was unwilling, however, to come forward as the accuser of one who was incapable of defending himself. Lord Grenville, who had been informed of Pitt's state by Lord Wellesley, and had been deeply affected by it, earnestly recommended forbearance; and Fox, with characteristic generosity and good nature, gave his voice against attacking his now helpless rival. "Sunt lacrymæ rerum," he said, "et mentem mortalia tangunt." On the first day, therefore, there was no debate. It was rumoured that evening that Pitt was better. But on the following morning his physicians pronounced that there were no hopes. The commanding faculties of which he had been too proud were beginning to fail. His old tutor and friend, the Bishop of Lincoln, informed him of his danger, and gave such religious advice and consolation as a confused and obscured mind could receive. Stories were told of devout sentiments fervently uttered by the dying man. But these stories found no credit with anybody who knew him. Wilberforce pronounced it impossible that they could be true; "Pitt," he added, "was a man who always said less than he thought on such topics." It was asserted in many after-dinner speeches, Grub Street elegies, and academic prize poems and prize declamations, that the great minister died exclaiming, "O my country!" This is a fable; but it is true that the last words which he uttered, while he knew what he said, were broken exclamations about the alarming state of public affairs. He ceased to breathe on the morning of the 23d of January 1806, the twenty-fifth anniversary of the day on which he first took his seat in Parliament. He was in his forty-seventh year, and had been, during near nineteen years, First Lord of the Treasury, and undisputed chief of the administration. Since parliamentary government was established in England, no English statesman has held supreme power so long. Walpole, it is true, was First Lord of the Treasury during more than twenty years, but it was not till Walpole had been some time First Lord of the Treasury that he could be properly called Prime Minister.

It was moved in the House of Commons that Pitt should be honoured with a public funeral and a monument. The motion was opposed by Fox in a speech which deserves to be studied as a model of good taste and good feeling. The task was the most invidious that ever an orator undertook; but it was performed with a humanity and delicacy which were warmly acknowledged by the mourning friends of him who was gone. The motion was carried by 288 votes to 89.

The 22d of February was fixed for the funeral. The corpse having lain in state during two days in the Painted Chamber, was borne with great pomp to the northern transept of the Abbey. A splendid train of princes, nobles, bishops, and privy councillors followed. The grave of Pitt had been made near to the spot where his great father lay, near also to the spot where his great rival was soon to lie. The sadness of the assistants was beyond that of ordinary mourners. For he whom they were committing to the dust had died of sorrows and anxieties of which none of the survivors could be altogether

without a share.   Wilberforce, who carried the banner before the hearse, described the awful ceremony
with deep feeling.   As the coffin descended into the
earth, he said, the eagle face of Chatham from above
seemed to look down with consternation into the
dark house which was receiving all that remained of
so much power and glory.

All parties in the House of Commons readily
concurred in voting forty thousand pounds to satisfy
the demands of Pitt's creditors.   Some of his admirers seemed to consider the magnitude of his embarrassments as a circumstance highly honourable
to him; but men of sense will probably be of a
different opinion.   It is far better, no doubt, that a
great minister should carry his contempt of money
to excess than that he should contaminate his hands
with unlawful gain.   But it is neither right nor
becoming in a man to whom the public has given
an income more than sufficient for his comfort and
dignity to bequeath to that public a great debt, the
effect of mere negligence and profusion.   As first
Lord of the Treasury and Chancellor of the Exchequer, Pitt never had less than six thousand a
year, besides an excellent house.   In 1792 he was
forced by his royal master's friendly importunity to
accept for life the office of Warden of the Cinque
Ports, with near four thousand a year more.   He
had neither wife nor child; he had no needy relations: he had no expensive tastes; he had no long

election bills. Had he given but a quarter of an hour a week to the regulation of his household, he would have kept his expenditure within bounds. Or, if he could not spare even a quarter of an hour a week for that purpose, he had numerous friends, excellent men of business, who would have been proud to act as his stewards. One of those friends, the chief of a great commercial house in the city, made an attempt to put the establishment in Downing Street to rights; but in vain. He found that the waste of the servant's hall was almost fabulous. The quantity of butcher's meat charged in the bills was nine hundredweight a week. The consumption of poultry, of fish, of tea, was in proportion. The character of Pitt would have stood higher if, with the disinterestedness of Pericles and of De Witt, he had united their dignified frugality.

The memory of Pitt has been assailed, times innumerable, often justly, often unjustly; but it has suffered much less from his assailants than from his eulogists. For, during many years, his name was the rallying cry of a class of men with whom, at one of those terrible conjunctures which confound all ordinary distinctions, he was accidentally and temporarily connected, but to whom, on almost all great questions of principle, he was diametrically opposed. The haters of parliamentary reform called themselves Pittites, not choosing to remember that Pitt made three motions for parliamentary reform, and that, though he thought that such a reform could not safely be made while the passions excited by the French Revolution were raging, he never uttered a word indicating that he should not be prepared at a more convenient season to bring the question forward a fourth time. The toast of Protestant ascendency was drunk on Pitt's birthday by a set of Pittites who could not but be aware that Pitt had resigned his office because he could not carry Catholic emancipation. The defenders of the Test Act called themselves Pittites, though they could not be ignorant that Pitt had laid before George the Third unanswerable reasons for abolishing the Test Act. The enemies of free trade called themselves Pittites, though Pitt was far more deeply imbued with the doctrines of Adam Smith than either Fox or Grey. The very Negro-drivers invoked the name of Pitt, whose eloquence was never more conspicuously displayed than when he spoke of the wrongs of the Negro. This mythical Pitt, who resembles the genuine Pitt as little as the Charlemagne of Ariosto resembles the Charlemagne of Eginhard, has had his day. History will vindicate the real man from calumny disguised under the semblance of adulation, and will exhibit him as what he was, a minister of great talents, honest intentions, and liberal opinions, pre-eminently qualified, intellectually and morally, for the part of a parliamentary leader, and capable of administering with prudence and moderation the government of a prosperous and tranquil country, but unequal to surprising and terrible emergencies, and liable, in such emergencies to err grievously, both on the side of weakness and on the side of violence.

THE END.

PRINTED BY R. AND R. CLARK, EDINBURGH.

www.ingramcontent.com/pod-product-compliance
Lightning Source LLC
Chambersburg PA
CBHW060559030726
47498CB00005B/1466